Gerald Massey

A Tale of Eternity

And other Poems

Gerald Massey

A Tale of Eternity
And other Poems

ISBN/EAN: 9783744765428

Printed in Europe, USA, Canada, Australia, Japan

Cover: Foto ©Andreas Hilbeck / pixelio.de

More available books at **www.hansebooks.com**

A  Tale of Eternity

. AND OTHER POEMS.

BY

GERALD MASSEY.

BOSTON:
FIELDS, OSGOOD, & CO.
1870.

CONTENTS.

HYMNS, AND OTHER LYRICS.

SONGS, AND OTHER BREVITIES.

CONTENTS.

A RHYME FOR THE READER.

SINGER sang in sleep, and, sleeping, dreamed
    He sang divinely, while his spirit seemed
So far in Music's heaven to soar and sing,
They could not follow who stood listening !
For him, the soul of sweetness found a voice.
For them, the Singer only " made a noise."

Such is the difference in the uttered strain,
From that fine music passing through the brain.
Such sumless treasures we possess in dreams,
To find at waking only mirrored gleams.
No revelation of the written word
Will render all the spirit saw and heard.

So fresh they breathed ; so faded now they look ;
My few poor withered flowers shut in a book.
Gone is the glory that once gleamed from them ;
The Spirit of Light imprisoned in the gem !
Now the winged life hath settled down in words,
These are but stuffed instead of Singing Birds.

Feelings brimful of warmth as is a rose
Of its June-red, have lost their perfumed glows ;

The heaven-revealing thoughts that star-like shone,
The daily kindlings of eternal dawn, —
All darkened down, like Meteors that have birth
In Heaven, to flash and quench them cold in earth.

We grasp at diamonds visible in the dew,
And open empty tear-wet hands to you !
We clasp at heart the daughters of the skies,
Their shadow stays with us ; the substance flies.
Glimpses divine will peep ; pictures will pass,
And leave no likeness on the Seer's glass.

The Poet's best immortally will lurk
In that rare motion of his soul at work.
Bee-like, he brings you one gold honey-drop ;
But the full-swing, high on the flower-top,
'Twixt Heaven that rained itself in sweetness down,
And Earth — all bloom for him — is ne'er made
          known.

MY poem was in the making.   These are your
Warmth-needy nurslings, Reader ! mine no more.
The life I gave will no more fill my breast
Than the flown birds come back to last year's nest.
And if these live again, 't is you must give
The reflex thrill to them by which they live.

You must make out the music from the hint
Prelusive : I but tune the instrument.
The glory or the gladness or the grace
Must shine for me re-orient in your face.
The seed, that in my life took secret root,
In yours must bud, and flower, and bear the fruit.

A TALE OF ETERNITY.

I

"Among the rest, a small unsightly root,
   But of divine effect, he culled me out;
   The leaf was darkish, and had prickles on it,
   But in another country, as he said,
   Bore a bright golden flower." — MILTON.

"Now a thing was secretly brought to me, and mine ear received a little thereof, in visions of the night, when deep sleep falleth on men, fear came upon me, and trembling; then a spirit passed before my face and the hair of my flesh stood up: an image was before mine eyes; there was silence, and I heard a voice." — BOOK OF JOB.

"He maketh His angels spirits; His ministers a flaming fire." — PSALMS OF DAVID.

"Millions of spiritual creatures walk the earth
   Unseen, both when we wake and when we sleep."
                                        MILTON.

"I've seen some men, veracious, nowise mad,
   Who have thought or dreamed, declared and testified
   They heard the Dead a-ticking like a clock
   Which strikes the hours of the eternities,
   Beside them, with their natural ears, — and known
   That human spirits feel the human way
   And hate the unreasoning awe which waves them off
   From possible communion.   It may be."
                                        MRS. BROWNING.

A TALE OF ETERNITY.

S One who, in a strange and far Country,
In presence of his future Bride may be,
That keeps the secret of her face con-
cealed,
Until, as Wife, the Maiden stands revealed :
And who doth make blind guesses at the face ;
Its wealth of nature and its gifts of grace :
Much marvelling if the form beneath the folds
Be like the picture that at heart he holds :
And who, as chance befall, doth furtively
Feel the hid features that he may not see —
Trying to gather, at a Lover's touch,-
The least of all he longs to know so much :
Even thus, before the Next World's face I stand,
And o'er its clouded features pass my hand ;
Groping to get where mortal sight doth fail,
Some inkling of the face behind the Veil !
It is the voice of Vision in the night :
I learned in darkness what I speak in light.

Perchance such ne'er attains the perfect True
And yet may utter meaning for the few,
As sandiest desert wastes reflect afar
Light from our Sun to some benighted Star!

PART I.

NIGHT after night I wakened with a start;
　　The coldness of a gravestone at my
　　　　heart;
　　As though I had been nearly caught by
　　　　Death
Who imaged Sleep to kiss away my breath!
The silence lookt so ominous, the gloom
Just losing shape and feature in the room.
Had I but wakened sooner, without doubt,
I should have found some dreadful secret ont.
Nothing to grapple with; nothing to see;
Yet something fearful there must somewhere be;
Grim shadows grew from out their hiding-nook;
A strange life lurked in the familiar look
Of innocent things, as though upon the eve
Of issuing, terrible as its prey perceive
The *Mantis* in the likeness of a leaf,
Changed in a moment to a Murderous Thief.
I peered out of the window, nothing there
But the vast heavens with all their loneness bare —
The phantom presence of Immensity
That from behind its dumb mask whispered me:

At times a noise, as though a dungeon door
Had grated, with set teeth, against the floor:
A ring of iron on the stones ; a sound
As if of granite into powder ground ;
A pickaxe and a spade at work ! sad sighs
As of a wave that sobs and faints and dies.
And then a shudder of the house ; a scrawl
As though a knife scored letters in the wall.
About the room a gush and gurgle went,
As if the water-pipe got sudden vent ;
Drop after drop, I heard it plop, and ping,
Into some vessel with metallic ring.
Yet, on these very nights there was no rain !
And then, betwixt the ear's suspense and strain,
A faint voice crying in the air or brain.

The wind would rise and wail most humanly
With a low scream of stifled agony
Over the birth of life about to be.
Through all the house its coldest wave hath rusht,
Although a moment since the night was husht.
And ere the hurried gust had ceased to moan,
The dreaming dog would answer with a groan.
On nights of wind and rain the sounds were worst ;
More live the portent the black midnight hearst.

At times I seemed to waken at a call
And rose up listening for the next footfall

Which never came, as though it could not keep
Tho step with that my spirit caught in sleep,
For I, in waking, must have crossed the line
Bounding the range of spirit-life from mine.
I felt tho Presence on that other side
Grope where some secret door might open wide.
I knew the brain might strike the electric spark
Which should make live this phantom of the Dark.
Once as I woke I could have sworn I saw
A white face from the window-pane withdraw!
But, softly in its place the curtain slid,
Even in the uplifting of the swift eyelid.

Sometimes I woke with lashes wet and bright
With a strange glory of delicious light,
As though an Angel had shone my shut eyes through
And filled my soul with heaven, as Dawn the dew:
A fragrance from afar with me would stay
And at my work my heart sang all next day.

I am no Coward; never could believe
That spirits do their hell or heaven leave
To walk by night in the old human ways.
For forty years this was my creed o' days.
Somehow the dark another tale doth tell:
We are so fearful of the Unfathomable!
The Infinite is full of whisperings;
With mortal tug the wildered spirit clings

To its known shore of firm reality,
Yet feels drawn outward — like the ebbing sea
That hugs its beach so closely and in vain —
In this vast ebb of Being to its main.

And it is eerie in the night to lie
Lonesome, all naked to the awful sky —
This secret spawning-time of hell on earth
When mist and midnight give the toad-stools birth,
And worlds of shy leaf-shadowed life steal forth, —
What time the Powers of Darkness have their day ;
Our world asleep and Heaven so far away :
When in the shroud-like stillness there may be
Shapes moving round us that we do not see !

Our little sphere of life is darkly rimmed
In the wide universe of Being brimmed
With life perhaps inimical to us !
Nor could we live if all were luminous.
But is it certain we have lost the sight
They had of old in watches of the night,
Who heard the voices, saw the shape that stood
Before them in God's own similitude ?
They saw with eyes of spirit — Heaven keep
The veil of flesh about me dark and deep !

What does the Darkness matter ?   Is it Death
That makes the light burn bluer with his breath ?

Was that a creaking of the stair? a Rat
Nibbling the wainscot? did a flittering Bat
Flap at the window?   Floors will crack for sure,
But may not unseen feet be on the floor?
Spirits stand rapping at Life's outer gate,
And, if we dare not open, will they wait?
Was that the Death-Watch ticking in the wall?
One's hair — alive — begins to coldly crawl.
Is there some Whispering-gallery of the ear,
In which the other world we overhear?
The very Mirror is a doorway, through
Whose dark another face may look at you!
It haunts you, gliding as the Moonbeams glide,
Like waters wan that counsel suicide.

Who knows with what those ghostly gleams are rife
In spectral semblance of our sunlit life?
What Night hath shielded from pursuing Day
In sanctuary darkness, hid away,
As Paramour of hers in some foul play?
What viewless horrors in the wind may lurk,
That fill the mind with Shadows eerie and murk;
Perhaps the Devil audibly at work?
Maybe the voices of a sunless world
That in the eclipse of night is doomward hurled:
What groping outcasts of ignoble soul
Are working through the darkness, like the mole,
Crouching in dreams to steal on sleeping Men.

Red-handed spirits that flung life back again
To Him who gave, and hide their murder-mark,
In any secret corner of the dark:
What phantom shapes forlorn may meet and march
In long procession under Night's dark arch,
Stretching their arms to us, worm-fretted, all
Hueless and featureless and weirdly tall:
What rootless strays of life are ever blown
About like floating ghosts of thistle-down
That seek a foothold and are whirled away:
Dead leaves a-dancing — vanishing sea-spray;
Night-wandering souls, without a house or shore,
That roam life's border-world forevermore
Homeless, as drifted clouds are driven past
Their heaven forever, by the hurrying blast.

And now we come to think, may we not hold
Ghost-hands in ours, that turn them icy cold?
A ghostly presence whitens in the cheek
And makes the blood run water, — wan and weak
The swooning life from out us faintly fleets,
And turns to drops at the chill touch it meets.
The walls of flesh are waxing all too thin
To keep the world of spirits from crowding in.
We wrap the clothes about us; but, still bare
In soul, we feel a wave of chillier air,
Like that which brings the dawn, but that's a breath
Of sweet new life, this hath an odor of death!

The spirit spiracles all open wide
And life seems drowning in the flooding tide;
We cannot cry, the Unseen world doth strive
To seal the mouth and bury the soul alive.
I must believe in Ghosts, lying awake
With them o' nights, when flesh will pimple and
      quake,
And lustily one pulls the Bell of Prayer,
From this thick snow of spirits to clear the air.

No marvel that the Birds salute the Dawn,
For all the dangers of the dark withdrawn;
Break into singing with their first free breath,
That they have swum the dim, vast sea of death,
And hymn the resurrection of the Light,
In praise to Him who kept them through the night
And cared for his least little feathered things,
Encompassed with the safety of His Wings;
While those, that cannot warble, twittering tell
Of darkness passed once more and all is well.

With what a thankful heart I 've often heard
The blessed cry of Morning's earliest Bird!
How eagerly watcht the weird and waning Night
Turn deathly pale and pass away in light.
Yet, I believe that God is master still.
He reigneth; He whose lightest breath could thrill
The universe of worlds like drops of dew,

And if the Spirit-world hath broken through
It cannot be unknown, unseen by Him;
It must be with His will, not their mere whim.
And if our world of breath be set aflood,
Swimming in supernatural neighborhood,
There is a soul within will not be drowned,
Even though a sea of spirits surges round :
An inner infinite with power to reach
The level of its outer ocean-beach !
Therefore I trust Him ; shut mine eyes and say
" Lead on, O Lord, Thou only know'st the way !
Father in Heaven, take my hand in Thine ;
Be at my heart, and in my countenance shine.
Then, all unfearing, shall I face the gate
At which the Powers of Darkness lie in wait."

PART II.

NCE on a time, the ancient story saith,
　　Some foolish Mummers danced a
　　　masque of Death.
　　They bore his emblems, trying, every
　　　one,
To out-parody the bony Skeleton;
And, as the merriment grew, there glided in
Grim Death Himself, mocking with ghastly grin
At their poor make-believe; as who should say
" This is the real thing and no mere play."

" Talk of the Devil," say we, " and he 's here,"
Sudden as thunder-claps, when skies are clear.

'T was thus all fears and phantoms of the past,
Shaped into something palpable at last.

One night, as I lay musing on my bed,
The veil was rent that shows the Dead not dead.

Upon a Picture I had fixed mine eyes,
Till slowly it began to magnetize.

So the Ecstatics on their symbol stare,
Until the Cross fades and the Christ is there!
Thus, while I mused upon the picture's face,
A veil of white mist wavered in its place;
And to a lulling motion I sank deep,
With spirit awake and senses all asleep,
Down through an air that palpitatingly
Breathed with a breath of life unknown to me ;
And when the motion ceased, against the gloom,
There lived another Form within the room,
Suddenly, strange and horrible, as rise
The Torturers that stare in dying eyes :
Or, as the Serpent — ere a leaf be stirred —
Looks through the dark on some bewildered bird :
A face in which the life had burned away
To cinders of the soul and ashes gray ·
The forehead furrowed with a sombre frown
That seemed the image, in shadow, of Death's
      crown ;
His look a map of misery that told
How all the under-world in blackness rolled.
A human face in hideous eclipse ;
No lustre in the hair, no life on lips ;
The faintest gleam of corpse-light, lurid, wan,
Showed me the lying likeness of a Man!
The old soiled lining of some mortal dress :
A Spirit sorely stained with earthiness.

But, almost ere I could have time to fear,
I saw what seemed an Angel standing near,
With face like His who wore the old thorn crown ;
In whose dear person very Love came down.
And on his face a smile for my relief:
A dream of glory in my night of grief,
Shedding an influent mildness through the awe,
Pleasant to feel, as was the smile I saw :
Indeed, methought he breathed a fragrance faint,
That overcame some rotting tomby taint.
He wore a purple vesture thin as mist,
The Breath of Dawn, upon the plum dew-kissed.
No flame-hued, flame-shaped, Golden-Holly tree
Ere kindled at the sun so splendidly
As that self-radiant head, with lifted hair
A-wave in many a fiery scimitar.
We think of Shades as native to the night;
We photograph the other world in white,
That will not paint its tints upon our sight. ·
But there are Colors of the Eternal Light,
And this was of them ; pulsing such live glows
As never, reddened blood or ripened rose :
No Mist from the past life as we have deemed
The Dead to be ; no pallid shadow dreamed
By Greeks of old, but Life itself this seemed.
And such a light was in the Angel's face
It made a glory round about the place
To see by : as you mark in the gold ray

The Motes that dance invisibly in the gray.
But, deep in shadow of his inner night,
The Dark Shape stood and sinned against the
        Light.

As men have felt, when earth rockt underfoot,
Their trust in it was wrencht up by the root;
The firm foundations of all things had given,
And any instant they might be in heaven :
As one midway across a wide, white road,
In winter, when all night the skies have snowed,
Learns 't is not earth but frozen stream beneath,
And he is leaning on the arms of Death :
So did I feel to find our earthy bound
Of Substance was no longer safe or sound;
That spirit-springs make quicksand of firm ground;
That spirit-hands withdraw our curtains round ;
That spirit between particles can pass
Surely and visibly, as light through glass ;
With power to come and go, stand upright, loom
Dense to the eye, outlined against the gloom.

The Dark Shape on me turned its eyes of guile,
Sullen yet fierce.   I read the wicked smile
That sneered — *" Behold the cause of all your fear !*
You need not shudder though while He is near."
And then he spoke, or seemed to speak, in words,
Although I saw his thoughts like murderous swords,

Or toothëd wheels, go whirling round within
The fearsome face so shadowy and thin,
And did not always need the speech to know
What dreadful thing it was he had to show.

" Lo ! I am one of those doomed souls who dwell
In Heaven's vast Shadow which the Good call Hell.
Lo ! I am he, the gloomy sneak, who did
The deed of darkness, fancying all was hid :
The Awful eyes being on me all the while,
And Devils pointing at me with their smile.
I carry such a hell within my breast,
That all about me throbs with my unrest,
As though the heavens were shaken, or the earth
Were overtaken in the throes of birth;
Doors tremble open, walls disintegrate,
And through the sense the soul keeps open gate !
With such a pulse of power my pangs awake
At midnight, that from sleep they sometimes shake
You !   Matter, with Mind's thrillings, doth so quake
That atoms from their fellow atoms start,
As though they felt the heave of some live heart."

Then seeing the questioning wonder in my look,
He answered, as my turn of thought he took.

" Yes, it is true, all true, the thing you dreamed ;
Most real is the life that only seemed.

Soul 's no mere shadow that gross substance throws ;
Our passions are not pageantary shows,
Exhaled from Matter, like the cloud from cape,
They are the life's own lasting final shape.
This scheme of things with all the sights you see,
Are only pictures of the things that be.
What you call Matter is but as the sheath,
Shaped, even as bubbles are, by spirit-breath.
The mountains are but firmer clouds of earth,
Still changing to the breath that gave them birth.
Spirit aye shapeth Matter into view,
As Music wears the forms it passes through.·
Spirit is lord of substance, Matter's sole
First cause and forming power and final goal."

And who is this, I asked, that in his face
Doth image humanly celestial grace ;
That calms my soul as when the Moon looks
      forth,
Whose smile in heaven makes stillness on the
      earth ?

" One of those Ministers who are sent below
To walk the earth, patrolling to and fro,
As sentinels on guard, night after night.
That in the darkness make a watch-fire light,
Lest sleeping souls be helplessly surprised
By mad wild beasts of worlds not realized."

I lookt, the shining face serenely smiled
Away all terror like a thing beguiled.

" One of the dreadful Angels of the Lord,
Who are his fiery-flaming two-edged sword,
That at each door and window waves and burns
Until the Angel of the Dawn returns.
They are with you, watching through the murkest hour,
And seen, or unseen, hold us in their power,
That when the devil rages in us, lo !
We strike and strike and yet there falls no blow.
They mesmerize us standing there behind,
And, as in dreams, we struggle bound and blind.
The sharpest tortures that I have to bear
Are when I feel His presence hovering near.
A ray from heaven turns to a sword in hell;
The flash is maddening, we so darkly dwell !
The heat of heaven is like the blazing ring
Of fire that makes the Scorpion try to sting
Itself to death ; an air of Heaven's breath
Is poison ; hell is spiritual death :
And this awakes us, with its stir and strife,
Like tinglings of the drowned recalled to life."

I glanced again : I saw the look arise
As of a drawn Sword in the Angel's eyes.

"We have met here for years.   He comes to see
Me digging nightly ; grope for my lost key ;

Gives me his countenance, and but for him
I might work hidden in the shadows dim.
His presence kindles round me such a light,
All heaven can see me prowling through the night;
All hell make merry at the grewsome sight.

" I never told my secret in your world
I kept it at the heart too closely curled;
There, at my life-springs, did I nestle and nurse
The hidden snake, my bosom's clinging curse,
My worm of torment biting bitterly,
And fed it fat for all eternity.
And no eye saw it writhe in my white face,
Or heard it hiss in its dark hiding-place,
When any voice of secret murders told,
And in its might it wantoned and grew bold.
It gnawed my heart as with hell-fire for years.
Drink would not drown it, nor a sea of tears
Quench it, nor all the waters of the land   ·
Whiten my soul, or wash my red right hand!
Whate'er I did my heart with hell-fire burned;
Mine eyes with redness swam where'er I turned.
I dared not slumber soundly, lest asleep
The unsleeping secret from my lips should leap
In dreams, and I on waking might have found
Myself had turned Informer, and was bound
In handcuffs, with the accusing faces round.

" And so, at last, I pricked the bubble of breath,
I plunged to hide me from Myself in death :
I found the hell-hole in the wild whirlpool ;
Plucked the cold hand down on my brain to cool ;
I grovelled out my own deep grave ; I fell
Right through it, into open arms of hell.

" I fancied, when I took the headlong leap,
That death must be an everlasting sleep ;
And the white Winding-sheet and green sod might
Shut out the world, and I have done with sight.
Cold water from my hand had washt the warm
And crimson carnage ; safe the little form
Lay underground : the tiny trembling waif
Of life hid from the light ; my secret safe.
In vain.   You cannot hide a deed like this,
With all the heavens a cloud of witnesses :
Useless to blot the blood out with the dust,
When it hath eaten with its ruddy rust
Into your spirit's hand, where, visibly
The murder-stain leers through eternity !
Look there."

I lookt and saw what seemed a hand
Of blood-stained shadow, kindling like a brand
When breathed on ! it so brightened as he sighed ;
Plucking it from his breast where he did hide
Its guilty red.

" That hand once gripped the knife

That slew my child.   This is its ruddy life,
Red-hot; on fire of hell !   In burning rings,
The blood my fingers clutcht, forever clings,
And clamps them with relentless ache and smart
So closely that they will not pull apart.
Once only, while I wept and almost prayed,
They yielded just a little: then was played
A trick of Demons on me ; all between,
They shone, thin-webbed with gore, and clearly seen
As through a window, through the web, there smiled
Up in my face the face of my dead child.
Better to bear this fiery grip of pain,
Than they should open on that sight again.

" The whirling world had flung my life from it.
And I felt falling through the Infinite,
For weeks and months, and years on years of nights
Innumerable, from stupendous heights ;
For, as a minute's slumber may be all
As one with that of a million years, my fall
So quickened being, that a minute's fears
Made instantaneous a million years.
No God to call upon, no power to stay,
No hand to clutch at on my endless way !
When just as I was plunging in a cloud
That lightened with the laugh of Hell and showed
It made of devilish faces which grew glad
And kindled at my coming, and all had

A gap-toothed wicked grin, as though each one
Saw in my face the kindred of his own, —
All the dark host rejoicing as I came ;
All making sure as Marksman of his aim,
When lo ! a Hawk swoops from its height unheard,
And from before his gun bears off his Bird !
So, while their claws for cruel welcome spread,
I was caught up ; borne swiftening overhead,
By one on wings of light, with lightning shod,
And then I knew that I was going to God ;
That life but sets in life still more profound,
As sunset into sunrise the world round ;
That all who enter by the gate of breath,
Must pass before the Awful eyes in death,
And stand all naked to the searching mien.
I could not shrivel away nor slink unseen !

" To me the vast and horrible Unknown
Was one dread face and all the face one frown !
Pain, sternness, pity eternal in a look
That read my life, wide-open as a book.
Not that the leaves turned over one by one
Revealing, page by page, all I had done, —
The Sense is as a scroll where manifold
Indelible things are day by day uprolled
And treasuried for the Memory to recall ;
Maps of the mental world hung on the wall :
But Life is more than Letter or than Law,

And deftly as the brain may take or draw
Its daily tallies, never can it keep
In fixĕd figure all the fathomless Deep
Of Consciousness conceals, whose restless sea
Ripples on changing sands unceasingly.
Spirit is one.   It is the crystal book,
Clear through and through : read at a single look.
To all the thoughts that ever passed through us
In life, in death we grow diaphanous.
We do not think what we have been, we ARE
Past, present, future, without near or far.
A glimpse of this is lightened, when the blind
Is raised, in drowning, from the seeing Mind!
So the electric flash, thrown on the wheel
Revolving swift in darkness, will reveal
Each whirling spoke distinct as standing still.
In spirit-world at once you find the whole
Of life contemporary with the soul.

" There is strange writing of the somewhile guest
Featured upon the form it leaves at rest,
Which men in some dim-wise may read, but here
Is the live Chronicler himself! the clear
Truth naked — brain and body were but dress —
Quickened by the Eternal consciousness.

" So, when before that face, I felt the frown,
There was no need of hell to drag me down,

*I could have welcomed wafts of burning flame
To clothe my nakedness of deadly shame.
I lifted to my brow one shading hand,
But snatched it burning from the Murderer's brand.
The other to mine eyes I pressed; 't was red
And wet and dropping with the blood I shed.
I tried to cover up my aching sight
And found myself all eye to pitiless light.*

*" In olden times, it was the wont, they say,
To bring the Murderer where his victim lay,
And at his touch, as to his slaying knife,
The wound would flush: Death speak with lips of
      Life.*

*" So, from the frown, a golden-headed Child
Lookt out on me and innocently smiled !*

*" I shrieked my guiltiness at sight of it,
And downward plunged, for hiding in the Pit.
' Curse God and die,' the Devil said of old.
I curse, and back the curses crowd tenfold.
Against the cold Heaven strikes my burning breath,
To fall in drops of wrath, far worse than death.
And still I curse and still I cannot die ;
And still I watch for Death with pleading eye,
To find that he will nevermore draw nigh !
Would that the Mighty One had spit on me
And wiped the blot from his eternity !*

PART III.

Y Temptress lives on still.

She is a Wife

And Mother; lives an unsuspected life.
She hath grown fat and flourished on the ill,
The poison, that should naturally kill.
That cruel stain of Murder seemed to pass
From off her face of life as breath from glass.
I sometimes play the devil in her dream
And plague her with a glimpse, one lurid gleam
Of all my torment; her thick veil I tear
And lay the unholy of unholies bare,
Else were her heart untroubled, deaf and blind.
With her things out of sight are out of mind,
And should she hear a voice from the Unknown
She takes it for an echo of her own.

" Ah, Mistress, did you know we have to stand
Together yet, as equals, hand in hand,
Like Eve and Adam, shivering side by side,
Where not a leaf our nakedness can hide;
Our secret blazoned, as a flag unfurled
High on the housetops of another world!

" *She was a buxom beauty!   In her way*
Imperious as the Thane's Wife in the Play.
A woman who upon the outside smiled,
Burnished like beetles, inwardly defiled;
With hair that like a thunder-cloud, black-brightening,
Caught the sunlight and flasht it back in lightning.
The Devil never toyed with worthier folds,
About a comelier throat, to strangle souls;
A face that dazzled you with life's white-heat,
Devouring, as it drew you off your feet,
With eyes that set the Beast o' the blood astir,
Leaping in heart and brain, alive for her;
Melted the sword of soul within its sheath:
The knee-joints loosened, smitten by her breath
Until you bowed, as the strong beast boweth,
When taken captive by the dark of death:
Lithe, amorous lips, cruel in curve and hue,
Which, greedy as the grave, my kisses drew
With hers, that to my mouth like live things clung
Long after, and in memory fiercely stung:
A dainty morsel of the Devil's meat
To roll beneath my tongue, as poison sweet!
Had not the Mother ate forbidden food,
This was the Daughter among Women that would.

" *But what avails to cast on her the blame?*
I will not: Will not name her by her name.
The deed is done; the sin is sinned; the brand
Is on my brow; the blood burns on my hand.

" I must have been a beast myself from birth.
We lived as Beasts in that old burrow of earth
They called a House; the Cot where I was born;
One of those dwellings Poets will adorn
Outside with Honeysuckle and climbing Rose,
But where, within, no flower of Heaven blows
With sweetening breath, for want of air and light,
And in the wild weeds crawl the things of night :
Where any life-warmth quickens the dark slime
Of hovelled sin to swarm in shame and crime.

" My pastoral home was one wherein are grown
Boys for the Hulks; girls for the pitiless Town
That 'flaunts beneath the gaslights on the highway,
The full-blown flowers of many a filthy byway !
Where Virtue had no safeguard, Vice no veil;
The Devil sowed his seed, never to fail —
With such a soil — in growing harvest meet
For him, as sure as corn is grown to eat.

" I should have been the beast that Nature binds
To beaten ways and with her blinkers blinds.
But, was a Beast with scope to work all ill ;
Treat Wife and dumb things cruelly — sin — kill
And go to Hell by freedom of the will.
And yet I knew not — such the curse of sin ! —
Until the fall came, what was ripe within ;
What demon I had nurst past suckling-time,
To find that he could go alone in crime.

" She came to me, her great black eyes aglare
Like stars of bale, yet with the hunted stare
Of wild things ; such as made me stare to see
What danger followed her and threatened me.
I knew that Nemesis was drawing near,
And in the beating of my heart could hear
The hovering wings that bow strong men with fear.

" ' What is it ? ' I asked.   What need for her to tell ?
'T was writ all over her.   I knew too well.
And still I stared beyond, as if that way
The blackness rose that blotted out the day.
For days, and weeks, and months, her secret lay
Safe-nestled, unsuspected by her friends.
But one day all disguise in sinning ends,
And every wayside hiding-place is past.
She had to leave her home and fly at last —
Mad with the misery of a Mother's pain,
She ran to me, through fire, and hail, and rain,
And mire below, and thunder overhead ;
Ran lightning-dazed, and drencht, till nearly dead.

" Well I remember that LAST DAY.   I see
It lightning-lit.   I feel it stamped in me,
As with the black seal of Eternity.
It was about mid-spring, when suddenly
The rear of beaten winter turned in ire,
And there was battle fierce of Frost and Fire.

The Birds stopped singing; all the golden flame
O' the Sun went out; the Cattle homeward came
With a forerunning shiver rusht the breeze,
And, in the Woods, the husht and listening trees
That had been standing deathly-dark and still,
Wind-whitened sprang, with every leaf athrill.
I watched the anguisht clouds go hurrying by,
Rackt with the rending spirit of prophecy:
Like Pythonesses in the pangs, they tost
And writhed in shadowy semblance of the Lost:
They met, they darted death, they reared, they roared,
And down the torrent of the tempest poured!
Through heaven's windows the blue lightnings gleamed,
And like a fractured pane the sky was seamed:
Hailstones made winter on the whitened ground,
And for two hours the thunder warrayed round.
And then I heard the Thrush begin again,
With his more liquid warble after rain.

" Tearing through all the fearful storm she came:
Worse storm within, and in her eyes hell-flame
Had broken loose to kindle, past control,
In huge dare-devilry of reckless soul.
As springs a Madman, dancing upon deck,
Who hath fired the Ship, and glories in the wreck;
As at a Prison-window one may stand
Who fired the house, and waves the lighted brand,
Her spirit sprang at me.   Her looks were wild.

She had come to me, she said, to bring the child,
For no one had a greater right to it!
This was God's truth, not merely meant for wit.
She swore that she had come there and would stay
Till it was born, and safely put away.
And even while I cursed her pangs grew worse,
And stopped me with an everlasting curse.

" 'Good God! this is too bad,' I thought; and laught
A laugh as bitter as the cup I quaft.
I had been married just a month! my Wife
Knew nothing of this dead love come to life.
As Fate would have it, she had gone from home:
I knew that any hour she might have come.
With desperate voice the woman made me writhe,
Harsh as the whetstone on the Mower's scythe
She rasped me all on edge; the hell-sparks flew,
Till there seemed nothing that I dared not do.
'Kill it, you Coward! Why not kill us both?'
She taunted me; and I felt little loath.
The Devil whispered, ' Why not kill them both?'
I said I would, and clenched it with an oath."

Now, while he spake, there came a frightful change
Upon him with transfiguration strange,
And slowly he assumed his mortal dress
With a last look of dying consciousness:
The eyes turned stony in a sightless stare,

And of all presence he grew unaware :
Clouded and lost within his dreadful dream
He went; a Man once more, each pore a stream
Of inner agony ; his body shook,
And from his mazèd face did " MURDER " look.
It was as when in dreams you see a dumb
Mouth shaped to cry it, though no sound will
      come.
While in his hand he grasped a gleaming knife,
So keen, you saw it thirst for a drink of life !
And, as he passed into his haunted gloom,
His dreadful purpose drew him from the room.

So terrible the scene, I should have cried
For help in the death-eddies, — must have died
But for the strong calm Spirit at my side,
Who took me by the hand and turned on mine
His cordial face with comfortable shine.
And then the darkness gave a sudden sigh,
And a wind rose that went lamenting by.
" *Listen,*" he said.   I leaned, all ear, to hark ;
I felt the quake of footsteps through the dark,
Heavily hurrying down a distant stair,
And caught a piteous wail faint on the air.
The Dog howled his lone cry, as he would fain
Give warning, knowing it was all in vain.
Then came the liquid gurgle and the ring
Metallic, with the heavy plop and ping,

Heavier than largest water-drops that fall
From melting icicles on house-eaves tall.
I knew them now; this resurrection night
Sounds were translated into things of sight.
These were the innocent drops a father shed.
They had the weight of blood, fell heavy as lead.
And now again I felt the griding sound
O' the grating door; the digging underground;
The shudders of the house; the sighs and moans;
The ring of iron dropped upon the stones;
The cloudy presence groping near; the quake
Of walls that vibrate with the parting shake;
Then the relief.   As they who stoop with dread,
While the Simoom goes withering overhead
Like iron red-hot, look up and breathe at last,
So felt I when that thing of Night had passed

'T is but a dream, methought, and I shall wake
Erelong and from its dread embraces break.
And if I could but only wake, I knew
By light of day these things could not be true!
How many a dream before had wraith-like gone
To nothing at the sceptic smile of Dawn.
And still I could not wake, nor wake my Wife;
And still the dream went on, and like as life
There stood the Angel in it; overshone
The well-known room.
                    And then the voice went on.

" The nether world hath opened at your feet,
And you have seen ascending from the Pit
The torment-smoke, where furnace-fires of Crime
Have crackt the crust of this your world of Time.

" It was an awful hour of storm and rain
And starless gloom in which the Child was slain.
Wild, windily the Night went roaring by,
As if loud seas broke in the woodlands nigh,
Or all the blasts of Heaven at once were hurled
To stop the onward rolling of the world.
The firmament was all one flash, and red
The lightning laught, as Hell were overhead.

" He had dug his grave amid this war of storm.
He bore the murdered Babe upon his arm
For burial, where no eye should ever mark.
Just then Heaven opened at him with the bark
Of all the Hell-hounds loosed.   And in the dark
Out went the light, and down he dropt the key,
That was to lead to safety secretly.
He was alone with Death, and paces three
Beyond the door an open grave gaped, free
For all the daylight world to come and see ;
And he was fastened.
     Like the luckless wight
Who wagered he would enter a Vault at night
In some old Graveyard, and, in proof he did,

Would leave his dagger stuck in a Coffin-lid. —
He ventured: bravely dashed the weapon down
And turned to triumph, when, by the student gown
He was held fast, as if the living tomb
Had closed upon him; clutched him in the gloom.
He had pinned his long robe to the coffin!   Fright
Came on him like a snow-fall!   Weirdly-white
His hair turned, and the youth was a forlorn,
Old, gray-faced, gibbering Idiot next morn.

" The Murderer did not madden thus, but he
Was stamped that moment for Eternity.
He stooped with his dead child, he groped and found
The key, and got the corse safe underground,
And out of sight had hid his murder-hole,
Ere Dawn looked ghostly on his guilty soul,
And on his hands no man could see the stain
His madness went beyond the burning brain;
His was the frenzy of a soul insane.

" The hour came when he lost the key again.
As the death-rattles thundered in his throat,
And earth was rushing past his soul afloat,
And pain had fiercely throbbed itself to rest,
And Time stopped ticking in the brain and breast,
It gleamed and vanisht from his fading sight,
While cracked his eye-strings straining through the night.
Thenceforth it was his hottest hell to be

Living the moment when he lost that key:
Hell that is permanent insanity !

" There was a man who died ages ago,
And 't is his madness still to wile his woe
At work forever, perfecting the plan
That should have, must have shown his fellow-man
How innocent he was of that old crime
He died for justly — had he thought in time.

" Even so this lost soul whirls and eddies round
The grave-place where the lost key must be found,
If the mad motion would a moment cease
And he could only get a moment's peace;
He often sees it, but he cannot touch
It; like a live thing it eludes his clutch —
Gone like that glitter from the eyes of Death
In the black river at night that slides beneath
The Bridges, tempting souls of Suicides
To find the promised rest it surely hides.

" For seven years it was his curse to come
At midnight and fulfil his dreadful doom,
Looking for that lost key, lest it revealed
The secret he so cunningly concealed;
Feeling at times he could endure his hell
If in one world of torment he might dwell.
And still from world to world he had to go

(*A rootless weed the wave swings to and fro !*)
Wandering with incommunicable woe ;
Well-knowing that, for every moment lost,
His soul would be in treble anguish tost,
While every storm of wind and rain would beat
Upon him, kindle hell to tenfold heat,
And make him hurry to your upper air,
Lest it should wash and blow the bones all bare.
For often will a wind of God arise
At midnight, and the voice of Murder cries
From it, and bones of murdered babes are found ;
Earth will no longer be their burial ground.
And so on stormy nights his pangs are worst :
More dread the gnashings of that soul accurst.

" For seven years he came, unseen, unheard.
'T was but the other day the bones were stirred,
As men were delving heedless underground.
They broke in on them, scattered them around :
Not guessing they were human.
      Lower in hell
His spirit sank, like waters in a well
Before there springs the Earthquake. Tremblings sore
Shook him with vengeance never felt before.
He came ; he found the murder had leaped out ;
The grave was burst ; the bones were strewn about
For all the world to find !
      It mattered not

To him that no one knew them; they might rot
To undistinguishable dust in peace;
That Death had signed his order of release
From this world's law, Death had no shadows dim
Enough to hide the blacker truth from him.
He was the Murderer still, who had to hide
The proofs of murder on the human side!
The Child was his; these were its tender bones,
Blown with the dust and dasht against the stones.
And all his care, his self-enfolded pain
And midnight watchings lone, were all in vain.

" The worms that in the dead flesh riot and roll
Are poor faint types of those that gnawed his soul!
Forever beaten now; though he should find
And grasp the key he lost when he went blind
In death: in vain he mounts upon a wind
Of hell and tries to fan the dry dust over them
With endless toil; no sooner doth he cover them
Than there 's an ominous muttering in the air,
And in an instant all the bones lie bare;
While lurking devils grin through masks at him,
In likeness of his Child's head, gorily grim!

" It comes upon him, almost with a gleam
Of comfort, when he 's rapt into the Dream
You saw him change in, and he passes through
His night of murder; lives it all anew,

So vividly each sound is heard by you ;
Each particle of Matter set afloat
Upon a Mind-wave, tossing like a boat
The Spirit rides.
                    For, as, upon his brain,
The sounds one midnight smote in a ruddy rain,
Till sense had dyed the spirit with their stain,
And Memory was branded deep as Cain,
So now his spirit echoes back again
The fixed ideas of a soul insane,
Till Matter taking impress of his pain,
Reverberates the sounds within your brain."

PART IV.

MUSED and mused in great astonish-
ment,
While on, and on, the growing wonder
went
Within, without, on wings that widelier spread
"*How many things,*" oft to myself I had said,
"*I have to ask, if one came from the dead.*"
And now I had my wish.   My thought could rise
No fleeter than the answer filled his eyes
And flasht electric utterance with tho whole
Illumined figure of a living soul !
And, ere I shaped my question, what was dim
And dumb in me shone clear as light in him.

"*More Laws than Gravitation keep us down
To the old place from whence the soul had flown.
Not every one in death can get adrift
Freely for life.   Some have no wings to lift
Their weary weight: the body of their sin
Which they so evilly have labored in.
Others will touch as 't were the window sill*

To flutter back upon the ground-floor still.
Others yet grovel like the beast belogged
In the old ways, to which they are self-clogged.
Just as the spirits of an earlier race
Of Man in dwarfhood, kept their dwelling-place
On earth and, revelling in the moon's pale rays,
Were seen as Wee Folk in old wondering days.

" A-many wander this side of the grave
To get the last glimpse they can ever have
Of those they loved, who will be lost in light,
While they go darkling and are lost in night.
They see them sometimes in the world of breath ;
They part forever at the second death.
Others would blot from out the book of Time
The published proofs of their long-secret crime
That glare so guiltily to spirit sight.
Teachers who called Good evil ; darkness light ;
Who see more clearly in the unclouding day,
Strive to recall the souls they led astray,
And find the world, that once hung on their breath,
Goes by them now, heedless and deaf as Death.
Some, who have done a wrong that, unperceived,
Ran to a sea of sin, are sorely grieved,
And ready to spend a lifetime shut from bliss,
Might they but right the wrong they did in this :
So clear, so awful, when the past is seen,
Grows the dark mystery of might-have-been.

" You know the Mill upon the windy hill,
That stands all day so desolate and still;
A weary, dreary, dark, deserted Mill,
Whose loneliness doth all the horizon fill,
With outspread arms appealing to the sky
And one dim window like a blinded eye?
I see those long arms tossing through the night,
While from the window gleams unearthly light
And furtive forms will dimly flit before,
With feet that stir no dust upon the floor.
These are the Ghosts of those who robbed the Poor
In old dead years !   And now, by window and door,
We catch their faces, wearing such a look
Of prayer as Men have when a ship has struck.
But no one comes to take his own again, .
And there is none to ease them of their pain.
Repentance woke so late, their toil is vain.
Night after night upon the haunted hill
In that old desolate, doom-stricken Mill.

" This happened beneath the broad shining day,
Right in the rush of life that makes its way
Through London streets.
                          Slowly, 'mid that swift throng,
A thoughtful man went mooningly along;
More lonely in that wilderness of men.
And at a corner where the Devil's den
Is palace-fronted now — all gilt and glass —

Illuminating nightly all who pass
By the broad way to hell with gin and gas,
And souls are sloughed, like city sewage, down
Dead-seaward, through the sink-holes of the town.
He heard a pitiful voice that took strange hold
Of him; ran through his blood in lightnings cold;
Mournful, remote, and hollow, as if the tomb
Had buried a live spirit in its gloom,
Monotonously sounding on below
A vast unutterable weight of woe;
A voice that its own speaker would not know!
As if unbreathing life were doomed to bear
Shut down on it the load of all the air.
He stopped.
        A woman clothed in rags he saw
With fixed beseeching eyes begin to draw
Him to her; left no power to say them nay.
With one stretcht arm she begged; on the other lay,
Soft in a snow of gold, a Cherub Child!
So have you seen a Glowworm on the wild
Bleak moorland; all the dusk a moment smiled.

" For the babe's sake he thrust a coin of gold
Into her hand! but, it fell through, and rolled
Ringing along the stones: he followed, found
It, brought it back and lookt around:
There was no woman waiting with her hand
Outstretcht, no Child, where he had seen them stand.

In vain he searched each by-way round about;
Through life even, never made the mystery out.

" The truth is, he was one of those who see
At times side-glimpses of eternity.
The Beggar was a Spirit, doomed to plead
With hurrying wayfarers, who took no heed,
But passed her by, indifferent as the dead,
Till one should hear her voice and turn the head;
Doomed to stand there and beg for bread, in tears,
To feed her child that had been dead for years!
This was the very spot where she had spent
Its life for drink, and this the punishment;
Feeling she had let it slip into the grave,
And now would give eternal life to save:
Heartless and deaf and blind the world went by,
Until this Dreamer came, with seeing eye;
The good Samaritan of souls had given
And wrought the change that was to her as Heaven.

" It is not Crime alone brings Spirits back
To pull beside you in the wonted track.
Shadows of mortal care will cloud the brow
That should have shone as clear as sunlit snow:
And those who hindered here must help you now.
Not always can the soul forgive in heaven
Itself for deeds that God hath long forgiven.

" A wedded couple, bedded, snug as birds
In nested peace, one night must needs have words
Of strife before they slept.   A foolish thing
Had on a sudden set them bickering ;
Some wild-fire wisp had dropt a subtle spark
That kindled at a breath blown through the dark,
And all their passion burst in tongues of flame :
Their anger blinding each to personal blame.
She had been pillowed on his beating heart,
And in an instant they had sprung apart !
The arm that wound about her he withdrew,
And Night, with dark divorce, came 'twixt the two.

" A little thing had plucked them palm from palm ;
A little thing had broke their happy calm ;
A little thing fall'n in the pleasant path
Of their life-stream, that turned to bubbling wrath !
And little might have made them yield and cling
Repentant ; yea, a very little thing.
A touch would have sufficed to make the stream
Flow free once more ; dream out its happy dream.
A kiss have fused them into one again,
And saved them many a year of piteous pain.
'T was such a little thing they had to do ;
Both yearned to make it up, and this both knew.
If one could but have said ' Good night,' scared Love
Would have come down to brood like Holy Dove.
And, being done, all would have been so well.

Not being done, it left the rift for Hell
To break through, and another triumph win.
Ever the worst of Traitors are within.
But neither spoke, though long upon the wing
Love waited lingeringly listening !

" Waking, he heard her in her slumbers weep,
And then he slept, and in the guise of Sleep
Death came for him, nor gave him time to say
' Good night,' ' Good by,' and at his side she lay
A Widow !   And upon that dark no day
Hath broke for her.   For him, nor hell nor heaven
Will open; praying still to be forgiven,
Night after night at her bedside he stands,
Wringing his soul as one may wring the hands ;
By natural law of grievëd love ; not sent
In vengeance and unnatural punishment.

" The unslain shadows of the Martyrs slain,
Rise on their fields of old heart-ache and pain,
To fight their battle over and over again.
Half-buried hands, still thrust up through the sod,
From fields of carnage, prayerfully to God,
Will grasp the weapons of immortal war.
Freed spirits make their conquering battle-car
Of human hearts : they did but hold their breath
To smite unheard in their dark cloud of death.
They work for Freedom still, though out of sight ;

They are torch-bearers in your mortal night.
The Tyrants may destroy the body; drench
The life out with the blood, but cannot quench
The spirit, nor put out the lofty light
O' the stars that in their courses 'gainst them fight!

"Wide as the wings of Sleep by night are spread,
Are Freedom's Exiles scattered, and her dead .
Have lain their bodies down 'neath God's great dome.
But every banisht spirit hurries home,
Soon as the free, long-fettered life upsprings
Awave one day on mighty warrior-wings.
Each soul, let out, fights with the strength of seven,
Under God's shield, and on the side of heaven.

"The secret meaning of the marvels told .
Of wars in heaven and visions seen of old, —
When, with a fiery cloud of witnesses,
The other world made its dumb-show to this
And drew vast plans of battle on the air,
Alive with death and lit with vengeful glare, —
Was, that the heavens on their huge scroll unfurled
The imagery of war in spirit world;
Reflecting, on the ceiling of the night,
The shadowy forms embattled beyond sight.

The other world is not cut off from this:
Forgetfulness is not the gate of bliss.

At times the buried dead within you rise
To look out on their old world through your eyes;
They touch you with the waving of their wing,
Lightly as airs of heaven the Æolian string.
At times as Comforters above you stoop,
To lift the burden from you when ye droop!
As parents on their little ones may peep
Ere going to rest, they bend to bless your sleep.
With fruit from our Lord's Garden dear ones come
To bring ye a foretaste; try to lure you home.

"With clap o' the shoulder, friends behind you steal
The old glad way, though ye no longer feel:
They watch you as ye watch the darkened mind
Of some arrested spirit; try to unwind
A way to it; with drops of pity melt
The clod about it; have their fondness felt!
Even as ye turn your thoughts to them above,
Do they return to you; look back for love.

" They left you standing still at gaze upon
The cloud they entered, where the light last shone.
And while the wet eyes watch, and wait, and yearn,
As if by that same way they might return,
And through the dark ye stretch the ungrasped hand,
There, at some window of the soul, they stand
All whitely clothed with immortality;
Closer to you than flesh and blood can be.

" *Old loves are with you in your dreams; but fear*
Lest they should make their presence felt too near;
The face of Love in Heaven they dare not show;
For with its glory they might set aglow
Your earthly love, which leaps to embrace a bliss
That lives and dies in a consuming kiss.
So warm Laodamïa wooed her dead
Dear Husband's Shade, as if they were new wed!

" *And certain spirits are perplexed to find*
How like their life to that they left behind
In natural nearness to their darlings here,
Who lose them just because they are so near
In life that grows impenetrably dear!

" *Many that tossed together on the sea,*
And parted in the storm; lost utterly,
Find they were only wreckt to meet again,
Safe on the same shore, after all the pain.
God hath so many ways by which we come
To Him; through many a door He draws us Home.

" *Others are horribly startled at the change*
Revealed in death, all is so ghastly strange!
So many Masters in the realms of breath
Serve at the feet of those who are crowned in death.
So many weeds, your blind world flung aside,
Are gathered up as flowers, thrice glorified.

4

The Invisible dawns!   The sleepers wake to find
Less death in dying than in living blind:
And now the eyes their earthy scales let fall,
They see that they have never lived at all.

" I 've known a follower of the strictest faith,
Whose dead religion rested on a death,
And frequent praying in the market-place,
With proclamation of his private grace;
Who sat among the loftiest Self-Elect,
But had not learned through life to walk erect —
Strait-waistcoated in stony pieties —
And when Death came — the Iconoclast who frees —
He could not stand without their rigid stay.
The Maker's image had but stamped the clay.
On earth he wore the mask of Man awhile,
But when the Searchers, with their slow, calm smile,
Had stripped him, the soul shrank from man's disguise:
It fled, and fell, and wriggled, reptile-wise.

" I 've seen the foolish slaves of luxury,
Who loll at ease and live deliciously;
In Pleasure's poppy-garden drowse and press
With amorous arms my Lady Idleness;
Who, floating downward in voluptuous dream,
Just lean to catch the sparkles from Life's stream
That runs with Siren-sound and dizzying dance,
And hides its wrecks with winking radiance, —

Who, risen from life's feast, came reeling thence
Immortals, drunken with the fumes of Sense;
I 've seen them in a pleasure-seeking group,
At Death's low door with mock politeness stoop,
And wantonly they went, nodding the head,
As though to lightsome music they were led:
Heedless the merry madcaps came before
The awful gate, as 't were a Playhouse door.
It opened, and the darlings entered in
As to the secret Paradise of Sin!
But in a moment what a change there was.
In front of them there rose a mocking glass
In place of drop-scene — this was not a Play —
In which they stared, and could not turn away,
But still stared on, in silence one and all,
To see their finery fade, their feathers fall;
In which grim moulting of the plumes of pride
They had to lay all ornaments aside;
And on the face of every Woman and Man,
Like wet paint on a mask, the colors ran;
The skin grew writhled, and within the head
Their eyes lookt like gray ghosts of hopes long dead.

" The naked image of their own selves they see,
Stripped in the mirror of eternity;
Worm-eaten through and through with thoughts that prey
On life itself and rot the soul away.
Wine-cups await them; though well kept for years

The wine, it had been made of human tears,
And tasted bitter!   Fruit was given to eat,
The fruit of their own life; so smiling-sweet
It lookt! like Apples when the shining round
Is made of rose-leaf on a golden ground;
The crimson and the golden melting through,
Right to the core, in one delicious hue.
But these were Apples of the Dead-Sea shore;
Ashes without, and maggots at the core.
Saluting their fine nostrils Odors rise;
The scent of lifelong human sacrifice!
The brother's blood, that climbs to them and cries.
Then are they led where healing waters wait
To wash the soilëd soul; repristinate
The image of God so earthily concealed;
But while they lave find, more and more revealed,
Deeper disfigurement and deadlier stain,
As wetted marble shows the darker grain.

PART V.

HE dim world of the dead is all alive;
All busy as the bees in summer hive;
More living than of old; a life so deep,
To you its swifter motion looks like sleep.
Whether in bliss they breathe, in bale they burn,
His own eternal living each must earn.
We suck no honey-comb in drowsy peace,
Because ennobling natural cares all cease;
We live no life, as many dream, caressed
By some vast lazy sea of endless rest —
For there, as here, unbusy is unblest.

" Man is the wrestling-place of Heaven and Hell,
Where, foot to foot, Angel and Devil dwell,
With both attractions drawing him.   This gives
The perfect poise in which his freedom lives.
No one so near to heaven to lack for scope;
No one so near to hell to lose all hope.
Whichever way he wills, to left or right,
Lets in a flood of supernatural might.
He flames out hellward, and all hell is free,
Rejoicing in the gust of liberty,

To rush in on him, work its devilry!
In strength of faith, or feebleness of fear,
He bows and bends the highest heavens near.
The brightness upon Prayer's uplifted face
Reflects some spirit-presence in the place.

" Each impure nature hath its parasites,
That live and revel in unclean delights.
Like moths around a flame they swim and swarm,
Or flies about a horse, that ride the warm
And reeking air which is their atmosphere,
Their breath of life, the ranker the more dear.
They glory in the grossness of the blood,
For, reptile-like, they lay their eggs in mud.
In every darksome corner of the mind
They hang their webs, the wingèd life to bind;
Weaving the shadow of the Evil One
To darken 'twixt the spirit and its sun.

" If those blind Unbelievers did but know
Through what a perilous Unknown they go
By night and day; what furtive eyes do mark
Them fiercely from their ambush of the dark;
What motes of spirit dance in every beam;
What grim realities mix with their dream;
What serpents try to pull down fallen souls,
As earth-worms drag the dead leaves through their holes
What cunning sowers drop the seed by night

That flames to fatal flower in broad daylight ;
What foul birds drop their eggs in innocent nests,
To win their heat from warmth of innocent breasts :
What snaky thieves o'ermount each garden wall ;
On life's fresh leaves what caterpillars crawl ;
What cool green pleasaunces and brooding bowers
Are set with soul-traps hid among the flowers ;
What Tempters in the Chamber of Sleep will break,
And with insidious whisperings keep awake
The Soul !   How, toad-like, at the ear will lurk
The cunning Satan, wickedly at work :
What evil spirits hover in amorous hate
Round him who nibbles at the devil's bait,
Or him who dallies, fingering the sharp edge
Of peril, or sits with feet over the ledge,
By some dark water, with his face ash-wan,
Until they urge him over ; a doomed Man !
What cruel demons try to break a way,
Through weak brains, back to the lost world of day,
And from some little rift in nature yawns
A black abysm of madness, and Hell dawns :
What starvelings seek to drink Corruption's breath
From rosy life, more rich than rot of death ;
What ghosts of drinkers old would quench their drouth
At the wine-bibber's dreaming stertorous mouth ;
What Sirens seek to kindle at your fire
Of passion some live spark of dead desire —
They would be ready even to doubt God's power

To shield their little life from hour to hour,
And many would be going, with idiot-grin,
Out of their mind to let the marvel in.

" But do not think the Devil hath his will.
Whate'er he doth he is God's servant still.
And in the larger light of day divine
The spark of his hell-fire shall cease to shine.
God maketh use of him; what he intends
For evil Heaven will shape to its own ends.
With subtle wile he tries to circumvent
The Lord, and works just what the Master meant.
He hangs the dark cloud round this world of yours;
. God smileth, and a rain of good down-pours.
He dug Christ's tomb so deep there sprang and swirled
Waters of life to baptize all the world.
He strove to found the Empire of the Slave,
It crumbled in : he had but delved its grave.

" He stole upon a Nation, in disguise
Of thieves that prowled by night; day-lurking spies;
Plotters who privily set their eyes to mark
Her weakness, and garroted her by dark!
The face of Freedom frightfully they scarred,
That men should know her not, so sadly marred,
And, seeing her in the dust, misjudge her stature;
And, finding she grew calm, mistake her nature!
They built about her; dreamed not she would stand

Up, terribly tall once more ; and, in her hand —
Clencht, till the knuckles whiten with their grip —
The sword set sharp as is her red-edged lip :
And in her eyes the lightnings that should break
In blinding, black, irreparable wreck : —
Rending their roof to heaven, their walls to earth,
(The sorer travail the more glorious birth !)
An Earthquake crash ! the edifice is crowned,
And there 's a heap of ruin on the ground !
Arise, to sweep them from her onward path,
Stern as the Spectre of God's whitest wrath.
Even while they clutcht the gains of their foul play
And parted them, I heard the Avengers say, —
' They plant in dust a breath will blow away,
Although they wet it well with blood to-day.

" ' Ay, Traitor, mount your topmost pinnacle.
·The merry-making heavens would mark you well,
Where all the gazers of the world may see .
You throned upon the peak of infamy ! '
So croped the implacable ministers of Fate,
Standing in shadow where they watch and wait.

' " ' Well done.   Now place the crown upon your
         brow,
With its brave glitter all eyes dazzle now :
Lost in its splendor is that frightful stain
Branded beneath ; the murder-mark of Cain ! '

So crooned the implacable ministers of Fate,
Standing in shadow where they watch and wait.

"' Well done. Now fold the Imperial Purple
        round,
And let a Pope's Anointed, robed and crowned,
Thus glorify the blood so basely spilt;
Thus image to all time the loftiest guilt.'
So crooned the implacable ministers of Fate,
Standing in shadow where they watch and wait.

"' Well done, thou faithful servant, Hell shall rise
From half her thrones to offer you their prize,
And greet your coming; meet you with a kiss
Of benison, for such a deed as this !'
So crooned the implacable ministers of Fate,
Standing in shadow where they watch and wait."

"Was Satan sent from heaven to ruin earth?"
I asked, "or what the story of his birth?"

"*Both heaven and hell are from the human race,*
And every soul projects its future place:
Long shadows of ourselves are thrown before,
To wait our coming on the eternal shore.
These either clothe us with eclipse and night,
Or, as we enter them, are lost in light.

" *There is no Devil such as Milton saw;*
No fallen Angel's eyes divined the flaw
In God's work, whereby Man might be accurst.
The Devil was a murderer from the first,
Our Saviour said.   But he was softly nurst
Up from a babe in arms.   A little seed
Of sin was sown that grew with little heed.
By door or window little sins will win
A way that widens for the larger sin,
As tiniest lichens climbing up the wall,
May lend a hand to help the Ivy crawl
That is to tower a conqueror over all
The house in ruin, crumbling to the fall.
Once life is set in motion there upspring
Infinite issues from the smallest thing.
A finger's breadth in swerving as we start
May land us in the end two worlds apart.

" *Our parents were not tempted by a Tree*
That hung out luscious fruitage, visibly
Held in God's hand, on purpose to beguile
Their simpleness with its suggesting smile.
That is the symbol of a world within;
There was the serpent born, there bred the sin.
The trees that midmost in the Garden stood,
Took root in soul and blossomed in the blood.
Nor were they left without the inward light,
The starry presence shining through your night,

That shows the wrong while it reveals the right ;
The magnet in the soul that points on through
All tempests and still trembles to be true.

" *The still small voice within cried,*

'Do not this

Or it will lead from me, and ye will miss
The innocent brightness of your morning bliss,
And long in a wild wilderness will stray,
Farther and farther from the primal way,
Until ye lose me, darkling in a cloud
Of your own making, winding like a shroud
About the life I gave; nor feel me near
When ye do call and think there 's none to hear.'

" *And yet they dallied with the thought of wrong*
Until they did it : looking down too long,
Like him who, on a perilous mountain ledge,
Gazes upon the gulf, dark o'er the edge,
Till he grows dizzy and, with brain a-swim,
Forgetting to look up — drops !   Or, like him
Who stood and watched that Titan, face to face,
The vast Steam-Hammer, with its monster mace,
Until the blows of its recurrent sound
Snapped his last trembling hold on things around ;
Mazed him and drew him nigher, slip by slip,
To thrust his hand into its crushing grip.

" They dallied with wrong-doing, and it grew
Too strong to wrestle with, and overthrew.
Eyes play with Pleasure!   Looking overmuch
Sets all the blood a-tingle for the touch!
How the fruit smiles, delicious to the eyes;
How quietly the Snake behind it lies,
With all his weight bending the branch down near;
The reptile music, sliding through the ear,
Winds round the soul, makes it a-tiptoe stand
With love-sick longing till it lifts the hand
To pluck, and feel, and smell, and taste just one
Ripe Apple, whose gold glistens so i' the sun!
But one step over the forbidden marge;
The sin so little, the delight so large!
And there's the old, old story of the Fall,
Eternally repeated for us all.

" Thus is the Devil born: born every day,
Harmless at first as toothless whelps at play;
Is born in thoughts which are the quick live seeds
That will be striving to take shape in deeds:
So would be born did any Pair begin   ·
Afresh; so form the protoplasm of Sin,
The pustule raised at just a prick of pin;
The nest-egg which the Devil is hatched in.
For Man, the outcome of Creation's past,
Is flower of all earth's life from first to last,
No lower life hath ever passed away

But left its larvæ in the human clay.
No reptile of the slime, no beast of prey,
But human passions personate to-day.
And these break loose to rend in deadly strife,
And will break loose, till, in the higher life,
The soul arisen to her immortal stature.
Leads, Una-like, these strong necessities of Nature.

" The sin that sprang, equipped for death, in Cain,
Was gathering life for many years ; had lain
In childhood nestled to the parent breast,
Who dreamed not of the wild beast he caressed
So gently ; fed on his own life, with pride,
The strength that gored him in mad fratricide !
Such little sins are fibres to the root
Of that which bears ripe murder for its fruit.

" To picture what I mean : see here, a Wife,
With bosom just a-brood o'er life-in-life,
Who in a fury-fit snatched up a knife   .
And drove it at her husband.   'T was a miss
Though near enough to hear Death's arrow hiss !
She had not dyed her hand in human blood,
But she had dipped her Unborn in a flood
Of wrath that surged and smoked and flashed hell-flame ;
Given her babe baptism in the Devil's name :
Stained the pure thing of heaven a lurid hue
With fume o' the pit, the white star reddened through.
And from that Mother-stricken life there grew
A Murderer whose own hand that Mother slew.

" *The ghosts of our own crimes long-buried will*
Live after us and haunt our children still.
Our vices, hid for generations past,
Break out and tell their secret tale at last.

" *Cain slew his brother.   In that deed the Devil* '
Took visible shape; stood forth erect, as Evil
Full-statured, from the serpent form of sin
In which he had wormed a way and wriggled in,
Before he made a foothold on the earth.

" *The Murderer died, and spirit-world gave birth*
To a thing that stained the stainless in a cloud
So black it made the clear heaven thunder-browed;
Death at the heart, Destruction on the wing!
This was the spirit of Cain, still hovering
Over the world, to rain in ruin down.
So Tyrants climb to wear the fatal crown
That sets them on a vantage-ground, to tread
A people's life out — deal death overhead.

" *From 'Earth sprang Satan, clothed with plumes of*
       power.
But, as a Bird, in the death-pangs, will tower
To fall, his exultation dropped to see
The loneliness of his eternity!
The old world-wall no longer hemmed him round;
The Boundless was his spirit's only bound;

The conscious stillness ached upon the ear;
No breath of being stirring far or near.
A Waste no wing had wandered, foot had trod
No print upon; a world left out by God.
And he the only life-beat of the whole
Illimitable solitude of soul.

"What wonder he should turn to Earth again
And feel his way back to the human; fain
To win a partner that would share his pain?

" The worst of Devils feel a little ease,
Shedding their poison; giving their·disease
To uninfected souls.   And soon he saw
How he might take advantage of the Law
That seems to work so blindly, while Men draw
Their lots as blindly; lets the sunshine fall
On just and unjust: gives one chance for all,
Nor spares the innocent when the guilty fall;
How beauty broods with its thrice-glorious glow
Where Death is lurking quietly below!
How Providence looks on the side of Wrong
Nine times in ten if it be only strong:
How unperceived God works by common light,
Nor cleaves his cloud to lighten through our night;
How much Man has to trust Him — even for breath
To feed his life and faith to live through death.
Rare mischief may be done ere God appears

Himself in miracle.   He so often hears
The cry unanswered, save in His own way
And season.   Here was scope enough to play
The devil with the appearances of things;
Keep out of sight and pull the puppet-strings.

" And, at the thought, he waved abroad his wings
For larger flight, to spread himself between
Man and his Maker; weave his web unseen,
Right in the dazzle of the heavenly light;
Beat down the prayers and yearnings in mid-flight;
Make shadows in the mind to curtain day
From the dim world in which poor wretches stray:
Put out in tears the trembling inner ray
And lure them with a Will-o'-the-wisp at play
Among the quagmires waiting by the way;
Ventriloquize the voice of God within
The soul and in a guise Angelic win
From Heaven, by mirroring that heaven in
Death's stream; make spirits take the leap for love
Of that false reflex of the beauty above!

" First Man-Slayer, He reached his ghastly goal,
And then became first slayer of the soul.

" And doing evil grew a dear delight,
And so he built his kingdom of the night
And proudly waxed in power; his business thrived;

For soon the Murderer with a Murderess wived,
Whom he had wooed in secret many a day
And dragged at last along the same byway,
To share with him the same blood-guilty fate,
And with fit offspring crown the loves of Hate.

" The Devil is no more the single soul
Of that first Murderer ; it is the whole
Vast aggregate of evil spirits lost ;
The cruel wreckers on that hell-bound coast.
Just as the person of the Holy Ghost
May mean the presence of a heavenly Host !
Or as ye say one spirit moves them when
One cry awakens from ten thousand men.

PART VI.

THIS world is not the Devil's merry-go-
    round
The Angels of the Lord are ever found
Encamped about the soul that looks to Him:
They are an inner lamp when all is dim
Without, and light poor souls through horrors grim.
Even as a myriad sunbeams hour by hour
Melt to make rich one little summer flower;
Or as a myriad souls of flowers fleet
Away to make a single summer sweet —
So many spirits make one smile of God
That feeds your life transfiguring from its clod.
There is no lack of Angel carriers
When mortals post to God their fervent prayers!
And these are happy in their work, for still
They find their heaven in doing the Father's will.
I have a meat, said Christ, ye know not of.
So these — they carry heaven in their love.
Not that the Blessèd leave their happy seat
When they draw near ye upon silent feet.
They do not need to thread their starry way
Through worlds of night, or wilderness of day

Spirit to Spirit hath not far to run,
Because in God all souls are verily one
Throughout all worlds : there are no walls of Space
Where all eternity is dwelling place.

" Distance is nothing in the world of Thought ;
And in the world of Spirit it is naught.
You hear of dying men whose souls have been
Present with distant friends ; most surely seen
Before the breathing ceased ; for they were there
In Thought so fixed, intense, that, on the air,
Their lineaments the utter yearning wrought,
In spiritual apparition of their thought,
Till they grew visible.   This Murderer dwells
In Spirit where his Thought is — hottest Hell 's
For him where his infernal deed was done !
The blood so safely hidden from the sun
Hath stained right through beyond this world of time,
Red to the other side, with his old crime.
He does not merely come and go ; he is
All presence to the proofs and witnesses.

" Spirits may touch you, being, as you would say,
A hundred thousand million miles away.
Those wires that wed the Old World with the New,
Are not the only links Mind lightens through !
The Angels, singing in their heaven above,
Feel when ye strike the unison of love.

A TALE OF ETERNITY.

The prayers of heaven fall in a blessëd rain,
On souls that parch in purgatorial pain.
And prayers from earth lift, with a sense of wings,
Poor souls that drift as helpless outcast things.

" A luminiferous ether of the soul
Pervades the universe, and makes the whole
Vast realm of Being one; — all breathing breath
Of the same life that is fulfilled in death.
And human spirits, from their earthy bound,
Can thrill the Immortals, in their crystal round,
Like flames that rise and answer a sweet sound:
And set the furthest heavens vibrating,
As air will dance close to a live harp-string.

" Thus Jesus warned you that His Little Ones —
Nestled like smallest planets next their Suns —
Are nearest God's great Angels, whose high place
Permits them to behold the Father's face,
With whom there is no distance known to sense.
Heaven is most near to utmost innocence.

" God, the Creator, doth not sit aloof,
As in a picture painted on the roof,
Occasionally looking down from thence.
He is all presence and all providence;
Sentient in whatsoever life may draw
Breath from Him, and, beyond, sentient in law.

He doth not sit at one end of the chain
Of Being, thrilling it now and again;
He who is Being and doth bound and bind
Its particles in the Eternal Mind.
Outside His providence we cannot stand.
His presence makes the smallest room expand
Wider than wings of day and Night e'er fanned.
I who am here, his Messenger, to-night,
But bring that presence to a point in light.
We are the agencies, the living laws,
Whereby creation is eternal Cause.

" This human life is no mere looking-glass,
In which God sees His shadows as ye pass.
He did not start the pendulum of Time,
To go by Law, with one great swing sublime;
Resting Himself in lonely joy apart:
But to each pulse of life is beating heart.
And, as a Father sensitive, is stirred
By falling sparrow, or heart-wingëd word.

" As the Babe's life within the Parent's, dim
And deaf, ye dwell in God, a-dream of Him.
Ye stir and put forth feelers which are claspt
By airy hands and higher life is graspt.
As yet but darkly.   Life is in the root
And looking heavenward, from the ladder-foot,
Wingless as worms, with earthiness fast bound,

Up which ye mount but slowly, round on round.
Long climbing brings ye to the Father's knee;
Ye open gladsome eyes at last to see
That face of Love ye felt so inwardly.

" In this vast universe of worlds no waif
Of spirit looks to him but floateth safe.
No prayer so lowly but is heard on high ;
And if a soul should sigh, and lift an eye,
He keeps that soul from sinking with a sigh.

" All life, down to the worm beneath the sod,
Hath spiritual relationships to God —
The Life of Life, the love of all, in all;
Lord of the large and infinitely small.

" Birds find their home across the pathless sea
By no hereditary memory.
From land to land they move, their way illumed
By the inflowing Love that bore them, plumed
For flight, through which the Mother Bird is taught
To know which youngling had the last worm brought ;
The Insect led to garner food in nook
For young, on which it never lives to look.

" The veriest atoms, even as worlds above,
Are bridal chambers of creative Love,
Quick with the motion that suspends the whole

Of Matter spiral-spinning toward Soul.
And nothing is, but groping turns to Him,
Like babe to bosom, though the sight be dim :
Nothing but what reflects in some faint wise
The image that is God in Angel eyes —
The Infinite One, whose likeness we but see
Glassed in the Infinite of variety:
Just as the waters fix a fluttering beam,
Caught in this chamber, and, with golden gleam,
Throw on the ceiling, limned in little, one
Pale image of the glory of the Sun !

" No seed of life blown down a dark abysm
Of earth or sea but feels the magnetism
That draws us Godward !   Flowers sunk in mines,
Or plants in ocean, where no sunbeam shines,
Will blindly climb up toward THEIR Deity,
Far off in Heaven, whom they can never see.

" There is a Spirit of Life within the Tree
That's fed and clothed from Heaven continually,
And does not draw all nourishment from earth.
It puts a myriad tender feelers forth,
That breathe in heaven and turn the breath to sap :
In every leaf it spreads a tiny lap
To take its manna from the hand of God
And gather force for fingers 'neath the sod
To clutch the earth with ; moulds, from sun and rain,

Its leaves ; with spirit-life feeds every vein
And through each vein makes wood for bough and bark :
Girth for the bole and rootage down the dark.

" So Man is fed by God and lives in Him :
Not merely nourished by his rootage dim
In a far Past ; a dead world underground,
But spirit to spirit reaches Heaven all round.

" Creative heat is current in the soul
From ages past, like sunshine in the coal,
Some fire of heaven in fossil stored away,
But spirit-life yet kindles at the ray
Warm from our Sun that shines in heaven to-day !

" Not in one primal Man before the Fall
Did God set life a-breathing once for all.
He is the breath of life from first to last ;
He liveth in the Present as the Past.
But ye, like rowers, turn your eyes behind ;
Ye look Without and vainly feel to find
Raised in relief, like letters for the blind,
The substance of that Glory in the mind.

" Hints of the higher life, the better day,
Visit the human soul, outlining aye
The perfect statue now rough-cast in clay ;
And with a mournful sigh ye think and say

' This is the type that was, and passed away ! '
God holds a flower to you, it only yields
The fragrance fading from forgotten fields.
' Ah, only Eden cóuld have wafted it ! '
Immortal imagery His hand hath writ
Within ye is with revelation lit
. By secret shinings of the Infinite.
'These are but glimmers of a glory gone ! '
I tell you they are prophecies of dawn
And glimpses of a life that still goes on.
Man hath not fall'n from Heaven, nor been cast
Out from some Golden Age lived in the Past !
His fall is from the possible Life before him :
His fall is from the Crown of Life held o'er him.
Ye stoop by Corpse-light, groping on the ground,
And lo ! the living God, a-shine all round !
Even while I speak there is a quickening,
The unrest of a world that feels the spring ;
The crust o' the Letter cracks ; new life takes wing ;
A strong ground-swell will heave, a wave will break,
The Eternal grows more visibly awake.

" Upon the verge of sunrise ye but stand —
The door of life just open in your hand.
Behind you is the slip of space ye passed ;
Before you an illimitable vast.
Not backward point the foot-prints that ye trace
Of those who ran the foremost in the race,

With light of God full-shining on their face!
Look up, as Children of the Light, and see
That ye are bound FOR immortality,
Not passing FROM it: Heirs of Heaven ye,
Not Exiles.   God reverses human growth
For spirits; they go ripening toward youth
Forever.   The fair Garden that still gleams
Across the desert, miraged in your dreams,
Smiles from the spirit, rather than the sod,
Wherever hallowed feet of Love have trod;
Wherever souls yet walk and talk with God.
And Heaven is as near Earth now as when
The Angels visibly conversed with Men.
The Holy Dove that came to brighten down
Over the head of Christ, a heaven-dropt crown,
Now broods within; it is the bosom-dove, —
It croons the music in the voice of Love.
'Neath human roofs still stoopeth the Divine
Closer than ever; makes the heart its shrine.

" God hath been gradually forming Man
In His own image since the world began,
And is forever working on the soul,
Like Sculptor on his Statue, till the whole
Expression of the upward life be wrought
Into some semblance of the Eternal Thought.
Race after Race hath caught its likeness of
The Maker as the eyes grew large with love.

But in one face alone ye look to see
The possible image smiling perfectly.

" Christ's was a conscious Birthday of the Soul.
Thenceforth the world on a broader gauge could roll
Out of old ruts : Man glimpse his glorious goal,
And leave the desert byways, darkly trod,
Heart-haunted by some gory ghost of God,
And Faith, exulting on its heavenward way,
Feel every dark should end at last in day.
No more vain searchings through the starry dome,
With vague blind yearnings for one hint of Home !
In Him ye see the Type Man climbs up to ; ·
The Model God is working from through you !
In Him ye have the nearest likeness given
On Earth of that hid face which is in heaven.

" You ask me ' how the lamp of life burns on
When all that visibly fed the flame is gone ? '

" Man does not live alone by visible breath,
And He who brings to life will lead through death.
Wait yet a little while and ye shall see
The flame was breathed on ; fed invisibly :
And that its motion springs with force seven-fold
When the life-heat is clasht against Death's cold.

" You think of spirit as prison-walled about
By substance, wondering how it can get out !

But to my vision radiates the soul
Through body; by its pulses lights the whole
With life, and makes it luminous as the glass
Through which you see but only in spirit pass.
The wee babe nestled in the Mother's lap,
Feels her soul radiate in love and wrap
It softly in the very heart of bliss,
And draw all heaven through it in a kiss.

" As chalk is formed at bottom of the sea
From life that sheds its shell continually;
As bones are built up out of life's decay,
The body is shaped of substance sloughed away
From soul in ripening: 't is a husk which yields
The earthy scaffold whereby spirit builds
Its heavenly house, that stands when the world-crust
Is made of dropt and perisht human dust.
Spirit is Lord and Master at the death,
As in beginning, of its house of breath.

" Man does not live alone by hunger and drouth,
But by the breath which kindles from God's mouth:
'T is breathing spirit makes the body breathe,
And sets in outer type the life beneath.
So print makes visible the unseen thought
To pass away, the miracle being wrought.
Life is an inner energy, unfurled
In visible shows from an invisible world;

Still fed and fed from that almighty force
Of which no science yet hath grasped the source,
Whose infant germ from the dead seed reborn,
Is greater than a realm of ripened corn.
Like worlds warmed into being by their Sun,
Ye are embodied by the rays that run
Mysteriously across a gulf of night;
A bridge of spirit laid in beams of light.
And that which is the centre of the blaze
Travels in life unseen along the rays.
The book will pass; the living Mind work on;
The Visible fades; still shines the Eternal sun.

" I tell you these things are: I may not show
You how: there's much the senses cannot know.
Who knows the links of that invisible chain
Which runs from soul to soul, from brain to brain,
Whereby thought passes into other thought,
And out of sound its silent shape is wrought ?
You see the miracle done before your eyes,
And in the flash of spirit to spirit dies
The common daylight: visual sense is blind
To see how Matter is made quick by Mind.
And there's a power in the hidden soul
To pass in at the eyes and print its whole
Self, in a picture finished infinitely
Beyond the portrait that the eyes can see.
Eyes ne'er behold your own souls face to face:
Your real selves invisibly embrace.

" *You know not how a prayer ascends to God.*
You saw no ladder Angel-feet e'er trod
In answer; hear no door turn on the hinge
When heaven opens, or the hells impinge
Upon the soul with their suggestion dark.
The Devil tempts, but how you cannot mark:
The bridge is still invisible that doth span
Your known and unknown: reach from God to Man.

" *With labors infinite your Science seeks*
Footing on inaccessible cloud-peaks.
Yet, must the Climbers know that there are things
Only attainable at last with wings.
That skies will not be scaled howe'er they clasp
The solid rock; that heaven still mocks their grasp.
On these they may not speak the final word.
On these the great Hereafter must be heard.
At best Man doth but darkly draw his light:
Each step ye take, each secret wrest from Night,
Must furnish food for faith as well as sight.

" *The more ye feel the chain whereby ye are spanned,*
The more its missing links elude the hand.
So Saturn's perfect rings, when, closer seen,
Are broken with dark gaps of night between!
Nor can ye more than mark the Visible shine
And in the gloom accept the Hand Divine.

" *Live fruitfully the life ye may possess*
With rootage beyond reach of consciousness,
And wait till the Unseen in flower blows.

" *To find what gems lie hidden where it grows*
Ye must not pluck the plant up by the root.
Wait till its treasures hang in precious fruit.

" *There is no pathway Man hath ever trod*
By faith or seeking sight but ends in God.
Yet 't is in vain ye look Without to find
The inner secrets of the Eternal Mind,
Or meet the King on His external Throne.
But when ye kneel at heart, and feel so lone,
Perchance behind the veil you get the grip
And spirit-sign of secret fellowship ;
Silently as the gathering of a tear
The human want will bring the helper near .
The very weakness, that is utterest need
Of God, will draw Him down with strength indeed.

" *Enough to know ye live because He lives !*
And love, because in love Himself He gives !
The gift is ever held sufficient sign
There is a Giver !   And if it be Divine
And like the Heaven ye dream, but may not see,
Giver Divine and Heaven there must be.

" Lean nearer to the Heart that beats through night:
Its curtain of the dark your veil of light.
Peace Halcyon-like to perfect Faith is given,
And it can float on a reflected Heaven
Surely as Knowledge that doth rest at last
Isled on its ' ATOM ' in the unfathomed vast
Life-ocean, heaving through the infinite,
From out whose dark the shows of being flit,
In flashes of the climbing wave's white crest;
Some few a moment luminous o'er the rest ! "

The voice ceased : the form faded in the beam
Of dawn, that swam down like the gladsome gleam
Of heaven to him who struggles, nearly drowned,
And draws him lifeward from the gulf profound,
And melts to a gold mist the dim green round.

6

PART VII.

WHO hath not marked how graciously the
    Dawn
Comes smiling when some stormy night
    hath gone ?
As Beauty lifts the heaven of her eyes
Full on you large with their serene surprise
That you should dream such gentleness could
    dart
The looks that hurt you to the very heart !
Calm eyes, that through luxurious reaches roll
The richness of their rest on the vext soul.

So comes the Morning ; new heavens rise above,
And open wider arms of larger love
Than ever : glad blue Ether, with the bliss
Of sunshine, laughs and kindles at its kiss.
There lie the tears of tempest, softly-bright
As Heaven had only rained in drops of light.
The air, an overflow of Heaven's own balm,
Naught but Earth's music breaks the divine calm.

Yet that same Morning looks on ruin and wreck,
And soothes a sea that lifeless swept the deck

Of some proud ship, and glorifies the wave
That landward heaves the mariner's glassy grave;
Playfully rippling, shoaling goldenly o'er
Dead seamen dimly drifting to the shore !
Terribly innocent, Morning laughs on high,
While Ocean rocks them with its lullaby.

So came the Morning, smiling, crowned with calm,
After my night of trouble, breathing balm.
Fair Earth with all her night-long tearful eyes
A-sparkle with the soul of the sunrise !
On every blade there hung a drop of dew,
And every drop a live star shimmered through :
All phantoms of the night by shadowy stealth
Retired with Darkness from our world of health;
All life unshrouded, to Heaven's influence bare,
Took wings of morning in the open air.
Our world, a warm safe nest of happy souls,
Basked in the brightness as the lily lolls
Her bosomed softness on the sunny stream,
Whose ripples lip her where she lies a-dream.
The stream, that crept a river of death by night,
Full of dark secrets, ran a river of light !
Such sense of rest to all glad things was given,
As earth were cradle of the peace of heaven.
A more than common freshness fed the breath
Of sweet new life; there was no taint of death.
My nightmare over, I would dream no more

Of murder and the charnel at life's core ;
Or nameless creatures that may haunt old graves
Bat-like, and flit from out lone, twilight caves.

Green earth, glad heaven, gayly vied to win
Thought out-of-doors, yet would it brood within.
Sullen and shy as fish that will not rise
To any tempting lure of feathered flies,
But haunt the pool where, horribly quiet, lies
A dead child, with its wide-awake blue eyes.

Lonely I wandered in my garden-ground,
Musing on Life, the Death's-head rosily crowned,
And of the mystery that clouds us round,
And of the mournful possibility
That, in some blindness, we may lose the key
Which to the keeping of each soul is given
To ope the door, and so be shut from Heaven ;
Raking the ashes and the dust of death,
Long after we have done with human breath ;
And of the features printed on my brain
In vision that would evermore remain,
And, any instant, sinister and swart
From out the light, at turn of eye, might start ;
And I should see him ! as 'neath the Tunnel's arc,
Where, down the shaft, day lightens through the
      dark,
Some chosen victim momently may mark

His murderer, with those snaky eyes at work
Fixed on him ; in whose spark malignant lurk
Cold fires of death drawn inward for the spring ;
The dagger flash leaps in their glittering !

So, till its horrors almost lived to sight,
My spirit brooded o'er the bygone night ;
Reflecting all the strife in upper air,
As you have seen, by some sea-margin, where
The circling sea-bird hovers, dreamily slow,
In likeness of the wave that sways below,
The Spirit of its motion on the wing :
Over that night my mind kept hovering.
At length the growing image of my thought
To some such final shape as this was wrought—

From end to end of things we may not see,
Nor square the circle of Eternity ;
But, I cannot believe in endless hell
And heaven side by side.   How could I dwell
Among the saved, for thinking of the Lost ?
With such a lot the Blest would suffer most.
Sitting at feast all in a Golden Home,
That towered over dungeon-grates of Doom,
My heart would ache for all the lost that go
To wail and weep in everlasting woe :
Through all the music I must hear the moan,
Too sharp for all the harps of Heaven to drown.

I cannot think of Life apart from Him
Who is the life, from cell to Seraphim :
And, if Hell flame unquenchably, must be
The life of hell to all eternity !
A God of love must expiate the stain
Of Sin Himself, by suffering endless pain ;
Sit with eternal desolation round
His feet; his head with happy heavens crowned.
From Him the strength immortal must be sent,
By which the soul could bear the punishment.
I cannot think He gave us power to wring
From one brief life eternal suffering :
If this were so the Heavens must surely weep,
Till Hell were drowned in one salt vast, sea-deep.
Forgive me, Lord, if wrongly I divine ;
I dare not think Thy pity less than mine.

I cannot image Heaven as Triumph-Car,
That rolleth red and recking from the war,
Upborne on wheels of torture whirling round
With writhing souls forever broke and bound !

God save me from that Heaven of the Elect,
Who half rejoice to count the numbers wreckt.
Because, such full weight to the balance given,
Sends up the scale that lands them surely in heaven,
And the proud Saved, exulting, rise the higher,
The lower that the Lost sink in hell-fire.

I think Heaven will not shut forevermore,
Without a knocker left upon the door,
Lest some belated Wanderer should come
Heart-broken, asking just to die at home,
So that the Father·will at last forgive,
And looking on His face that soul shall live.
I think there will be Watchmen through the night,
Lest any, afar off, turn them to the light;
That He who loved us into life must be
A Father infinitely Fatherly,
And, groping for Him, these shall find their way
From outer dark, through twilight, into day.

I could not joy for Harvest gathered in,
If any souls, like tares and twitch of sin,
Were flung out by the Farmer to the fire,
Whose smoke of torment, rising high and higher,
Should fill the universe forevermore,
While we with glad feet trod the crystal floor
Through which the damned lookt up at Paradise,
Forever fixed, like fishes frozen in ice.

I could not sing the song of Harvest Home,
Thinking of those poor souls that never come;
Such mournful eyes from out their night would
     gleam
And haunt forever all my happy dream!
Such tears, — lost jewels that flash God-ward, in
The dark, down-trodden Toad-like head of sin!

The New World's poorest emigrant will lend
A kindly hand to help a poorer friend.
And I must pray to God from out my bliss
For those who were beyond all help but His, —
Pray and repray, the same old prayer anew;
Forgive them, Lord, they know not what they do.
Because they were so utterly accurst,
Self-doomed, that bitterness would be the worst.
O, look down on them, from Thy place above,
The look of pity, Lord, half-way to love!

Mere human love, in this, its narrow sphere,
Can never think of those it once held dear,
Who, down the darkened way will pull apart,
But with a pitying eye; an aching heart,
And still, as less the beckoning hand they heed,
The strength of Love grows with their greater need;
The less they heed, the more it yearns to save.
And shall this love be dwarfed beyond the grave,
To lose, on wings, its feet-attainëd height?
Better its blindness, than the eye of light
That coldly down, on endless hell could glance,
With all its mortal sympathies in trance.

Or will some Lethean wave the soul caress,
And numb it into dull forgetfulness;
Washing away all memory of distress
That others feel, while we but lift the hand

To pluck and eat the lotus of the land,
And those far wailings of the world of tears
Come mellowed into music for our ears,
With just the zestful dash of discord given,
That   makes   the   pleasure   pungent — perfects
        Heaven ?

'T is hard to read the Handwriting Divine;
The vanishing *up-stroke* so invisibly fine !
There must be issues that we do not see.
The whole horizon of Futurity
Is nowise visible from where we stand ;
We are but dwellers in a lowly land.
We think the-sun doth set, the sun doth rise,
And yet our world 's but turning in the skies.
Seen from our lower level there must pass
Mysteries, so high and starry, we but glass
Them darkly, as we strain our mortal sight,
While 'twixt our souls and them there stands the
        night.
And then we scratch upon our window-pane,
Dimming its clearness, and we are so fain
To read our own imaginations fond,
For the true figures of the world beyond.
We model from the human life, and so
Feature the future from the face we know.
'T is always sunless one side of our globe,
And thus we fashion the Eternal's robe

God made Man in His image, but our plan 's
To mould and make God's image in the Man's,
And if my thought be human as the rest,
At least the likeness shall be Man's at best.
Too long hath Calvin's spectrum sacrificed,
Smoke-hued with hell, the pure white light of
      Christ !

Our Science grasps with its transforming hand ;
Makes real, half the tales of wonder-land.
We turn the deathliest fetor to perfume ;
We give decay new life and rosy bloom ;
Change filthy rags to paper virgin white ;
Make pure in spirit what was foul to sight.
Even dead, recoiling force, to a fairy gift
Of help is turned, and taught to deftly lift.
How can we think God hath no crucible
Save that Black Country of a burning Hell?
Or the great ocean of Almighty power,
No scope to take the life-stream from our shore,
Muddy and dark, and make it pure once more ?

Dear God, it seems to me that Love must be
The Missionary of Eternity !
Must still find work, in worlds beyond the grave,
So long as there 's a single soul to save ;
Must, from the highest heaven, yearn to tell
    Thy message ; be the Christ to some dark hell ;

That all divergent lines at length will meet
To make the clasping round of Love complete ;
The rift 'twixt Sense and Spirit will be healed,
Ere the Redeemer's work be crowned and sealed ;
Evil shall die like dung about the root
Of Good, or climb converted into fruit !
The discords cease, and all their strife shall be
Resolved in one vast peaceful harmony :
That all these accidents of Time and breath
Shall bear no black seal of a Second Death :
That, freed from branding heats that burn in Time,
The lost *Black Race* shall whiten in that clime :
All blots of error bleacht in Heaven's sight ;
All life's perplexing colors lost in light :
That Thou hast power to work out every stain,
That purifying is the end of Pain ;
And, waking, we shall know what we but dream
Dimly, that punishment is to redeem ;
And here, or There, the penitent thrill must leaven
The earthiest soul and wing it toward Heaven ;
That when the angel-Reapers shall up-sheave
The harvest, Angel-Gleaners will not leave
One least small grain of good — and there are
    none
So evil but some precious germ lives on, —
The grimiest gutter crawling by the way
Still hath its reflex of the face of Day ; —
And all the seeds divine foredoomed by fate

To bear blind blossoms here shall germinate
And have another chance, in other place,
Where tears of gratitude and dews of grace
Shall warm and quicken to the feeblest root,
Till in Thy garden they are ripe for fruit.
So shall we find the Dark of our old Earth
Twin with the eternal Daylight from the birth,
And trodden in the grave-dust we shall see
This serpent-symbol of Eternity
That only maketh ends meet, head and tail,
A world all blessing with a world all bale.

Thus, in its maze, my mind went round and
          round, —
Like him, lost in the Bush, who thought he found
The pathway that he sought, because he beat
His track with constant tread of his own feet. —
As round the dew-drencht garden-walks I went
Till, pausing, all unconscious of intent,
Nigh where a greenery of Syringas grew
And, shedding shadow round, there leaned a Yew, —
Sombrely ancient watcher by the tomb !
A Nest of Thrushes the live heart o' the gloom ;
I saw the earth was crackt, where recent rain
Had crusht and crumbled in a new-made drain,
And human bones were plainly peering through,
As if Death grinned and showed a tooth or two !
I searcht, and, ere the ghastly work was done,

Had gathered half a tiny skeleton,
That had been once a Child.

                  And then it came
On me that in my dream I saw the same,
And had been warned to calcine them in flame,
And pound them small as is the finest rust,
And on the winds of heaven fling the dust.
I did it, and, although that soul accurst,
Still walks the darkness, we had passed the worst,
And there was peace o' nights at the Haunted
      Hurst.

THE ARYAN MOTHER.

Behold a phantom-form appears, majestic in its gloom!
Mournfully it looks across a Chasm deep as doom:
A quivering heartache seems to move its withered, wordless
    lips;
Familiar eyes are kindling through their wan light of eclipse:
It is the Ancient Mother rising, Sphinx-like, 'mid her sands,
To plead with those who will not hear. She wrings her
    wrinkled hands;
Yearns over both. As Brothers long ago she brought them
    forth,
Her dusky Indians and her great white Heroes of the North!
The Children have no memories of the Morning-Land, and
    yet
The Mother's heart remembers, though all the world forget.

HAVELOCK'S MARCH.

E look with horror, when the blood
    grows cold,
  On that which stung us hotly enough
    of old;
Blame me not wantonly: I do but draw
Faintly the thing we felt; the sight we saw!

THE REVOLT.

" Come hither, my brave Soldier-boy, and sit you
      by my side,
To hear a tale, a fearful tale, a glorious tale of
      pride ;
How Havelock with his handful, all so faithful
      and so few,
Held on in that far Indian land, to bear our Eng-
      land through
Her pass of bloodiest peril, and her reddest sea
      of wrath ;
And strode like Paladins of old on their avenging
      path.
Though clothes were drencht, and flesh was parcht,
      and bones were chilled with cold,
The gallant hearts never gave up ; they never
      loosed their hold ;
But fought right on, and triumphed, till our eyes
      rained as we read
How proudly every place was filled, with living
      and with dead.

" The stillness of a brooding storm lay on the
      Eastern land ;
The dark death-circle narrowed round our little
      English band :

The false Sepoy stoopt lower for his spring, and
  in his eye
A bloody light was burning on them, as he glided by :
Old Horrors rose, and leered at them, from out
  the tide of time, —
The peering peaks of War's old world, whose
  brows were stained with crime !
The conscious Silence was but dumb, a cursëd
  plot to hide ;
The darkness only a mask of Death, ready to slip
  aside.
Under the leafy palms they lay, and through their
  gay green crown
Our English saw no Storm roll up : no Fate
  swift flaming down.

" At last it came.　The Rebel drum was heard
  at dead of night :
They dasht in dust the only torch that showed the
  face of Right !
Once more the Devil clutches at his lost throne
  of the earth,
And sends a people, smit with plague of madness,
  howling forth.
As in a Demon's dream they swarm from horrible
  hiding-nooks ;
Red Murder stabs the air, and lights their way
  with bloody looks !

Snuffing the smell of human blood, the cruel
    Moloch stands;
Hearing the cry of '*Kill! Kill! Kill!*' and claps
    his gory hands.
At dead of night, while England slept, the fearful
    vision came,
She lookt, and with a dawn of hell the East was
    all aflame.

" Stern tidings flasht to Havelock, of legions in
    revolt:
'*The traitors turn upon us, and the eaters of our salt,*
Subtle as death, and false as hell, and cruel as the
    grave,
Have sworn to rend us by the root; be quick, if ye
    would save ;
The wild beasts bloody and obscene, mad-drunk with
    ·gore and lust,
Have wreaked a horrible vengeance on our England
    rolled in dust.'
And such a withering wind doth blow, such fear-
    ful sounds it brings,
The soul with shudders tries to shake off thoughts
    like creeping things.
A vast invisible Terror twines its fingers in the
    hair,
With one hand feeling for the throat; a hand that
    will not spare.

7

" They slew the grizzled Warrior, who to them
    had been so true;
The ruddy stripling with frank eyes of bonny
    English blue;
They slew the Maiden as she slept; the Mother
    great with child;
The Babe, that smiled np in their face, they stabbed
    it as it smiled.
The piteous, pleading, hoary hair they draggled in
    red mire;
And mocked the dying as they dasht out, frantic
    from the fire,
To fall upon their Tulwars, hacked to death; the
    bayonet
Held up some child; the devils danced around it
    writhing yet:
Warm flesh, that kindled so with life, was torn,
    and slowly hewn,
To daintiest morsels for the feast where death
    began too soon.

" Our English girls, whose sweet red blood went
    dancing on its way,
A merry marriage-maker quick for its near wed-
    ding-day, —
All life awaiting for the breath of Love's sweet
    south to blow,
And budding bridal roses ripe with secret balms
    to flow, —

They stripped them naked as they were born;
    naked along the street,
In their own blood they made them dip their deli-
    cate white feet!
With some last rag of shelter the poor helpless
    darling tries
To hide her from the cruel hell of those devouring
    eyes;
Then, plucking at the skirts of Death, she prayer-
    fully doth cling,
To hide her from the eyes that still gloat round her
    in a ring.

THE AVENGERS.

" ' Now, Soldiers of our England, let your love arise
    in power ;
For never yet was greater need than in this awful hour :
Together stand like old true-hearts that never fear nor
    flinch ;
With feet that have been shod for death, never to
    yield an inch.
Our Empire is a Ship on fire, before a howling wind,
With such a smoke of torment, as 't would make high
    heaven blind !
Wild Ruin waves his flag of flame, and ye must
    spring on deck,

And quench the fire in blood, and save our treasures
    from the wreck.'
Many a time has England thought she sent her
    bravest forth;
But never went more gallant men, or more heroic
    worth.

"Hungry and lean, through rain and mire, our
    war-wolves ravening go
On their long march, that shall not mete the red
    grave of the foe:
Like winter trees stripped to their naked strength
    of heart and arm,
That glory in their grimness as they tussle with
    the storm!
Only a handful few and stern, and few and stern
    their words;
Strange meaning in their eyes that meet and strike
    out sparks like swords!
And there goes Havelock! leading the Forlorn
    Hope of our land;
The quick heart spurring at their side; the banner
    of their band:
Kindled, but calm, along their ranks his steady
    eye doth run,
As marksman seeks the death-line down the level
    of his gun.

" Beneath the whitening snows of age his spirit-
    ardors glow,
As glow the fragrant fires of spring in flowers
    beneath thc snow.
Look in his grave and martial face, with God's
    dear pity toucht;
A savior soul doth sanctify the sword his hand
    hath clutcht:
A little while his silent thoughts have gone within
    to pray,
And send a farewell of the heart to the dear ones
    far away.
He prays to God to light him through the perilous
    darkness, when
He grapples with the beasts of blood, and quells
    them in their den.
And now his look is lifted in the light of some far
    goal;
His lips the living trumpet of a gray-haired seer's
    soul.

" On the house-tops of Allahabad black, scowling
    brows were bent,
In hate, and deep, still curses, on our heroes as
    they went
To fight their hundred-days-long fight; all true as
    their good steel,
The Highlanders of Havelock, the Fusileers of
    Neil !

A falling firmament of rain the heavens were ponr-
  ing down ;
They heeded not the drowning heavens, nor yet the
  foeman's frown :
Forward they strained with hearts afire, and gallantly they toiled
Till darkness fell upon them : then the Moon up-
  rose and smiled.
A little thing ! and yet it seemed at such a time to
  come
Just like a proud and mournful smile from the
  very heart of Home.

" That night they halted in a snipe-swamp; hungry, cold, and drencht ;
With hearts that kept the blitheness of brave men
  and never blencht.
Through flooding nullah, slushy sand, onward they
  strode again,
Ere Dawn, a wingëd glory, alit upon the bur-
  nisht rain,
And mists up-gathered sullenly along the rear of
  flight,
Slowly as beaten Bellooches might lounge from
  out the fight.
Then heaven grew like inverted hell; a blazing
  vault of fire !
The Sun pursuing pitiless, to bring the brain-
  strokes nigher ;

With sworded splendors fierce in front, and dart-
    ing down all day,
Intently as the eyes of Death a-feeding on his prey.

" All day long, and every day, with patience con-
    quering pain,
Our good and gallant fellows with one purpose for-
    ward strain ;
For there is that within each heart nothing but
    death can stop ;
They hurry on, and hurry on, and hurry till they
    drop ;
Trying to save the remnant ; reach the leaguered
    place in time
To grasp, with red-wet slaughtering hands, the
    workers of this crime.
They think of all the dead that float adown the
    Ganges' waters :
Those noble Englishmen of ours ; their gentle
    wives and daughters !
Of Fire and Madness broken loose, and doing
    deeds most pitiful ;
And then of vengeance dealt out by the choked
    and blackened city-full.

" They think of those poor things that climb each
    little eminence ;
As, from the deluge of the dark, when day is
    going hence,

The sheep will huddle up the hill, and gather there
    forlorn;
So gather they in this dread night, to wait the far-
    off morn.
Or, crouching in the jungle, they look up in Na-
    ture's face,
To find she has no heart, for all her rectilinear
    grace!
Each leaf a sword, or prickly spear, or lifted jagged
    knife!
No shields of shelter like our leaves; but threat-
    ening human life,
With ominous hints of blood; and there the roots
    go writhing round,
Like curses coiled upon the spring, that rest not
    underground.

"They find sure tokens all the day! and starting
    from their dream
At night, they hear the Pariah dogs that howl by
    Ganges' stream,
Knowing the waters bear their freight of corpses
    stiff and stark,
Scenting the footfalls on the air; as Death comes
    down the dark;
Only the Lotus with ripe lips, and arms caressing
    clings.
The silence swarms with ghastly thoughts; each
    sound with ghastly things.

There, stands the plough i' the furrow; there the
    villagers have flown !
There, Fire ran dancing over roofs that underfoot
    went down !
There, Renaud hung his dangling dead, with but
    short time for shrift, .
He caught them on their way to hell, and gave
    them a last lift.

"They saw the first sight of their foe as the fourth
    dawn grew red ;
Twenty miles to breakfast marched ; and had to
    fight instead.
The morning smiled on arms up-piled, and weary
    wayworn men,
But soon the assembly sounded, and they sprung
    to arms again ;
The heaviest heart up-leaping light, as flames that
    tread on air.
The Rebel line bore down as they had caught us
    unaware ;
But Maude dasht forward with his guns, over
    the sandy mire,
And little did they relish our bright rain of rifle
    fire :
Quickly the onward way was ploughed, with heaps
    on either hand ;
They broke the foe, then broke their fast, that
    dauntless little band.

"Again they felt our withering fire, by Pandoo
    Nuddee stream;
Again they feared the crashing charge, and fled
    the vengeful gleam:
Small loss was his in battle when the Conqueror
    lookt round;
But many fell from weariness, and died without a
    wound.
Soft, whispering flowery secrets, came a low wind
    of the west
That eve, like breath made balmy with the sweet
    love in the breast;
Breathing its freshness through the groves of
    Mango and of Palm;
But the sweetest thing that wind could bring was
    slumber's holy balm,
To bless them for the morrow, and give strength
    for them to cope
With those ten thousand men that stood betwixt
    them and their hope.

"It must have been a glorious sight to see them as
    they went,
With veteran valor steady; sure of proud accom-
    plishment,
When Havelock bade his line advance, and the
    Highlanders swept on;
Each one at heart a thousand; a thousand men as
    one;

Linked in their beautiful proud line across the
    broken lands,
Straight on ! they never paused to lift the weapon
    in their hands ;
Silent, compact and resolute, charged as a thunder-
    cloud,
That burst, and wrapt the dead and living in one
    smoky shroud ;
One volley of Defiance ! one wild cheer ! and
    through the smoke,
They flasht ! and all the battle into flying frag-
    ments broke.

"When night came down they lay there, gashed
    all over, side by side,
The gray old warrior, and the youth, his Mother's
    darling pride !
Rolled with the rebel in the dust, and grim in
    bloody death ;
And over all the mist arose, dank as the grave-
    yard's breath.
But light of heart we took the hill, and very proud
    that night
Was Havelock of his noble men, and Cawnpore
    was in sight.
The men had neither food nor tent, but the red
    road was won :
And very proud were they to hear their General's
    ' *Well done* ' ;

Not knowing how their triumph-cheer had rung a
    fatal knell;
Nor what that wretch had wrought who has no
    match this side of Hell.

CAWNPORE.

" Cawnpore was ghastly silent, as into it they
    stepped;
There stood the blackened Ruin that the brave old
    Soldier kept !
Where strained each ear for the English cheer, and
    stretcht the wan wide eyes,
Through all that awful night to see the signal-
    rocket rise;
No tramp, no cheer of Brothers near; no distant
    cannon's boom;
Nothing but Death goes to and fro betwixt the
    glare and gloom.
The living remnant try to hold their bit of blood-
    stained ground;
Dark gaps continual in their midst; the dead all
    lying round;
And saddest corpses still are those that die, and do
    not die;
With just a little glimmering light of life to show
    them by.

" Each drop of water cost a wound to fetch it from
    the well ;
The father heard his crying child and went, but
    surely fell.
They had drunk all their tears, and now dry agony
    drank their blood ;
The sand was killing in their souls ; the wind a
    fiery flood ;
Oh, for one waft of heather-breath from off a
    Scottish wold !
One shower that makes our English leaves smile
    greener for its gold !
Then life drops inward from the eyes ; turns np-
    ward with last prayer,
To look for its deliverance ; the only way lies
    there !
And then triumphant Treachery made leap each
    trusting heart,
Like some poor Bird called from the nest, up-pois-
    ing for the dart.

"' *Come, let us pray,*' their Chaplain said. No
    other boon was craved :
No pleading word for mercy sued ; no face the
    white flag craved ;
But all grasped hands and prayed, till peace their
    souls serenely filled ;
Then like our noble Martyrs, there they stood np,
    and were killed.

Only one saved !
    He led our soldiers to the house of blood ;
An eager, panting, cursing crew ! but stricken
    there they stood
In silence that was breathlessness of vengeance
    infinite ;
A-many wept like women who were fiercest in the
    fight :
There grew a look in human eyes as though a
    wild beast came
Up in them at that scent of blood and glared de-
    vouring flame.

" All the Babes and Women butchered ! all the
    dear ones dead ;
The story of their martyrdom in lines of awful red !
The blood-black floor, the clotted gore, fair tresses,
    deep sword-dints ;
Last message-scrawl upon the wall, and tiny finger-
    prints :
Gathered in one were all strange sights of horror
    and despair,
That make the vision blood-shot, freeze the life, or
    lift the hair.
Faces to faces flasht hell-fire ! O, but they felt
    't would take
The very cup of God's own wrath, that gasping
    thirst to slake :

For many a day ' *Cawnpore* ' was hissed, and, at
    its word of guilt,
The slaying sword went merciless right, ruddy to
    the hilt.

" There came a time we caught them, with a vast
    and whelming wave,
And of their grand Secunder Bagh we made a
    trophied grave.
Once more the 'Highlanders pressed on with stern,
    avenging tread,
And Peel was there with his big guns, and Camp-
    bell at their head :
A spring of daring madness ! and they leapt upon
    their prey
With hungry hearts on fury fed, for many and
    many a day.
For hours and hours, they slew, and slew, the
    devils in their den :
' *Ye wreaked your will on women weak, now try it
    with strong men.*'
The blood that cried to heaven long in vapors
    from our slain,
Fell hot and fast upon their heads in a rich ruddy
    rain.

" That day they saw their delicate white marbles
    glow and swim ;

There rose a cry like hell from out a slaughter
    great and grim:
And as they claspt their hands and sued for mercy
    where they fell,
One last sure thrust was given for that red and
    writhing Well.
And there was joy in every heart, and light in
    every eye,
To see the traitor hordes that fled, make a last
    stand to die!
While from the big wide wounds, like snakes, the
    runlets crawled along
And stole away; the reptiles who had done the
    cruel wrong!
A terrible reprisal for each precious drop they
    spilled.
Seventeen hundred coward killers there were brave-
    ly killed.

THE RELIEF.

"England's unseen, dead Sorrow doth a visible
    Angel rise;
The sword of justice in her hand; Revenge looks
    through her eyes:
Stern with the purpose in her soul right onward
    hastens she,

Like one that bears the doom of worlds, with
    vengeful majesty ;
Sombre, superb, and terrible, before them still she
    goes !
And though they lessen day by day, they deal such
    echoing blows,
That still dilating with success, still grows that
    little band,
Till in the place of hundreds, ten thousand seem
    to stand.
With arms that weary not at work, they bear our
    victor flag,
To plant it high on hills of dead, a torn and
    bloody rag.

" And Lucknow lies before them, — all its pageant-
    ry unrolled ;
Against the smiling sapphire gleam her tops of
    lighted gold.
Each royal wall is fretted all with frostwork and
    with fire,
A glory of color jewel-rich, that makes a splen-
    dor-pyre,
As wave on wave the wonder breaks, the pointed
    flames burn higher,
On dome of mosque and minaret, on pinnacle and
    spire ;

8

Fairy creations, seen mid-air, that in their pleas-
    aunce wait,
Like wingëd creatures sitting just outside their
    heaven-gate.
The City in its beauty lies, with flowers about her
    feet ;
Green fields, and goodly gardens, make so foul a
    thing seem sweet.

The Bugle rings out for the march, and, with its
    proudest thrill,
Goes to the heart of Havelock's men and works its
    lordly will,
Making their spirits thrill as leaves are thrilled in
    some wild wind ;
Hunger and heartache, weariness and wounds, all
    left behind.
Their sufferings all forgotten now, as in the ranks
    they form ;
And every soul in stature rose to wrestle with the
    storm.
All silent ! what was hid at heart could not be
    said in words :
With faces set for Lucknow, ground to sharpness,
    keen as swords !
A tightening twitch all over ! a grim glistening in
    the eye,
' *Forward !* ' and on their way they strode to dare,
    and do, and die.

" Hope whispers at the ear of some, that they shall
    meet again,
And clasp their long-lost darlings, after all the toil
    and pain ;
A-many know that they will sleep to-night among
    the slain ;
And many a cheek will bloom no more for all the
    tearful rain :
And some have only vengeance ; but to-day 't is
    bitter sweet;
And there goes Havelock ! his the aim too lofty
    for defeat ;
With steady tramp the column treads, true as the
    firm heart's-beat ;
Strung for its headlong murderous march through
    that long fatal street.
All ready to win a soldier's grave, or do the daring
    deed !
But not a man that fears to die for England in her
    need.

" The masked artillery raked the road, and ploughed
    them front and flank ;
Some gallant fellow every step was stricken from
    the rank ;
But, as he staggered, in his place another sternly
    stepped ;
And, firing fast as they could load, their onward
    way they kept.

Now, give them the good bayonet! with England's
    fiercest foes,
Strong arm, cold steel will do it, in the wildest,
    bloodiest close :
And now their bayonets abreast go sternly up the
    ridge,
And with a cheer they take the guns, another,
    clear the bridge.
One good home-thrust! and surely, as the dead in
    doom are sure,
They send them where that British cheer can
    trouble them no more.

"The fire is biting bitterly; onward the battle
    rolls ;
Grim Death is glaring at them, from ten thousand
    hiding-holes ;
Death stretches up from earth to heaven, spread-
    ing his darkness round ;
Death piles the heaps of helplessness face down-
    ward to the ground ;
Death flames from sudden ambuscades, where all
    was still and dark ;
Death swiftly speeds on whizzing wings the bul-
    lets to their mark ;
Death from the doors and windows, all around and
    overhead,
Darts, with his cloven fiery tongues, incessant,
    quick, and red :

Death everywhere, Death in all sounds, and, through
    its smoke of breath,
Victory beckons at the end of long dark lanes of
    death.

"Another charge, another cheer, another battery
    won!
And in a whirlwind of fierce fire the fight goes
    roaring on.
Into the very heart of hell, with comrades falling
    fast,
Through all that tempest terrible, the glorious rem-
    nant passed.
No time to help a dear old friend : but where the
    wounded fell,
They knew it was all over, and they lookt a last
    farewell.
And dying eyes, slow setting in a cold and stony
    stare,
Turned upward, see a map of murder scribbled on
    the air
With crossing flames; and others read their fiery
    fearful fate,
In dark, swart faces waiting for them, whitening
    with their hate.

"O, proudly men will march to death, when Have-
    lock leads them on :

Through all the storm he sat his horse as he were
  cut in stone !
But now his look grows dark; his eye gleams
  with uneasy flash :
' *On, for the Residency, we must make a last brave
  dash.*'
And on dasht Highlander and Sikh through a sea
  of fire and steel,
On, with the lion of their strength, our first in
  glory, Niel!
It seemed the face of heaven grew black, so close
  it held its breath,
Through all the glorious agony of that long march
  of death.
The round shot tears, the bullets rain; dear God,
  outspread thy shield !
Put forth thy red right arm, for them ! thy sword
  of sharpness wield.

" One wave breaks forward on the shore, and one
  falls helpless back :
Again they club their wasted strength, and fight
  like ' *Hell-fire Jack.*'*
And ever as fainter grows the fire of that intrepid
  band,
Again they grasp the bayonet as 't were Salvation's hand.

   * Soubriquet of Captain Olpherts.

They leap the broad, deep trenches, rush through
    archways streaming fire;
Every step some brave heart bursts, heaving deliv-
    erance nigher:
'*I 'm hit,*' cries one, '*you 'll take me on your back,
    old comrade, I
Should like to see their dear white faces once before I
    die;
My body may save you from the shot.*'
                    His comrade bore him on:
But, ere they reacht the Bailie Guard, the hurry-
    ing soul was gone.

"And now the Gateway arched in sight; the last
    grim tussle came.
One moment makes immortal! dead or living,
    endless fame!
They heard the voice of fiery Niel, that for the
    last time thrilled;
'*Push on my men, 't is getting dark*': he sat where
    he was killed.
Another frantic surge of life, and plunging o'er
    the bar,
Right into harbor hurling goes their whirling wave
    of war,
And breaks in mighty thunders of reverberating
    cheers,
Then dances on in frolic foam of kisses, blessings,
    tears.

Stabbed by mistake, one native cries with the last
    breath he draws,
' *Welcome, my friends, never you mind, it 's all for
    the good cause.*'

"How they had leaned and listened, as the battle
    sounded nigher;
How they had strained their eyes to see them com-
    ing crowned with fire!
Till in the flashing street below they heard them
    pant for breath,
And then the English faces smiled clear from the
    cloud of death;
And iron grasp met tender clasp; wan weeping
    women fold
Their dear Deliverers, down whose long brown
    beards the big tears rolled.
Another such a meeting will not be on this side
    heaven!
The little wine they have hoarded, to the last drop
    shall be given
To those who, in their mortal need, fought on
    through fearful odds,
Bled for them, reacht them, saved them, less like
    men than glorious gods.

DEATH OF HAVELOCK.

" The Warrior may be ripe for rest, and laurelled
    with great deeds,
But till their work be done, no rest for those whom
    God yet needs :
Whether in rivers of ruin their onward way they
    tear,
Or healing waters trembling with the beauty that
    they bear ;
Blasting or blessing they must on : on, on, for-
    ever on !
Divine unrest is in their breast, until their work be
    done.
Nor is it all a pleasant path the sacred band must
    tread,
With life a summer holiday, and death a downy
    bed !
They wear away with noble use, they drink the
    tearful cup ;
And they must bear the bitter cross who go with
    Christ to sup.

"Each day his face grew thinner, and sweeter,
    saintlier grew
The smiling soul that every day was burning keen-
    lier through.

And higher, each day higher, did the life-flame
    heavenward climb,
Like sad sweet sunshine up the wall, that for the
    sunset time
Seems watching till the signal that shall call it
    hence is given ;
Even so his spirit kept the watch, till beckoned
    home to heaven.
His work was done, his eyes with peace were soft
    and satisfied ;
War-worn and wasted, in the arms of Victory he
    died.
' *Havelock 's dead,*' and darkness fell on every up-
    turned face ;
The shadow of an Angel passing from its earthly
    place.

"In the red pass of peril, with a fame shall never·
    dim,
Died Havelock, the Good Soldier: who would not
    die like him ?
In grandest strength he fell, full-length ; and now
    our hero climbs
To those who stood up in their day and spoke
    with after times :
There on the battlements of Heaven, they watch
    us, looking back

To see the blessing flow for those who follow in
    their track.
He smileth from his heaven now; the Martyr with
    his palm;
The weary warrior's tired life is crowned with
    starry calm.
On many sailing through the storm another star
    shall shine,
And they shall look up through the night and con-
    quer at the sign.

"They laid it low, the old gray head, not only
    gray with years;
It had been bowed in Sorrow's lap and silvered
    with her tears;
Our England may not crown it, with her heart too
    full for speech;
The hand that draws into the dark, hath borne it
    beyond reach.
The eyes of far-away heaven-blue, with such keen
    lustre lit,
As they could pierce the dark of death, and, star-
    like, fathom it,
They may not swim with sweetness as the happy
    Children run
To welcome home the Reaper, when the weary
    day is done!

How would the tremulous radiance round the old
    man's mouth have smiled;
Our good gray-headed hero, with the heart of a
    little child.

" Honor to Henry Havelock ! though not of kingly
    blood,
He wore the double royalty of being great and
    good.
He rose and reacht the topmost height; our Hero
    lowly born :
So from the lowly grass hath grown the proud
    embattled Corn !
He rose up in our cruel need, and towering on he
    trod ;
Baring his brow to battle bold, as humbly to his
    God.
He did his work nor thought of nations ringing
    with his name,
He walkt with God, and talkt with God, nor cared
    if following Fame
Should find him toiling in the field, or sleeping
    underground ;
Nor did he mind what resting-place, with heaven
    embracing round.

" When swarming hell had broken bounds, he
    showed us how to stand

With rootage like the Palm amidst the maddest
    whirl of sand;
Undaunted while the swarthy storm around him
    swirled and swirled,
A winding-sheet of all white life ! a wild Sahara
    world !
The drowning waves closed over him, lost to all
    human view,
But, like an arrow straight from God, he cleft
    their twelve hosts through.
No swerving as he walkt along the rearing earth-
    quake ridge;
He made a way for Victory, his body was her
    bridge.
Grand in the mouths of men his fame along the
    centuries runs;
Women shall read of his great deed and bear
    heroic sons.

" He leant a trusting hand on heaven, a gentle heart
    on home;
In secret he grew ready, ere the Judgment hour
    was come.
War blew away the ashes gray, and kindled at the
    core
Live sparkles of the Ironside fire that glowed on
    Marston Moor.
Some Angel-Mute had led him blindfold through his
    thorny ways,

Till, on a sudden, lo, he stood, full in the glory's
    blaze.
Aloud, for all the world to hear, God called his
    servant's name,
And led him forth, where all might see, upon the
    heights of fame.
His arch of life, suspended as it sprang, in heaven
    appears,
Our bow of promise o'er the storm, seen through
    rejoicing tears.

" Joy to old England! she has stuff for storm-
    sail and for stay,
While she can breed such heroes, in her quiet,
    homely way :
Such martial souls that go with grim, war-figured
    brows pulled down,
As men that are resolved to bear Death's heavy,
    iron crown.
So long as she has sons like these, no foe shall
    make her bow,
While Ocean washes her white feet; Heaven kisses
    her fair brow.
If India's fate had rested on each single savior
    soul,
They would have kept their grasp of it till we
    regained the whole.
The Lightnings of that bursting Cloud, which
    were to blast our might,

But served to show its majesty clear in the sterner
    light.
" Our England towers up beautiful with her dilat-
    ing form,
To greater stature in the strife, and glory in the
    storm ;
Her wrath's great wine-press trodden on so many
    vintage fields,
With crush and strain, and press of pain, a ripened
    spirit yields,
To warm us in our winter, when the times are
    coward and cold,
And work divinely in young veins ; wake boyhood
    in the old.
Behold her flame from field to field on Victory's
    chariot wheels,
Till to its den, bleeding to death, Rebellion back-
    ward reels.
Her Martyrs are avenged ! ye may search that
    Indian land,
And scarcely find a single soul of all the traitor
    band.

" We 've many a nameless hero lying in his un-
    known grave,
Their life's gold fragment gleaming but a sunfleck
    on the wave.
But rest, you unknown, noble dead ! our Living are
    one band

Of England's power ; but, with her Dead she
    grasps into the land.
The flower of our Race shall make that Indian
    . desert bud,
Its shifting sands drench firm, and fertilize with
    English blood.
In many a country they sleep crowned, our con-
    quering, faithful Dead :
They pave our path where shines her sun of
    empire overhead ;
They circle in a glorious ring, with which the
    world is wed,
And where their blood has turned to bloom, our
    England's Rose is red.

" Your brother Willie, Boy, was one of Havelock's
    little band ;
My Son ! my beautiful brave Son, lies in that In-
    dian Land.
They buried him by the wayside where he bowed
    him down to die,
While Homeward in its Eastern pomp the Triumph
    passed him by.
And even yet mine eyes are wet, but 't is with that
    proud tear
A lofty feeling in its front doth like a jewel wear.
I see him ! on his forehead shines the conqueror's
    burning crest,

And God's own cross of Victory is on his martial
    breast.
I should have liked to have felt him near, when
    these old eyes grow dim,
But I gave him to our England; she had greater
    need of him."

9

IN MEMORIAM.

A RECORD of affectionate remembrance, inscribed to the
Lady Marian Alford on the death of her son, John William
Spencer, Earl Brownlow, as the Author's offering of sym-
pathy in the common sorrow.

The dear ones who are worthiest of our love
Below, are also worthiest above.
Too lofty is his place in glory now,
For hands like ours to reach and wreathe his brow:
A few poor flowers we plant upon his tomb,
Watered with tears to make them breathe and bloom.
The gentle soul that was so long thy ward,
Now hovers over thee, thine Angel-Guard:
And, as thou mourn'st above his dust so dear,
Thy happy Comforter draws smiling near.
Look up, dear friend, our Doves of Earth but rise,
Transfigured into Birds of Paradise.

"The idea of his life doth sweetly creep
Into my study of imagination ;
And every lovely organ of his life
Will come apparelled in more precious habit —
More moving delicate, and full of life,
Into the eye and prospect of my soul
Than when he lived indeed."

IN MEMORIAM.

PPARELLED richly in presence of the
    Gods,
  With crown upon his brow, the old
    Greek stood
And offered up his soul at Sacrifice.
Even then the tidings came, — "THY SON IS
DEAD."

They saw the sharp words pierce him through and
    through,
The firm lip quiver and the face grow white;
They saw the strong man tremble to the knees:
Slowly the big drops gathered in his eyes:
Slowly he took the crown from off his head,
And let it fall to the ground, as one who feels
Heart-broke all over, — for his pride of life
Hath faded, and his strength is spilled in dust.

Bnt, when the Messenger went on to tell
The exulting story — how the valiant youth

Had lost a life to win a Country's love :
How bravely he had borne him in the battle ;
How well he fought, how gloriously he fell ;
The weeping Father put his war-look on
And rose up with the stature of his soul —
All his life listening at the hungry ear —
Eyes   burning   with   the   splendor   of   quenched
          tears —
His pillared chin firm-set, his brave mouth clenched
In calm resolve to bear, and on his face
A smile as if of Sword-light !
                              Then he stooped,
And gently took the crown up from the ground ;
Softly replaced it on his brow, and wore
It proudly, as the visible symbol of
That other awful crown which darkened down.

So, when the word came that our friend was dead,
We bowed beneath the burden of our loss,
And could have grovelled straightway, prone in
          dust.
But looking on the happy death he died,
And thinking of the holy life he lived,
And knowing he was one of those that soon
Attain their starry stature, and are crowned,
We could not linger in the dust to weep,
But were upborne from earth as if on wings ;
A sunbeam in the soul dried up the tears,

In which the sorrow trembled to be gone;
For his dear sake we could afford to smile.

Why should we weep, when 't is so well with him ?
Our loss even cannot measure his great gain !
Why should we weep when death is but a mask
Through which we know the face of Life beyond ?
Grief did but bow us at his grave to show
Far more of Heaven in the landscape round !

For such a vestal soul as his, — so pure,
So crystal-clear, so filled with light, we lookt
As at some window of the other world,
And almost saw the Angel smiling through —
'T was but a step from out our muddy street
Of Earth, on to the pavement all of pearl !

Why should we weep ?   We do not bury love ;
We cannot seek that jewel in the grave !
The dust of earth but claims its kindred dust :
We do not bury life, and cannot feel
The grave-grass grow betwixt our warmth and
          him ;
Death emptieth the House but not the Heart :
That keeps its darlings safe though out of sight.

Let us uplift the eyelids of the Mind
And see the living Love who dwelt awhile

In that frail body, now a spirit of Light
All jubilant upon the hills of God.
This gloom we feel, this mourning that we wear,
Is but the Shadow of his lordlier height.

Why should they weep who have another friend
In death ; another thread to guide them through
Life's maze ; another tie to draw them home ;
A firmer foothold in the infinite ;
Another kinsman on the spiritual side ;
Another voice to greet them through the Void ;
Another face to kindle with its life
The pale impersonality of God ?

The dearest souls, you know, must part in sleep,
And death is but a little longer night.
A little while, and we shall wake to find
Our lost ones with us face to face, and feel
All years of yearning summed up in a kiss.

Why should we fear the Grave ?   It is the bed
Where the King lay in State with Angels round,
And hallowed it forevermore to us.
Why should we fear the Grave ?   It is the way
The Conqueror went, and made the very dust
Grow starry with the sparkle of his splendor,   .
And left the darkness conscious of His presence.
We can look down upon the Grave now He
Has plumbed it, spanned it, one foot on each side.

Through His dear love who hath abolished death,
We may shut up our Graveyards of the heart
That lookt so grim of old, and plant anew
This garden of our God to smile with flowers.

Why do we shrink so from Eternity?
We are in Eternity from Birth not Death !
Eternity is not beyond the stars —
Some far Hereafter — it is *Here*, and *Now!*
The Kingdom of Heaven is *within*, so near
We do not see it save by spirit-sight.
We shut our eyes in prayer, and we are *There*
In thought, and Thoughts are spirit-*things* —
Realities upon the other side.
In death we close our eyelids once for all
To pass forever, and seem far away.
And yet the distance does not lie in death :
Death 's not the only door of spirit-world,
Nor Visibility sole presence-sign :
The Near or Far is in our depth of love
And height of life : We look WITHOUT, to find
Our lost ones are beyond all human reach :
We feel *Within*, and lo ! they are nestling near.

Flow soft, ye tears, adown my Lady's face,
And bathe the broken spirit with your balm,
And melt the cloud about her into drops
That glister with the light of Heaven's own smile.

And thou, God, whisper as the tears do fall,
No cloud would rise to rain but for Thy Sun !
She sorroweth not as those who have no hope,
Nor is her House left wholly desolate.
O Grief, lie lightly on my Lady's brow :
She gave her best of life in love for him !
A crown of glory wears the dear bowed head
That hath grown gray in noble sacrifice.

Ah me, I know the heart must have its way.
I know the ache of utter loneliness ;
The distance between those that were so near ;
The silence never broken by a sound
We still keep listening for ; the spirit's loss
Of its old clinging-place, that makes our life
A dead leaf drifting desolately free :
The many thousand things we had to say ;
And on the dear still face that hushing look,
As though the sweet life-music still went on
Though too far off for hearing — (as it doth) !
Thrice have I wrestled and been thrown by Death,
Thrice have I given my dear ones to the grave ;
And yet I know — see it in spite of tears :
Say it, even while the heart breaks in the voice :
These are His ways to draw us nearer Him.
And we must climb by pathways of the cloud.

He breaks the image to reveal Himself !
He takes our dearest things to woo us with ;

Takes, for a little while, the gift he gave
Forever : but to better still our best.

Feeling for that which fled, our finite love
Is caught up in the clasp o' the Infinite,
Palpably as though God did press the hand
And make the heart well up and flood the eyes
With that proud overflow of a fuller Heaven !

O Lady, let mine be the song-bird's part,
That singeth after rain and shakes the drops
Down, with his thrillings, from the drooping spray,
And sets it softly springing nigher Heaven
That smiles out 'twixt the clouds with gladdest
        blue !
Your love-ties have but lengthened to let free
The shadowed soul that needed far more sun.
So the fair Lily,* growing down the dark
Beside her lover, yearneth towards Heaven
And lives up faster, till she springs afloat,
To sun her on the surface of the stream :
And now she draws up, even by the root,
Her Love left pining on the earth below,
Lifting him to her side again, full flower ;
And 't is his Heaven to die and get to her !

* The " *Valisneria*," the male and female flowers of which
appear on separate plants ; the latter blooming on the surface of the water, while the former tears its roots from the
soil to rise and blossom and die beside it.

What did we ask, with all our love for him,
But just a little breath of fuller life,
To float the laboring lungs ?   And God hath given
Him Life itself; full, everlasting Life !
What did we pray for ?   Rest, even for a night,
That he might rise with Sleep's most golden dews
Refreshed, to feel the morning in his soul ?
And God hath given him His Eternal Rest.
We could not offer freedom for one hour
From that dread weight of weariness they bear
Who try for years to shake Death's Shadow off:
And God hath made him free forevermore.

Before me hangs his Picture on the wall,
Alive still, with the loving, cordial eyes. —
How tenderly their winsome lustre laughed ! —
The fine pale face, pathetically sweet,
So thin with suffering that it seemed a soul :
We feared the Angels might be kissing it
Too often, and too wooingly for us :
The hands, so woman-white and delicate,
That day by day were gliding from our grasp :
They used to make my heart ache many a time.

I see another picture now.   The form
Ye sowed in weakness hath been raised in power;
A palace of pleasure for a prison of pain.
The beauty of his nature that we felt

Is featured in the shape he weareth now!
The same kind face, but changed and glorified;
From Life's unclouded summit it looks back,
And sweetly smiles at all the sorrows past,
With such a look as taketh away grief:
No longer pale, and there is no more pain.
His face is rosed with Heaven's immortal bloom
For he hath found the land of Health at last;
The One Physician who can cure all ills:
And he hath eaten of the Tree of Life,
And felt the Eternal Spring in brain and breast
Make lusty life that lightens forth in love.

Indeed, indeed, as the old Poet saith,
He was a very perfect, gentle Knight!
A natural Noble, by the grace of God:
Affection in the dearest human form.
Yet, gentle as he was, how gallantly
He bóre his sufferings, kept the worst from sight,
Having the heroic flash of English blood.
How freely would he spend his little hoard
Of saved-up strength with spirit lordly and blithe,
To enrich a welcome and make gladder cheer!

And to the Poor he was all tender heart.
The very last time that he talked with me
His trouble was to know how poor folks lived
Upon so small a pittance, and he sighed

For life, for strength to do more than he could,
And in his kingly eyes great sorrow reigned.

No sighs, no weakness now, in that glad world
Where yearning avails more than working here,
And to desire is to accomplish good :
For Wishes get them wings of power, and range
Rejoicing through illimitable life ;
And we shall find some Castles built in Air
Stand good ; are habitable after all !
To me, his life is like the innocent Flower
That springs up for the light and spreads for love ; ˙
Breathes fragrantly in gratitude to God,
And in sweet odors passes from our sight.
But there's no jot of all his promise lost : —
Each golden hint shall have fulfilment yet —
All that was heavenliest perfected in heaven.

All the shy modesties of secret soul
That breathed like violets hidden in the dusk ;
The folded sweetness, the unfingered bloom ;
The unsunned riches of his rarer self ;
Are shut up softly to be saved by Him
Who gave us of the Flower, but keeps the fruit.

The best his life could grow on earth is given ;
The rest can ripen till ye meet in heaven.

And dear my Lady, little can we guess
What God hath planned for those He loves so much,
And beckons home so early to Himself!
May some full foretaste of his perfect peace
Fall on you, solacing with solemn joy.
Of such as he was, there be few on Earth,
Of such as he is, there are many in Heaven;
And Life is all the sweeter that he lived,
And all he loved more sacred for his sake:
And Death is all the brighter that he died,
And Heaven is all the happier that he 's there.

So, one by one the dear old faces fade.
Hands wave their far farewell while beckoning us
Across the river, all must pass alone.
We stand at gaze upon their shining track,
Until the two worlds mingle in a mist,
And the two lives are molten into one:
Familiar things grow phantom-like remote;
Things visionary draw familiar-near;
The picture that we gaze on seems the Real
Looking at us, and we the Shadows that pass.

And yet 't is sweet to feel — as underfoot,
OUR path slopes for the quiet place apart;
Day darkens in the Valley of Death's shade —
Our best half landed in the better life;
The balance leaning to the other side;

The peaceful evening comes that brings all home,
And we are weaning kindly to leave go
Our hold of earth ; life in the Autumn-leaf
Loosens with every shower ; and as the gloom
Gathers, and things are growing all a-dusk,
We know our Stars are smiling overhead ;
In their eternal setting high and safe
Where they can look down on our passing night,
Glad in the loftier radiance of a sun
We may not see, with steadfast gaze of love
Unfathomable as Eternity :
Dear memories of Vesper gentleness
That are the Phosphor hopes of coming day,
And death grows radiant with our Shining Ones.

Blessëd are they whose treasures are in Heaven !
Their grief 's too rich for our poor comforting.
Let us put on the robe of readiness,
The golden trumpet will be sounding soon,
That bids us to the gathering in the Heavens !
Let us press forward to their summit of life
Who have ceased to pant for breath and won their
      Rest,
And there is no more parting, no more pain !

CARMINA NUPTIALIA.

10

The Story of all stories, sweet and old;
Sweetest to Lovers the last time 't is told.

CARMINA NUPTIALIA.

———◆———

WEDDED LOVE.

THIS little spring of life, that feeds the
        root
    Of England's greatness, giveth, un-
        derground,
Bloom to the Flower, and freshness to the Fruit ;
  Then wells and spreads, with golden ripples
      round,
In circling glory to a sea of might,
  Embracing Home and Country of our love ;
Half-mirroring the beauty beyond sight —
  Taking some likeness of the above abode.

THE WEDDING.

ALL Women love a Wedding ! old
　　　Or youthful; Mother, Widow, or
　　　　　Wife:
It lights with precious gleam of gold
　　　The river of poorest life :

For one, the gold is far and dim ;
　　For one, a glimpse of things to be ;
But here it sparkles, at the brim
　　　Of full felicity !

And they will cluster by the way ;
　　Crowd at this Eden-gate, with eyes
That run, and pray that this Pair may
　　　Keep their new Paradise.

Green is the garden, as at first ;
　　As smiling-blue the happy skies,
Where float the bubble-worlds that burst,
　　　And leave us smarting eyes.

They seem to think that these *must* clasp
　　The jewel turned to dew or mist :
The glamour they could never grasp,
　　　Though wedded lips have kissed ;

That this gold Apple of promise, crowned
With redness on the sunny side,
Will gradually grow ripe all round;
    That this new Lover and Bride

Must reach the breathing Magic Rose
Such cunning spirits hold in air,
On which our fingers could not close,
    Even when we knew 't was there !

This nest of hopes will bring forth young
Unto the brooding heart's low call —
Not merely pretty birds'-eggs, strung
    To hide a naked wall !

So many start thus, hand-in-hand —
Few only reach the blessèd goal ;
But *these* shall surely see the land
    Hid somewhere in the soul.

And delicate airs creep sweetly through
Old bridal-chambers dusty and dim :
Down from a far heaven warm and blue,
    The mellow splendors swim.

The Woman's eyes grow loving wet ;
They dazzle with the morning ray :
The Woman's longing will beget
    Her own dear wedding-day !

In his network of wrinkles, Age
   May veil their virgin beauties now ;
Faces be furrowed — a strange page
    Of writing on the brow :

The smiling soul cannot erase
   The sad life-lines it shines above ;
Yet, imaged in the dear old face,
    You see their own young love !

The sleeping Beauty wakes anew
   Beneath the touch of tender tears ;
The Flower unfolds, to drink the dew,
    That seemëd dead for years.

All hearts are as a grove of birds
   Spring-toucht and chirruping every one ;
And each will set the Wedding-Words
    To a music of her own.

Some withered remnant of old bliss
  ' Flushing on faded cheeks they bring,
Telling of times when Love's young kiss
    Was a fire-offering ;

And spirits walk in white, as starts
   This bridal-tint that blooms anew ;
And so, with all their Woman-hearts,
    They fling Good Luck's old shoe !

SERENADE.

 WAKE, sweet Love, for Heaven is awake,
And waiting to be gracious for thy sake !
All night I saw thy fairness gleam afar
With fresh, pure sparkle of the Morning-
    Star :
Awake, my Love, and let the veil be drawn
From Beauty bathëd at the springs of Dawn.

" Awake, sweet Love, for Heaven is awake,
And waiting to be gracious for thy sake.
    A touch upon some silver-sounding string,
    As all the harps of heaven were vibrating
    Within me, woke me, bade me rise and say
    ' Awake, my Love, this is our wedding-day.'

" Awake, sweet Love, for Heaven is awake,
And waiting to be gracious for thy sake.
    It is the tender time when turtle-doves
    Begin to murmur of their vernal loves :
    Spirits that all night nestled in the flowers
    Shake perfume from their wings this hour of hours.

" Awake, sweet Love, for Heaven is awake,
And waiting to be gracious for thy sake.

To feel thee mine my faith is large enough,
And yet the miracle needs continual proof!
One minute satisfied, the next I pine
For just one more assurance thou art mine.

" Awake, sweet Love, for Heaven is awake,
And waiting to be gracious for thy sake.
Thy presence sets my cloudland round about
Glowing as heaven were turning inside out :
And all the mists that darkened me erewhile
Are smitten into splendors at thy smile.

" Awake, sweet Love, for Heaven is awake,
And waiting to be gracious for thy sake.
Our great sunrise of life begins to glow,
And all the buds of love are ripe to blow ;
And all the Birds of Bliss are gayly singing,
And all the bridal-Bells of Heaven are ringing."

ARGUING IN A CIRCLE.

HEN first my true Love crowned me with
her smile,
Methought that heaven encircled me the
while !
When first my true Love to mine arms was given,
Ah, then methought that I encircled Heaven."

AN APRIL WEDDING.

APRIL Wedding,
    Sad-smiling, shadowy-bright;
The Grave at foot, and overhead
    The merry Bird of Light!

O April Wedding,
    The conscious ear at times
Detects the Bell that tolled the knell
    Among the Marriage-Chimes!

O April Wedding,
    Thy hues together run,—
Through wet eyes seen,—as Red and Green
    Dazzle till they grow one!

O April Wedding,
    Where Love is crowned in tears,
And on a ground of deepest gloom,
    Hope's brightest Bow appears!

O April Wedding,
    In glittering sun and showers
The very grave looks glad To-day,
    And dead hands offer flowers!

O April Wedding,
  Thy clouds go all in white;
Those that darkliest wept now smile
  Most glorified in light!

LEAVE – TAKING.

HEN the wings are feathered,
  The·birds forsake their nest;
So the Bride will leave her Home
  Leaning to her Lover's breast.
The tear was in her eye,
  But the soul was smiling through,
Brimful of sunshine
  As a drop of summer dew.

AS THEY PASSED

ITHIN Love's chariot, side by side,
  Sweetness and Strength did never ride
  More perfectly personified:
  One of the dearest Angels out
Of Heaven, the Bride was, beyond doubt;
And his a Manhood fit to be

The mortal Mansion of some deity.
All eyes, like jewels, on them hung
   Glowing with precious life,
As at her Husband's side she clung
   The nestled, new-made Wife!
Glad were they in the happiness they gave,
But in their own proud pleasure they were grave.

EVOÉ.

N the presence of Spring, *our* beautiful
     Spring,
   Blithe bird of the Bosom! the heart
     will sing.
A Spirit of Joy in the oldest breast
Is stirring, and making it young as the rest:
Wakes a new life to leap in each limb,
And laugh out of eyes that were wintry and dim;
So the old Wine stirs in his winter gloom,
And wants to waken, and climb, and bloom,
As he used to do in the world outside,
When grapes grew big in their purple of pride.
He would laugh in the light, he would flush in the
     foam;
In a care-drowning wave he would rosily roam;
For his blood is so mellow, so merry, so warm,

Into spirit of joy it would fain transform,
And in human life keep holiday—
Rioting ruddily, ripple and play;
Break on the brain in a luminous spray,
Tinting with heaven our earthly clay;
In a fiery chariot mount on its way,
With spirit-company, lordly and gay,
And pass like a soul that is lost in day.
So the Spirit of Joy in the oldest breast
Is stirring, and making it young as the rest;
Wakes a new life to leap in each limb,
And laugh out of eyes that were wintry and dim.
Blithe bird of the bosom! the heart will sing
In the presence of Spring, *our* beautiful Spring.

A FACT THAT FLOWERS DOUBLE.

ENGLISH John Talbot, Shakespeare's
terribly brave
Great Fighter, lay in his forgotten grave.
It was but yesterday they found his dust,
The sheath of that old Sword all gone to rust
In English earth; his burial-place recover
In lands owned by a certain Lordly Lover.
And, lo! a Rose had sprung from out his tomb,
And climbed about the Lover's life to bloom:

A peerless flower of the old Hero's stock —
The tenderest gush from that heroic rock.
Not oft doth Fate vouchsafe so plain a sign,
Prefiguring the lives that are to twine.
All sweetness to this wedded life be given ;
Its root so deep in earth, its perfect flower in heaven.

A WAYSIDE WHISPER.

EVEN years I served for you,
    To Love, our lord of life,
    Ere he made me a Master
      And I won you for my wife, —
So faithfully, so fondly,
    Through a world of doubts and fears,
Seven long years, Belovëd !
    Seven long years.

" Seven years you beaconed me —
    My leading, crowning star,
To climb the Mount of Manhood,
    And you drew me from afar :
You made my gray hours golden,
    You glistened through my tears,
Seven long years, Belovëd !
    Seven long years.

" *Sometimes you shined so near me —*
   Far as we dwelt apart —
I hardly sought you with my arms
   You were so safe at heart !
Sometimes you dwined *so distant*
   I bowed with solemn fears ;
Seven long years, Belovëd !
   Seven long years.

" *I built my Arch of Triumph*
   For you to ride through ;
I kept my lamps all lighted
   That the warring winds outblew :
I worked and I waited
   And I fought down my fears,
Seven long years, Belovëd !
   Seven long years.

" *Now the perils are all over,*
   And the pains all past,
My fortune's wheel full-circle comes
   In your dear eyes at last !
For such a prize the winning
   Most brief and poor appears,
Yet, 't was seven long years, Belovëd !
   Seven long years."

THE WELCOME HOME.

ARM is the Welcome! 't is our way to grasp
    The hand in love or greeting till it ache;
But to a tender heart our love doth take
The happy pair it doth so proudly clasp.

And very tender in its love To-day
    Is every heart toucht with a thought of Him
    Low-lying in the Cypress-shadow dim,
From which we came to waft you on your way.

And the still face, that looks from Ashridge towers
    With smile more regnant in its touching ruth,
    And sad hoar-frost upon the dews of youth,
And Widow's weeds to mix with bridal-flowers.

Through Him we lost, we have more love to give.
    As some fond Mother yearningly hath breathed
    Her life out in the new life she bequeathed,
Our dearest died that this great love might live.

These darling Violets, eloquently mute,
    Are rich in sadder bloom and sweeter breath,
    And that pathetic sanctity of death,
Because our buried joy was at their root.

These Roses blush with a more vital glow
   Of crimson — like pale buds, whose tips are red
   As though the flower's heart, in breaking, bled —
Because of looks so lately wan with woe.

These are our Jewels! tears that purged our sight
   Like Euphrasy; they lay above the Dead
   All drear and dim; but the sad drops we shed
Now live with twinkling lustres in Your light!

The love that darkly wept at heart hath risen
   Transfigured.   See its sunburst in each face!
   As Earth, with all her flowers, smiles embrace
To Spring, rejoicing from her wintry prison.

These Voices, mounting merry as Larks upspring,
   But now were praying on the low, cold sod:
   The night is past — they soar in praise to God;
They make the old English greeting rarely ring.

We lean and look to You, thinking of Him.
   Warm welcome for the sake of One that 's gone;
   Warm welcome for your own!   Pass on, pass on;
We wave our hands, and shout till sight grows dim:

And, ere the shouts cease ringing in your ears,
   We drink a health — all standing — drink to you,
   While in our eyes the tears are standing too:
Old tears, that wanted to be wept for years:

But keep a holy hush 'mid all the noise,
    To match the silent music your hearts make:
    Pass on into your faëry heaven, and take
Our gentlest blessing on your wedded joys.

The dawn *will* rise, though golden days be set;
    The birds sing merrily, in spite of Death;
    Young hearts will love while lasts this human
        breath;
Rainbows bridge Earth and Heaven for eyes tear-
        wet.

Pass *gayly* on in glory through the gate
    Of your new life, beneath this Bridal-Dawn;
    And when from future days the veil is drawn
All happy fortunes for you lie in wait!

And, looking on your bliss, with proudest flush
    May the dear Mother's face be glorified.
    We, now the sound hath ceased, will stand out-
        side
Your Portals—all hearts praying 'mid the hush.

11

THE BONNY BRIDELAND FLOWER.

N the Brideland sleeping,
  Nestled Beauty's Flower;
Came the Lover peeping
  Into her green bower;
On her face hung tender
  As a drop of dew;
With her virgin splendor
  Thrilling through and through.

Now, the shy, sweet maiden
  Softly droops her head:
All her heart is laden
  With his coming tread!
Now the new dawn breaketh
  In a blush of bliss;
The Belovëd waketh
  At her Troth-love's kiss.

In our dull gray weather
  We have seen her bloom;
Fain as Exiles gather
  Round some flower from Home;
Seen the face that never
  Fades away, but gleams,
With its still smile, ever
  Through the land of Dreams.

Fair befall the bonny,
   Bonny Brideland flower!
All things dear and sunny
   Bless her bridal bower!
Truest love e'er given
   Feed her new life-root;
And thou God in heaven,
   Crown the flower with fruit.

A LOVER'S SONG.

NE so fair — none so fair.
   In her eyes so true
Love's most inner Heaven bare
   To the balmiest blue!

" One so fair — none so fair.
   In the skies no Star
Like my Star of Earth so near —
   They but shine afar.

" One so fair — none so fair.
   All too sweet it seems:
Wake me not, O world of care,
   If I walk in dreams.

" One so fair — none so fair.
O my bosom-guest,
Love ne'er smiled a happier pair
To the bridal-nest.

" One so fair — none so fair.
Lean to me, sweet Wife:
Light will be the load we bear:
Two hearts in one life."

THE MARRIED LIFE.

 HAPPY love of weans and Wife,
    Ye make a man's heart dance;
Kindle the desert face of life
    With colors of romance:

A Land of Promise sparkles where
    Your rosier light hath shone;
Too distant to attain, but near
    Enough to tempt us on.

'T is here that Heaven striketh root
    To give the Immortal birth,
Man tastes the unforbidden fruit
    That deifies on earth.

All ye that such a Garden own,
  Of wingèd thieves beware,
And trifles, light as thistle-down,
  That sow the seeds of care.

Only in singleness of heart,
  Ye keep the heaven ye win!
When Wife and Husband pull apart
  The Serpent will slide in.

VIA CRUCIS VIA LUCIS.

PITE of the Mask Eternal Love doth
     wear
  At times, that makes us shrink from it
     in fear,
Because the Father's face we cannot find,
Nor feel the presence of His love behind,
Nature at heart is very pitiful.

How gentle is the hand doth kindly pull
The coverlet of flowers over the face
Of Death, and light up his dark dwelling-place!
With fingers and with footfall soft and low
She comes to make the quiet mosses grow:
Safe-smiling, draws the Snow-drop through the
     snow.

Busy in sun and rain, she strives to heal,
Doing her best to comfort or conceal :
With tenderest grass makes green the saddest
      grave,
And over death her flags of life *will* wave.
She is the Angel, waiting by the prison,
That saith, " *He is not here, he is arisen,*"
When lorn in soul we seek the face we knew,
And dream of buried sweetness coming through
The earth in spring-time, every flower a smile
Of that dear Presence we have lost awhile.

Thus, on our old Crimean battle-ground,
A poor, unknown, dead Soldier's bones were
      found, —
(*Known* with those noble Englishmen of ours!)
When the next May came with her sweet Wild
      Flowers,
Nestled they lay above-ground in a grave
Of tall, plumed grass, funereally a-wave
In the West-wind that breathed of Home : and
      tender
There rose from earth a dawn of such spring
      splendor,
As if the heavens were breaking through the tomb :
The Wild Flowers had so buried them in bloom.

And, if we lift our eyes up from the ground,
We see how surely life is compassed round

With the Divine, that doth so kindly bound
The pitiless blaze of fires that soon would scorch
To ashes and put out our tiny torch
Of being; veil the vastness of the Whole,
As with droopt eyelids for the naked soul.

The silent Ministers of Healing crowd
About the broken heart and spirit bowed,
To stay the bleeding with immortal balm,
And still the cries with wings of blessëd calm;
Out of the old death make the new life spring,
Our earthly-buried hopes take homeward wing;
And to each blinding tear that dimmed our sight,
They give a starrier self; a Spirit of Light.

No matter in what separate lives we range,
We feel a rootage deeper than all change.
We know the roses flower to fade : We know
The roses also fade again to blow.
Death is Life's Shadow !
                      Mute the music looks,
And dark and dead when shadowed in the books :
Do but interpret it, all heaven will roll
The Life of Music through the echoing soul.

So we grow friends, familiar friends, with Death;
Can look up in his face with firmer faith,
To see the frowning brows shade tender eyes,
Like sunny openings into Paradise.

Through all the gloom and stillness of distress,
With life all muffled up in silentness,
We voyage on — ice-locked, snow-blind, frost-
          bound —
Like Sailors with the Arctic winter round,
Who thought they stranded in the dark, and
          found
The solid water all one floating ground ;
And drifted through the night, divinely drawn,
Out to the open sea, where daylight shone.

The Shadow of Death is changed into the Dawn,
That radiant Angel of Eternity !
The mourners look up from the grave to see
The dark, that bowed them by its awfulness,
Fell from the Father's hands, spread out to bless.

So, in His own good season, God hath given
This beautiful Joy-Bringer from His Heaven,
To bear His benediction from above,
And be the smiling Presence of His love !

" I go, but I will send the Comforter ! "
The gracious promise is fulfilled in Her.
Though heaviness endureth for a night,
Joy cometh with the morning.   Lo ! the Light.
Gone is the winter from our spirit clime;
This is the herald of our golden time.

In all the beauty of promise, Spring is here —
Our Spring — that will be with us all the year.

O beautiful Joy-Bringer! everywhere
Happiness smiles around you, like an air
Of glory, which you dwell in — Phosphor-fair!
The lives that have in mourning darkling lain
Now gather color; sun them once again.
The tender shine that cometh after rain
Illumes the eyes of old heart-ache: the pain
Of loss transmuted to all-golden gain.

Just now we are in the shadow of coming change,
And faces darken, and old things grow strange;
And from the new Unknown a many shrink.
Our world is getting tilted,* Sages think.
" *The wine of life is drawn, and the mere lees* "
All that is left us.   Shame on fears like these!
Whate'er Eclipse may come, storm-signals threat,
There 's room for noble life in England yet.
As in the very heart of Hope we 'll ride,
Borne on the ninth wave of our triumph's tide,
That with its new life heaves Old England'
        breast,
Only be loyal to the Loftiest;
Arise and crown old sanctities anew,
By nobler conquest make your lordship true;

* Astronomically.

Awake the spirit in our English blood,
That slowly brightens to the fervid flood,
And does not flash till the leap comes that shows
Power all the lustier for its long repose.
And if the proudest Nobles have to bow,
Then let it be as Rowers bend to row
A sturdier stroke; and faint not, though we know
Not under what dark arch we have to go.
But win the nod of an approving soul,
Even though ye never reach your chosen goal.

O, young hearts, dancing to the rise and fall
Of life's most winsome tune at festival,
Looking on your new world wherein ye move
With all the large, sweet wonder of young love,
The moments thronging with the life of years;
Crowded with happiness and quick to tears;
New smiles of greeting in each minute's face;
New worlds of pleasure brimming every space;
This is no winter-withered earth to you.
Love comes, and life is deified anew!
And hearts grow larger than their fortunes are.
The horizon lifts around, sublime and far,
With god-like breathing-space, — an ample scope
For loftier life, and glorious ground for hope.

Turn, happy Lovers, turn on those below
A little of the light in which ye glow;

A little of your sunshine round you shed,
And make our old world blossom where ye tread.
Bring back a little seed from Eden-bowers
To sow onr fallows with immortal flowers.
Ah!   Nobles, what a chance is yours to be
The founders of a lordlier Chivalry!
And, with the proud old fire this people lead.
When they were weak, I threatened; now I plead,
Give eyes to their blind strength, for great the need.

The *Word* of *Life* is wellnigh preached to death;
The Flower of all Sweetness withereth
Crnsht in the grip of many that handle it,
As though they thonght Life would but yield its
          sweet
In giving up.the breath.
                         We want the Book
Translated into life, not the mere look
Of Life embalmed and shrouded in the Book.
We want the Word made Flesh to breathe once
          more
In likeness of the lineaments it wore
Living,—the life indeed, quick in the lives
Of Fathers, Mothers, Children, Husbands, Wives.
We need that maiden life of Christ fulfilled
In Marriage,—all its preciousness distilled.
We need the life itself—lived in the Home
On Week-days, ere the Sabbath-rest will come
To many a homeless hnngerer for home.

We pray "*Thy Kingdom Come.*" But not by
    prayer
Alone will it be built of breath in air.
In life through labor, must be brought to birth
The Kingdom; as it is in heaven, on Earth.

The light that left Heaven centuries ago
Hath not yet reached dark myriads here below:
Your lives might be the lamp that bears this light,
Still burning, as the stars through all the night.
Because ye are lookt up to, they would mark
Your shining!
       O, the spirits lying dark
To-day, as jewels waiting but the spark
Of splendor that to Love's dear smile is given,
To brighten with the best that brighten Heaven!
Look down, you Shining Ones, look kindly down,
And save them, set as jewels in your crown.

How beautiful upon the mountain height,
The feet of them that bring the Lowly light —
O'ershadowing, on wings of gentle Love,
The faults and failings that they soar above!
How beautiful the face of those whose smile
Doth make God's sunshine in the heart of Toil;
In low sick-rooms a presence as of Health;
The true Rich folk, in whom the Poor have wealth!
A beautiful life begets itself anew

In other lives, as perfume stealing through
The sense creates the flower to live again;
Its spirit re-embodied in the brain.

Heart full of shining love and singing hopes,
Come down where life, blindfolded, grovels and
     gropes.
We house the Poor to lie and die. But give
Them room to stand in; house the Poor to live;
A little touch of clasping hands might prove
Mightiest of all the languages of Love.
Give them a glimpse of kindlier, sweeter grace,
And be the model of a nobler race, —
The living Poem that we may not write;
The picture that we cannot paint to sight;
The music that we dream but do not get;
The Statue marble never mirrored yet.
Come down, and meet them, fellow-man to man
So much we might do, as it seems, to span
The ancient gulf that severs Rich and Poor,
In which Christ threw Himself; forevermore
To show His sorrowing Poor that God hath not
Forgotten those he seemed to have forgot!

And the gulf closes not, and He doth reach
On either side a piteous hand to each:
One are they by the message that He gave;
One by the life He lived; one by His grave;

One by the tears He wept — the love — the pain;
And still they stand apart, and He is torn atwain.

Now while the Thrush upon the barest bough
Sits singing high in azure, telling how
The Spring-wind wanders where the Children go
A-violeting by the warm hedgerow;
Daily more rich the Sallow-palms unfold
And change their silver into sunny gold;
" *Good by, old Winter,*" the blue heavens laugh;
" *The flowers shall write you a kindly epitaph,*"
Far on a sea of Light the twinkling Lark
Is launched, and floating like a heaven-bound bark,
In which some happy spirit sails and sings,
And stirs us in a dream of waking wings,
With homeward yearnings, heavenward flutterings,
As all about the inner life there plays
A breath of bliss from out old innocent days,
Now, while the Spring mounts somewhere up the
      blue,
We bring our firstling flowers to offer you!
Violets, dim and tender; glad Primroses,
That promise, ere the happy prospect closes,
Ye, hand in hand, through rosier days shall tread
Green earth, with richer glories garlanded;
Where the wild Hyacinths, all a-dreaming, lean,
In peeps of deep sea-azure through the green;
And Summer sets that Golden Age of hers

A-bloom, in mellow miles of yellow Furze;
While, smiling down the distance, Autumn stands,
The ripened fruitage glowing in his hands.

And, if among the flowers some few appear
Sacred to woe, and leaning with the tear
Still in the eyes, I did but seek the leaf
Of Healing — gather Heartsease for your grief:
Nor are they tears, but rather drops of dew
From heaven, that hidden Love is looking through.

As, after death, our Lost Ones grow our Dearest,
So, after death, our Lost ones come the nearest:
They are not lost in distant worlds above;
They are our nearest link in God's own love —
The human hand-clasps of the Infinite,
That life to life, spirit to spirit knit!
They fill the rift they made, like veins of gold
In fire-rent fissures torture-torn of old!
With sweetness store the empty place they left,
As of wild honey in the rock's bare cleft.

In hidden ways they aid this life of ours,
As Sunshine lends a finger to the flowers,
Shadowed and shrouded in the Wood's dim heart,
To climb by while they push their grave apart.
They think of us at Sea, who are safe on Shore;
Light up the cloudy coast we struggle for!

The ancient Terror of Eternity —
The dark destroyer, crouching in Life's sea
To wreck us — is thus Beaconed, and doth stand
As the Deliverer, with a lamp in hand.
We would not put them from us when we are sad;
We will not shut them from us when we are glad;
Nor thrust our Angel from the Marriage Feast,
Although he comes, not clothëd like the rest
In visible garment of a Wedding-Guest.

Now pray we.
    Lord of Life, look smiling down
Upon this Pair; with choicest blessings crown
Their love; the beauty of the Flower bring
Back to the bud again in some new spring!
Long may they walk the blessëd life together
With wedded hearts that still make golden weather,
And keep the chill of winter far aloof
With inward warmth when snow is on the roof;
Wed in that sweet forever of Love's kiss,
Like two rich notes made one in bridal bliss.

We would not pray that sorrow ne'er may shed
Her dews along the pathway they must tread:
The sweetest flowers would never bloom at all
If no least rain of tears did ever fall.
In joy the soul is bearing human fruit;
In grief it may be taking divine root.

Come joy or grief, nestle them near to Thee
In happy love twin for eternity !
They take our Darling's place ; long may they be
As glad and beautiful a hope as he
Hath left a bright and blessëd memory
Their day fulfil the promise of his dawn —
That, as with Thee, he may with us live on.

AN ORPHAN FAMILY'S CHRISTMAS.

I.

BLITHE old Carle is Christmas;
   You cannot find his fellow;
Match me the hale red rose in his cheek,
   Or the heart so mild and mellow;
The glitter of glory in his eyes,
  While the Wassail-cup he quaffs,
Or the humor that twinkles about his wrinkles
  As helplessly he laughs.

Of all High-Tides 't is Christmas
  Most richly crowns the year;
Right through the land there ripples and runs
  Its flood of merry good cheer.
Troops of friends come sailing down,
  Making a pleasant din;
Fling open doors! set wide your hearts!
  Christmas is coming in.

A happy time is Christmas,
  We gather all at home,

And like the Christmas fairies,
  With their pranks, our darlings come;
And gentle Sylvan Spirits hid
  In holly-boughs they bring,
To grow into good Angels,
  And bless our fairy-ring !

A jolly time is Christmas,
  For Plenty's horn is poured ;
Then flows the honey of the Sun,
  Our fruits all summer hoard !
Merry men tall march up the hall :
  They bear the meats and drinks ;
And Wine, with all his hundred eyes,
  Your hearty welcome winks.

A glorious time is Christmas ;
  Young hearts will slip the tether ;
Lips moist and merry, all under the berry,
  Close thrillingly together.
A gracious time ! the poorest Poor
  Will make some little show,
As ailing infants, seeing the fun,
  Will do their best to crow !

And O the Fire of Christmas,
  That like some Norse God old,
Mounts his log up-chimney, and roars
  Defiance to the cold !

He challenges all out-of-doors ;
    He wags his beard of flame ;
It warms your very heart to see
    Him glory in the game.

A hallowed time is Christmas,
    Of loftiest festival ;
For, eighteen hundred years ago,
    It opened Heaven to all.
'T was then our Father, in his arms,
    The Blessëd Babe held forth
. To win back wandering human love,
    And lure it up from Earth.

II.

But there are nooks in Poverty's dim world,
Where the high tide of richness never runs.
No drop of all its wealth for some who sit
And hear the river of bounty brimming by.
They see the Christmas shows of wealth and warmth,
At window, whilst at every door shut out !
The Plenty only flouts their poverty ;
The music mocks them with its merriment ;
They look into each passing face and find
No likeness of their own deep misery.

In one of these dark nooks, at Christmas time,
An Orphan family, with little fire,

And only light enough to see the gloom,
Together sat; two Sisters, and one Brother;
The youngest six years old; the eldest twelve;
An old Grandfather lying ill abed.
They knew that Christmas came, but not for them.
Thus had they often sat o' winter nights,
Shivering within, as the dark shuddered without,
And creeping close together for heart-warmth;
Poor unfledged nurslings with the Mother gone!
Knowing a Presence brooded over them,
In whose chill shadow they were palled and
      hooded;
So mournfully it kept the Mother's place!
Till flesh would creep as though about to leave
The spirit naked — bare to that cold breath
Which whispers of the grave — all lidless eye
To that appalling sight the helpless Dead
Lie looking on, in their amazement, dumb,
And petrified to marble! So they sat;
The Shadow in the house and on the heart;
The old Clock ticking through the lonely room,
With sounds that made the silence solemner,
And weird hands pointing to far other times;
Talking of merry Christmas coming in;
Of visionary futures, and old days,
With thoughts so far beyond their years! The life
In their young eyes gleamed supernaturally,
Betwixt the fire-shine, and the night-shadow,

As their old inmates of the heart stole forth
To walk and talk in the old ways once more.
And so, like those lorn pretty Babes i' the Wood,
That Robins buried when the talk was done,
They told each other stories ; sang their Hymns ;
By way of bribing·the grim Solitude,
Not to look down upon them quite so dreadful !
Poor darlings, with no Father, and no Mother.

III.

AY, me, dear Sister, gentle Brother,
   How soft the thought of a Mother lies
   At heart ; how sweet in sound 't will rise ;
And these poor Children had no Mother !

No Mother-arms, in secret nook
   To fold the sufferer to her breast,
   With love that never breaks its rest,
And Heartsease in her very look.

No Mother-wings to brood above
   The winter nest and keep them warm ;
   And shield them from the pitiless storm,
With the large shelter of her love.

No Mother's tender touch that brings
　A music from the harp of life,
　Like hovering heaven above the strife
'And precious tremblings of the strings.

No Mother with her lap of love
　Each night for heads that bow in prayer;
　Dear hands that stroke the smiling hair,
And heart that pleads their cause above.

No Mother whose quick, wistful eye,
　Will see the shadow of Danger near,
　And face, with love that casts out fear,
The blow that darkly hurtles by.

No Mother's smile ineffable,
　To stir the Angel in the bud,
　Till, into perfect womanhood,
The Flower blushes at the full.

No Mother! when the Darling One
　Bends with a grief that breaks the flower,
　To loose the sorrow in a shower,
And lift the sweet face to the sun.

No Mother's kiss of comfort near
　The River that Death overshades;
　Or voice that, when the dim face fades,
Sounds on with solemn words of cheer.

Ay, me, dear Sister, gentle Brother,
  How soft the thought of a Mother lies
  At heart; how sweet in sound 't will rise;
And these poor Children had no Mother.

IV.

YET, God is kind, and wondrous are His ways.
Affliction's hand, it seemed, had, at a touch,
Awoke the Mother in the young Child-heart
Of little Martha, who had now become
A wee old woman at twelve years of age,
With many motherly ways. Yea, God is kind.

The tiny Snowdrop braves the wintry blast;
He tenderly protects its confidence
That lifts the venturous head, safe in His hand:
And Martha, in her loneliness of earth,
And such a dearth of human fellowship,
And such companionship with solitude,
Had found a way of looking up to Heaven:
And oft I think that God in heaven smiled:
Holding his hand about her little life,   .
As one that shields a candle from the wind.
She had the faith to feel him nearest, when
The world is farthest off; and, in this faith,
Her spirit went on wings, or, hand-in-hand

With Love that digs below the deepest grave,
And Hope that builds above the highest stars.

In the old days before their sorrow came,
And vast Eternity oped twice to them,
And each time, following the lightning-flash,
They groped in darkness for a Parent gone,
She was the merriest of merry souls ;
The gay heart laughing in her loving eyes ;
The peeping rose-bud crimsoning her cheek ;
There was as quick a spirit in her feet,
As now had passed into her toiling fingers,
That match the Mother's heart with Father's hands
In their unwearied working for the rest.
In those old days the Father made a song
About his little maid, and sang it to her.

V.

" It is a merry Maiden,
   With spirits light as air ;
While others go heart-laden,
   And make the most of care,
She trips along with laughter :
Old Care may hobble after.

" A sunbeam straight from heaven,
   She dances in my room ;

The gladdest thing e'er given
To cheer a heart or home,
My stream of life may darkle,
She makes the brighter sparkle.

" Her smile is like the Morning
That turns the mist to pearls ;
All thought of sadness scorning,
She shakes her sunny curls ;
And, with her merry glancing,
She sets all hearts a-dancing."

VI. .

BUT now the Maid was changëd ; she had been
With Sorrow in its chilly sanctuary ;
Her look was paler, for it had been toucht
With that white stillness of the winding-sheet,
That smile forlornly sweet upon the face
When left forever widowed of the soul !
Henceforth her life went softly all its days
As if she felt the Grave-turf underfoot.
Her beauty was more spiritual ; not aged
Or worn ; less color, but more light.
It was a brier-rose beauty, tremulous
With tenderest dew-drop purity of soul.

I 've often seen how well their beauty wears
Whose sufferings are for others, not for Self;
How long they keep a fair unfurrowed face,
Whose tears are luminous with healing love,
Like pearly ears that bring good spirits down
To water and enrich their special flowers,
And do not come from cares that kill the heart;
They sere no bloom; they leave no snaky trail.
So Martha kept her face, and might have been
The younger sister of that lily Maid,
The lovable Elaine of Astolat.

VII.

WE write the tale of Heroes in the blood
They shed when dying where they nobly stood;
And the red letters gloriously bloom
To light the warrior to a loftier doom.
But there are battles where no cheers arise,
And no flags wave before the fading eyes;
Heroes of whom the wide world never hears;
Their story only writ in Woman's tears.
Yet that invisible ink shall surely shine
Brightest in Heaven, and verily divine.
And when God closes our world's blotted book,
To cast it in the fire with awful look,
It was so badly written, leaf on leaf
Thus lived might touch the Father's heart with grief.

And this Child-Mother's life may yield one story
That shall be told among the first in glory.

Her busy love and thoughtful care are such,
The others do not miss the Mother much.
From dawn to dark her presence lights the place
With many a gleam of reliquary grace.
Their few poor things in seemly order stand,
Bright as with last touch of the Parent's hand.
The clothes are mended, and the house is kept
Clean as of old; bravely hath Martha stepped
In Mother's footprints; her wee feet have tried
Their best to track the Parent's larger stride.
With household work her little hands are hard,
Her arms are chilled, her knees with kneeling
       scarred :
Dusty her hair that might have richly rolled
With warm Venetian glow of Titian's gold.
Great-hearted little woman ! she toils still,
Though the Grandfather, lying old and ill,
To her twin troubles adds a heavier third,
She works on without one complaining word.

VIII.

AND once a year she has her holiday;
One day of airy life in fairyland.
When young leaves open large their palms to catch

The gold and silver of the sun and shower;
Shy Beauty pusheth back her glittering hood,
To peep with her flower face; the Silver Birk
Shakes out her hair full-length against the blue;
The Fir puts forth her timid finger-tips,
Like shrinking damsel trying a cold stream
In which she comes to bathe.
                      In merry green woods
She rambles where the blue wild hyacinths
Smile with their soft dream-haze in tender shade:
Above, the lightsome dance of gladsome green;
Below, the whispering sweetness of the wood;
Birds singing, as for love of her, all round:
Or, by the Brook that turns some stray sunbeam
To a crooked scimitar of wavy gold,
Then to itself laughs at the elfish work!
With her large eyes, and eager leaping looks,
At Nature's living picture-page she glowers,
And gets some color in her own pale life.
Then home, with kindled cheek, when Eve's one
      Star
Stands, waiting on the threshold of the night,
In lively expectation of all heaven.

IX.

HOME when the happy day is done,
    Home comes my little Maid;

Her pleasure — golden in the sun —
  Now dewy in the shade.
Thoughts of the day will hover and bless
Her sleep with sacred balminess.

Through shutting eve the stars all peep,
  But still there comes no night;
'T is but the Day hath fallen asleep
  And smiles in dreams of light.
And Martha feels the heart of Love
Beat on in silent stars above.

X.

To-NIGHT they sit with sadder, lonelier thoughts
Than ever; closer comes the Wolf of Want,
And darklier falls their shadow of Orphanhood.
For now the old man keeps his bed, and seems
Death-stricken, with his face of ghastly gray;
His life all crowded in cold glittering eyes
Watching the least light movement that is made.
The Boy, a blithe and sunny godsend, gay
As singing fountain springing in their midst,
With loving spirit leaping to the light,
Is down at heart to-night, and sad and still.
While Dora, in whose purple-lighted eyes
There seems the shadow of a rain-cloud near,

With but a faint shine of the cheery heart;
.She longs to fly away and be at rest,
And gives her wishes wings in measured words
That win strange pathos from her sweet young
     voice.

" Come to the Better Land, that Angels know;
They walk in glory, shining as they go !
The King in all His beauty takes the least
To sit beside Him at the eternal feast."
Thus sings the voice that calls me night and day.
      " This is a weary world,
        Come, come, come away !
      Ah, 't is a dreary world,
        Come, come away."

" From old heartache, and weariness, and pain —
Sorrows that sigh, and hopes that soar in vain —
Come to the Loved and Lost who are now the Blest;
They dwell in regions of Eternal rest."
Thus sings the voice that calls me night and day.
      " This is a weary world,
        Come, come, come away !
      Ah, 't is a dreary world,
        Come, come away."

" Here all things change; the warmest hearts grow
     cold;
The young head droops and dims its glorious gold;

Where Love his pillow hath made on Beauty's breast,
The creatures of the Grave will make their nest."
Thus sings the voice that calls me night and day.
> *" This is a weary world,*
> > *Come, come, come away!*
> *Ah, 't is a dreary world,*
> > *Come, come away."*

" The dear eyes where each morning rose our light,
Soon darken with their last eternal night ;
The heart that beat for us, the hallowed brow
That bowed to bless, are cold and silent now."
Thus sings the voice that calls me night and day.
> *" This is a weary world,*
> > *Come, come, come away!*
> *Ah, 't is a dreary world,*
> > *Come, come away."*

" Nor fear the Grave, that door of Heaven on Earth ;
All changed and beautiful ye shall come forth,
As from the cold dark cloud the winter showers
Go underground to dress, and come forth Flowers."
Thus sings the voice that calls me night and day.
> *" This is a weary world,*
> > *Come, come, come away!*
> *Ah, 't is a dreary world,*
> > *Come, come away."*

" *Come to the Better Land, that Angels know ;*
They walk in glory, shining as they go !
The King in all His beauty takes the least
To sit beside Him at the eternal feast."
Thus sings the voice that calls me night and day.

" *This is a weary world,*
Come, come, come away !
Ah, 't is a dreary world,
Come, come away."

XI.

" NAY, Sister," says the cheery Martha, " though
Our lot be sad, your strain 's too sorrowful !
We cannot spare you yet.   Nor must we stoop
To make our Burden heavier ; hear me, love.

" *A little flower so lowly grew,*
So lonely was it left,
That Heaven lookt like an eye of blue
Down in its rocky cleft.

" *What could the little Flower do*
In such a darksome place,
But try to reach that eye of blue,
And climb to kiss Heaven's face ?

13

> *" And there 's no life so lone and low*
> *But strength may still be given*
> *From narrowest lot on earth to grow*
> *The straighter up to Heaven."*

Again she sang, and set them singing too.

> *" When He was with us, our Saviour said,*
> *Suffer the Children to come unto me :*
> *Still I see Him, with arms outspread,*
> *Waiting to gather us round his knee.*
> *And though there 's room for all the rest,*
> *I think He loves the Little Ones best.*

> *" Here we are poorest of God's Poor,*
> *Toiling for bread from day to day,*
> *But laid up in Heaven a treasure is sure,*
> *While Money is round and rolls away.*
> *And though there 's room for all the rest,*
> *I think He loves the Little Ones best.*

> *" Little hearts make merry, and sing*
> *How his love to Children warms !*
> *Little voices ripple and ring —*
> *How he takes them in his arms !*
> *And though there 's room for all the rest,*
> *I think He loves the Little Ones best."*

XII.

Then, silent Leonard lifted up his look,
Bright as a Daisy when the dews have dried;
A sudden thought struck all the sun in his face.
"*Martha and Dora, I know what I'll do!*
I'll write a Letter to our Saviour; He
Will help us if we put our trust in Him."
The sisters smiled upon him through their tears.

This was the Letter little Leonard wrote.

"*Dear, beautiful Lord Jesus,*
  Christmas is drawing near;
Its many shining sights we see,
  Its merry sounds we hear,
With presents for good Children,
  I know Thou art going now,
From house to house with Christmas trees,
  And lights on every bough.

"*I pray thee, holy Jesus,*
  To bring one tree to us,
All aglow with fruits of gold,
  And leaves all luminous.
We have no Mother, and, where we live,
  No Christmas gifts are given;

We have no Friends on earth, but thou
  Art our good friend in Heaven.

" *My Sisters, gentle Jesus,*
    They hide the worst from me;
But I have ears that sometimes hear,
    And eyes that often see.
Poor Martha's cloak is worn threadbare,
    Poor Dora's boots are old;
And neither of them strong like me,
    To stand the wintry cold.

" *But most of all, Lord Jesus,*
    Grandfather is so ill;
'T is very sad to hear him moan,
    And startling when he 's still,
Ah! well I know, Lord Jesus,
    If thou wouldst only come,
He 'd look, and rise, and leave his bed,
    As Lazarus left his tomb.

" *Forget us not, Lord Jesus,*
    I and my sisters dear;
We love thee! when thou wert a Child,
    Had we been only near,
And seen thee lying, bonny babe,
    In manger or in stall,
Thou shouldst have had our Home, our bed;
    We would have given thee all."

XIII.

THE Letter signed and sealed, their prayers are said,
And Martha lights the younger Bairns to bed.
With all a Mother's heart she bends above
Their rest, her eyes filled with a Mother's love.
For soon their voices cease ; life fades away
Into its quiet nest, till morrow-day :
As the lake-lilies shut their leaves of light
When down the gloom descends the hush of night.
In fear of what is passing, bow the head
Beneath the water, they shrink down in bed !
But soon the Angel Sleep doth smile all fear
Away with wooing whispers at the ear ;
And they will ope at morn eyes bathed in bliss ;
Their faces fresh from the good Angel's kiss.
But Martha sleeps not yet ; now they are gone,
Brave little woman, she must still work on,
And watch, to-night, for Grandfather is worse,
She thinks, with no one near, save her for nurse.

XIV.

'T is very sad to hear a man so old,
Talk of *his* mother who, beneath the mould,
Has lain an age, and see him weep young tears,

That have to pierce the crust of seventy years.
He turns and turns, incapable of rest,
Tossed on the billow that heaves in brain and breast;
A life that beats with all too weak a wave
To land him on the other side the Grave!
The old man mutters in his broken dream.
  " Last night I wandered in a world of moan;
  I saw a white Soul going all alone,
      Over the white snows of eternity;
      I followed far, and followed fast to see
  The face, and lo, it was my own."

And now he muses by some weird sea-side.

  " The tide is a-making its bonny Death-bed;
  The white sea-maidens rise ready to wed;
  Nearer and nearer, unveiling their charms,
  They toss for their lovers, long, shadowy arms!
  Dancing with other-world music and motion;
  Brides of dead Sailors; the Beauties of Ocean.

  " Wave after wave my worn, old Bark has tossed;
  One moment saved, another it seemed lost
  Forever, still it righted from each blow;
  But the great wave is coming on me now!
  I see it towering high above the rest;
  A world of eyes in its white glittering crest;
  See how it climbs, calm in its might, and curls

Ready to clasp me in the wildering whirls.
And when it bursts, in darkness, for last breath,
I shall be fighting, grappled fast with Death."

He sees an Image of Martha now, with dim
Wet eyes ; it moves in brightness far from him.

" I am like the hoary Mountain,
Gray with years, and very old ;
And your life, a sprightly fountain,
Springs, and leaves me lone and cold ;
Dancing, glancing on its way,
Down the valleys warm and gay.

" There you go, Dear, singing, sparkling,
I can see your dawn begin ;
While the night, around me darkling,
With its death-dews, shuts me in —
Hear you singing on your way
To the full and perfect day."

The suffering passes into weariness ;
The weariness fades into kind content ;
Faintly the tired heart flutters into stillness,
And he has done with Age, and Want, and Illness.

Gently he passed ; the little Maiden wept ;
Sank down o'erwearied by the dead, and slept,

With such a heavenly lustre in her face,
You might have fancied Angels in the place:
Companions through the day of our delight,
That watch as wingëd Sentries all the night.

XV.

NEXT day a group of serious silent men
Found a *Dead Letter* with strange life in it;
It was addressed to *Jesus Christ in Heaven.*
It called up their old hearts into their eyes,
For lofty meeting in a touch of tears.
At length it reached the Lady Marian.
And the Boy's letter had not missed its mark.

The child had called on Christ, and lo, He came :
In spirit loving, helpful, as of old !
In person of the Lady Marian ;
One of those representatives of His
Who help to make the Poor believe in Him :
Believe Him once a dweller on our earth
Because He hath some living likeness yet.

XVI.

THIS is my Lady Marian .
She walks our world, a Shining one !

A Woman with an Angel-face,
Sweet gravity, and tender grace ;
And where she treads this earth of ours,
Heaven blossoms into smiling flowers.
    This is the Lady Marian.

One of the spirits that walk in white !
Many dumb hearts that sit in night,
Her presence know, just as the Birds
Know Morning, murmuring cheerful words.
Where Life is darkest, she doth move
With influence as of visible Love.
    This is the Lady Marian.

Her coming all your being fills
With a balm-breath from heaven's hills :
And in her face the light is mild
As though the heart within her smiled,
And in her bosom sat to sing
The spirit of immortal Spring.
    This is the Lady Marian.

One of God's treasurers for the Poor !
She keepeth open heart and door.
That heart a holy well of wealth,
Brimming life-waters, quick with health ;
That door an opening you look through,
To find God our side of Heaven's blue.
    This is the Lady Marian.

" *We shall not mend the world ; we try,*
And lo, our work is vain ! " they cry.
With her pathetic look, she hears ;
You see the wounded soul bleed tears ;
But toward the dark she sets her face,
And calmly keeps her onward pace.
    This is the Lady Marian.

True picture of the Master of old !
Touches of likeness manifold !
The human sweetness in His face ;
Large love that would a world embrace ;
His heavenly pity in her eyes,
And all the soul of sacrifice.
    This is the Lady Marian.

XVII.

FROM out the blackness that took shape in Her,
Came Lady Marian on Christmas Eve,
Quick with maternal tenderness of soul,
Her starry smile so radiant through their night,
Her hands brimful of help, as was her heart
With yearnings to arise and go when first .
She read the letter little Leonard sent
In his confiding simpleness of faith.
And Martha knows that their worst days are done ;

In Dora's rich sad eyes a merry light
Soon dances !   Lady Marian will be
A Mother, sent of God, to all the three.
A trembling prayer had shook the Tree of Life,
And, golden, out of heaven the fruitage falls
Into the children's lap direct from God.

XVIII.

THE Master called a little Child,
   And placed it in their midst, to show
   The clearest mirror men could know,
In which the face of Faith e'er smiled :

A little Child, with eye unworn,
   Whose heart goes straightway for the light,
   Like buds that put forth all their might
To start up heavenward soon as born :

A little Child, that even in play
   The nearest path to heaven walks ;
   And in its innocent brightness talks
With God in the old wondrous way :

Friends of a failing faith, when your
   Lighthouses of eternal life
   Hold trembling lamps across the strife,
And darken, darken hour by hour :

While higher climb the waves that drench :
　　And on the rocks the breakers roar :
　　And Light in Heaven opes no new door,
And higher climb the waves that quench :

When timid souls that sail the sea
　　Of Time are fearful lest yon band
　　Of Cloud should not be solid Land,
When they step in Eternity, —

And faint hearts flutter 'twixt a nest
　　That is not sealed to wind and wet,
　　And one that is not ready yet,
With wandering wings, and find no rest :

Our Heaven-sealers in the dust
　　Sit, with their hopes dead or discrowned ;
　　Their splendid dreams all shivered round
And broken every reed of trust :

The Sheep are scattered, sore distressed ;
　　Their Shepherd miss with many alarms ;
　　While the young Lambs can feel His arms
Enfold them safely to His breast :

I 'll sit me down, no more beguiled
　　By those who are too serpent-wise,
　　And seek my Saviour through the eyes
And pure heart of a little Child.

Christ, give me but this little one's grace,
   With faith to feel in darkest night,
   How the good Father's heart of light
With that mild radiance fills Thy face.

LADY MARIAN.

I N her Ancestral tree's old smiling shade,
Spencer and Milton sang, and Shake-
speare played.
I cannot prophesy immortal fame,
And endless honor for my lady's name
Through my poor Verse; but it shall surely give
All that it has, and long as it may live.

She heard my children singing in the street,
And smiled down on them starry-clear and sweet,
But half-way up in Heaven, and far from me,
As Shakespeare's Juliet in her balcony;
A golden Creature, all too rare to stay,
With waving white hand she would pass away!

Now I have seen her; heard her voice To-day,
And toucht her hand; enricht my life for aye:
The thought in sunbeams radiantly upsprings,
To smile out in the saddest face of things.

After the gloom is gone, the worst is passed,
I know you, my good Fairy, found at last.

Though poor, and grim to tears, our life might be,
We had proud visions in our poverty !
My Princess too, with darkly sparkling e'en,
As I lay dreaming, over me would lean ;
And now the silken clew of hidden power,
Hath led me to her beauty in its bower.

Lady ! Giorgione should have painted you
With live warm flesh-tints golden through and
        through ;
The sun-soul making luminous its prison
With sunken splendors, rarer than have risen ;
Bird-peeps of brightness — dawn-dew — smiling
        fire —
Full of all freshness as a spring-wood quire ;

A glow and glory of impetuous blood ;
Brave spirits that crowd all sail to take the flood
Of large, abounding life, that in the sun
Heaves flashing, with a frolic fringe of fun ;
A happy wit ; creative genius, proved
In Pictures that Angelico would have loved :

A stately soul : yet with a laugh that brings
Echoes from Girlhood's heaven as it rings !

And that fine spirit of motion's airy charm,
Which hovers glancing round the flower of form :
A lofty lady of a proud old race,
Recklessly splendid in her gifts and grace.

Yet, as the life of some tall, towery tree
Climbs till atop it laughs exultingly
With all its leaves, using its pride of place
To look both earth and heaven full in the face !
Thus — np through bole and branch of wealth and
      blood,
Breaks ont her noble natural Womanhood.

No fear of England's great old Houses when
Such glorious women give us noble men,
And sway the heart o' the people sovereignly
As the Moon sways the heavings of the sea,
To touch its darkness with her lovelier light,
And mould to loftier shape its climbing might.

Their foes may rave, but, far off is their fall,
Whose glory is the heritage of all !
Who grew some grain we long shall save for seed ;
Who man the gap for England in her need.
All who love England think with holy pride
Of all who for her like De Norman died.

My Lady Marian, you are good, and trno ;
Most bountiful, and gracious as the dew :

And glad Hearts — winged with Blessings — fol-
    low you
Far as the Earth is green, or Heaven is blue;
But, dear my lady, there is work to do
In England yet, and royal work for you.

Why leave your own free air, and English Home,
For Paris — that Slave-Dancer — or for Rome?
With all their lustres, dazzlingly displayed,
They cannot match the sweetness of our shade;
Our leafier pathways cool with gladder green;
Our Hearts, whose heavings lift you up — our
    Queen.

Much Mother's Milk wants sweetening with the
    Balms
That you can bring; much need of more than
    Alms!
In eyes wide open souls lie fast asleep;
With daylight on the face hearts darkly weep;
Our world has many a ward where wounds and
    wails
Cry for a thousand Florence Nightingales.

I know that Knowledge through our Shire doth
    trail
With slow illumination of a snail!
But still we dream of some bright better day,

And while we sleep the great Dawn comes our
      way.
Think How long God's love brooded over Earth
Before she quickened for her noblest Birth!

O, they shall bless you down in pit and den, —
Transforming slowly into Women and Men;
And smile, as leaves out-smile in first spring-hours,
With livelier green, while fall the singing showers;
Or as the winter mosses round your trees
Look up and smile at their good influences.

Your pardon, Lady, if my unskilled word,
Like a bad player, should mistake the chord!
No churlish charge, no plea of parasite,
Is mine; but leal heart-service of a knight
Who in old days had fought for you and bled;
Going to death as 't were a bridal bed.

Our lost " Maid Marian " bore your name, and she
Yet works a very tender ministry;
And, somehow, when of her we sit and think
Our hearts touch you by an invisible link.
Sacred to her, my sadder verses take;
And kindly think of them for Marian's sake.

Room for my Sea-Kings too, your heart will make,
From young Sir William Peel, to old King Hake.

You have the spirit born of the salt spray
That snuffs the sea-breeze meadowy miles away;
The Norse blood running seaward round the world,
That leaves the Celtic round the Homestead curled.

You love our Heroes! and you might have been
In battle-need our Boadicea Queen!
And stood up to the full majestic height
In your war-chariot beckoning on the fight:
A famous victory you would have wrought,
Or with your heroes fallen as you fought.

AN OLD MAN-O'-WAR'S-MAN YARN.

Y, ay, good neighbors, I have seen
    Him! sure as God 's my life;
    One of his chosen crew I 've been;
    Have n't I, old good wife?
God bless your dear eyes! did n't you vow
  To marry me any weather,
If I came back with limbs enow
  To keep my soul together.

Brave as a lion was our Nel,
  And gentle as a lamb:
'Tell you it warms my blood to tell
  The tale — gray as I am —
It makes the old life in me climb,
  It sets my soul a-swim;
I live twice over every time
  That I can talk of him.

You should have seen him as he trod
  The deck, our joy, and pride!

You should have seen him, like a god
  Of storm, his war-horse ride!
You should have seen him as he stood
  Fighting for our good land,
With all the iron of soul and blood
  Turned to a sword in hand.

Our best beloved of all the brave
  That ever for freedom fought;
And all his wonders of the wave
  For fatherland were wrought!
He was the manner of man to show
  How victories may be won;
So swift, you scarcely saw the blow;
  You lookt — the deed was done.

He sailed his ships for work; he bore
  His sword for battle-wear;
His creed was " *Best man to the fore!* "
  And he was always there.
Up any peak of peril where
  There was but room for one :
The only thing he did not dare
  Was any death to shun.

The Nelson touch his men he taught,
  And his great stride to keep;
His faithful fellows round him fought

Ten thousand heroes deep.
With a red pride of life, and hot
   For him, their blood ran free;
They *"minded not the showers of shot,*
   No more THAN *peas,"* said he.

Napoleon saw our sea-king thwart
   His landing on our isle;
He gnashed his teeth, he gnawed his heart,
   At Nelson of the Nile,
Who set his fleet in flames, to light
   The lion to his prey,
And lead Destruction through the night
   Upon his dreadful way.

Around the world he drove his game,
   And ran his glorious race;
Nor rested till he hunted them
   From off the ocean's face;
Like that old war-dog who, till death,
   Clung to the vessel's side
Till hands were lopped, then with his teeth
   He held on till he died.

O, he could do the deeds that set
   Old fighters' hearts afire;
The edge of every spirit whet,
   And every arm inspire.

Yet I have seen upon his face
  The tears that, as they roll,
Show what a light of saintly grace
  May clothe a sailor's soul.

And when our darling went to meet
  Trafalgar's Judgment-day,
The people knelt down in the street
  To bless him on his way.
He felt the country of his love
  Watching him from afar ;
It saw him through the battle move :
  His heaven was in that star.

Magnificently glorious sight
  It was in that great dawn !
Like one vast sapphire flashing light,
  The sea, just breathing, shone.
Their ships, fresh painted, stood up tall
  And stately : ours were grim
And weatherworn, but one and all
  In rare good fighting trim.

Our spirits were all flying light,
  And into battle sped,
Straining for it on wings of might,
  With feet of springy tread ;
The battle light on every face ;
  Its fire in every eye ;

Our sailor blood at swiftest pace
  To catch the victory nigh.

His proudly wasted face, wave-worn,
  Was loftily serene;
I felt the brave, bright spirit burn
  There, all too plainly seen;
As though the sword this time was drawn
  Forever from the sheath;
And when its work to-day was done,
  All would be dark in death.

His eye shone like a lamp of night
  Set in the porch of power;
The deed unborn was burning bright
  Within him at that hour!
His purpose, welded at white heat,
  Cried like some visible Fate,
" *To-day we must not merely beat:*
  We must annihilate."

He smiled to see the Frenchman show
  His reckoning for retreat,
With Cadiz port on his lee-bow;
  And held him then half beat.
They showed no colors, till we drew
  Them out to strike with there!
Old Victory, for a prize or two,
  Had flags enough to spare.

Mast-high the famous signal ran ;
  Breathless we caught each word :
" *England expects that every man*
  Will do his duty."   Lord,
You should have seen our faces ! heard
  Us cheering, row on row ;
Like men before some furnace stirred
  To a fiery fearful glow !

'T was Collingwood our lee line led,
  And cut their centre through.
" *See how he goes in !* " Nelson said,
  As his first broadside flew,
And near four hundred foemen fall.
  Up went another cheer.
" *Ah, what would Nelson give,*" said Coll,
  " *But to be with us here !* "

We grimly kept our vanward path ;
  Over us hummed their shot ;
But, silently, we reined our wrath,
  Held on, and answered not,
Till we could grip them face to face,
  And pound them for our own,
Or hug them in a war-embrace,
  Till one of us went down.

How calm he was ! when first he felt
  The sharp edge of that fight.

Cabined with God alone he knelt;
  The prayer still lay in light
Upon his face, that used to shine
  In battle, — flash with life,
As though the glorious blood ran wine,
  Dancing with that wild strife.

" Fight for us, thou Almighty One !
  Give victory once again !
And if I fall, Thy will be done.
  Amen, Amen, Amen !"
With such a voice he bade good by ;
  The mournfullest old smile wore :
" Farewell ! God bless you, Blackwood, I
  Shall never see you more."

And four hours after, he had done
  With winds and troubled foam.
The Reaper was borne dead upon
  Our load of harvest-home —
Not till he knew the old flag flew
  Alone on all the deep ;
Then said he, *" Hardy, is that you ?*
  Kiss me." And fell asleep.

Well, 't was his chosen death below
  The deck in triumph trod ;
'T is well. A sailor's soul should go
  From his good ship to God.

He would have chosen death aboard,
  From all the crowns of rest;
And burial with the patriot sword
  Upon the victor's breast.

"*Not a great sinner.*" No, dear heart,
  God grant in our death-pain,
We may have played as well our part,
  And feel as free from stain.
We see the spots on such a star,·
  Because it burned so bright;
But on the side next God they are
  All lost in greater light.

And so he went upon his way,
  A higher deck to walk,
Or sit in some eternal day,
  And of the old time talk
With sailors old, who, on that coast,
  Welcome the homeward bound;
Where many a gallant soul we 've lost,
  And Franklin will be found.

Where amidst London's roar and moil
  That cross of peace upstands,
Like martyr with his heavenward smile,
  And flame-lit, lifted hands,
There lies the dark and mouldered dust;
  But that magnanimous
And manly Seaman's soul, I trust,
  Lives on in some of us.

OLD KING HAKE.

OT by the Sea on a rocky coast
    Was old King Hake;
Where inner fire and outer frost
    Brave virtue make!
He was a hero in the old
    Blood-letting days;
An iron hero of Norse mould,
    And warring ways.
He lived according to the light
    That lighted him;
Then strode into the eternal night,
    Resolved and grim.
His grip was stern for free sword play,
    When men were mown;
His feet were roughshod for the day
    Of treading down.
When angry, out the blood would start
    With old King Hake;
Not sneak in dark caves of the heart,
    Where curls the snake,

And secret Murder's hiss is heard
    Ere the deed be done.
He wove no web of wile and word;
    He bore with none.
When sharp within its sheath asleep
    Lay his good sword,
He held it royal work to keep
    His kingly word.
A man of valor, bloody and wild,
    In Viking need;
And yet of firelight feeling mild
    As honey-mead.

Once in his youth, from farm to farm,
    Collecting Scatt,
He gathered gifts and welcomes warm;
    And one night sat,
With hearts all happy for his throne —
    Wishing no higher —
Where peasant faces merrily shone
    Across the fire.
Their Braga-bowl was handed round
    By one fair girl:
The Sea-King lookt and thought, "*I've found
    My hidden pearl.*"
Her wavy hair was golden fair,
    With sunbeams curled;
Her eyes clear blue as heaven, and there
    Lay his new world.

He drank out of the mighty horn,
    Strong, stinging stuff;
Then wiped his manly mouth unshorn
    With hand as rough,
And kissed her; drew her to his side,
    With loving mien,
Saying, " *If they will make you a Bride,*
    I'll make you a Queen."
And round her waist she felt an arm,
    For in those days
A waist could feel: 't was lithe and warm,
    And wore no stays.
" *How many brave deeds have you done?* "
    She asked her wooer,
Counting the arm's gold rings: they won
    One victory more.
The blood of joy looked rich and red
    Out of his face;
And to his smiling strength he wed
    Her maiden grace.
'T was thus King Hake struck royal root
    In homely ground;
And healthier buds with goodlier fruit
    His branches crowned.

But Hake could never bind at home
    His spirit free;
It grew familiar with the foam
    Of many a sea;

A rare good blade whose way was rent
    In gaps of war,
And wore no gem for ornament
    But notch and scar.
In day of battle and hour of strife,
    Cried Old King Hake :
"*Kings live for honor, not long life.*"
    Then would he break
Right through their circle of shields, to reach
    Some chief of a race
That never yielded ground, but each
    Died in his place.
There the old Norseman towered tall
    Above the rest
A head and shoulders, like King Saul;
    They saw his crest
Toss, where the war-wave reared, and rode
    O'er mounds of dead,
Till all the battle-dust was trod
    A miry red.
For Odin, in the glad wide blue
    Of heaven, would laugh
With sunrise, and the ruddy dew
    Of slaughter quaff.

But, 't was the bravest, lordliest show,
    To see him sit,
With his Long-Serpent all aglow,
    And steering it

For the hot heart of fiercest fight.
    A grewsome shape !
The dragon-head rose, glancing bright,
    And all agape ;
Over the calm blue sea it came
    Writhingly on,
As half in sea, and half in flame,
    It swam, and shone.
The sunlit shields link scale to scale
    From stem to stern,
Over the steersman's head the tail
    Doth twist and burn.
With oars all moved at once, it makes
    Low hoverings ;
Half walks the water, and half takes
    The air with wings.
The war-horns bid the fight begin
    With death-grip good :
King Hake goes at the foremost, in
    His Bare-Sark mood.
A twelvemonth's taxes spent in spears
    Hurled in an hour !
But in that host no spirit fears
    The hurtling shower.
And long will many a mother and wife
    Wait, weary at home,
Ere from that mortal murderous strife
    Their darlings come.

Hake did not seek to softly die,
    With child and wife :
He bore his head in death as high
    As in his life.
Glittering in eye, and grim in lip,
    He bade them make
Ready for sailing his War-Ship,
    That he, King Hake,
The many-wounded, gray, and old,
    His day being done,
He, the Norse warrior, brave and bold,
    Might die like one.
And chanting some old battle-song,
    Thrilling and weird,
His soul vibrating, shook his long
    Majestic beard.
The gilded battle-axe, still red,
    In his right hand ;
His shield on arm, his helm on head,
    They helpt him stand,
And girded him with his good sword ;
    Then, so attired,
With his dead warriors all aboard,
    The ship he fired,
And lay down with his heroes dead,
    On deck to die ;
Still singing, drooped his gray old head,
    With face to sky.

15

The wind blew seawards; gloriously
          The death-pyre glowed;
On his last Viking voyage he
          Triumphing rode:
Floating afar between the Isles,
          To his last home,
Where open-armed Valhalla smiles,
          And bids him come.
There, as a sinking sunset dies
          Down in the west,
The fire flamed out; the rude heart lies
          At rest — at rest,
And sleeping in its ocean bed,
          That burial-place
Most royal for the kingly dead
          O' the old sea-race!
So the Norse noble of renown,
          With fearless pride,
His flaming crown of death pulled down.
          And so he died.

GARIBALDI.

THIS is the Helper that Italy wanted
　　To free her from fetters and grave-
　　　　clothes quite :
　　His is the great heart no dangers have
　　　　daunted ;
　His is the true hand to finish the fight.
Way, for a Man of the kingliest nature !
Scope, for a soul of the high Roman stature !
　　　His great deeds have crowned him ;
　　　His heroes are round him ;
On, on, Garibaldi, for Freedom and Right.

To brave battle-music up goes the smoke-curtain ;
　A Country arises all one should he call :
The sound of his trumpet is never uncertain ;
　He fights for his Cause till it conquer or fall.
His chariot-wheels do not spin without biting ;
And far better pointed for Freedom's red writing —
　　　His Rifles and Guns —
　　　Than their politic pens ;
Garibaldi, my Hero, best Man of them all.

When he sailed up our river, the frank hearty Sea-
      man,
  We saw how an English soul smiled from his face :
For Italy's savior we knew it was THE man,
  All hero, no matter what garb, or what place.
And we prayed he might have one more grip that
      was glorious !
Prophesied he should be leader victorious
     Of Italy, free
     From the Alps to the sea ;
Now breathless we watch while he runs the great
      race.

Fierce out of torment his fighters have risen,
  Shouting from hell where they tortured them
      dumb :
Maimed from old battle-fields, mad from the prison,
  Suddenly, strange as Cloud-armies, they come ;
With mouths that can shut like the Eagle's beak
      clasping ;
With hands that will grip like a bower-anchor
      grasping ;
     The flying foe feels,
     When they 're close at his heels,
That Death and the Devil are bringing his doom.

Not only living ! but dead men are fighting
  For him ! thus with few he can fight the great
      host ;

For each one they see an unseen foe is smiting ;
  Over each head an avenging white ghost !
All the young Martyrs they murdered by moon-
     light ;
All the dark deeds of blood done in the noonlight,
    Make their hearts reel
    With a shudder, and kneel
To lay down their arms and give all up for lost.

They tell the wild tales of him, gathered together,
  Turn pale at his shadow in midst of their speech ;
For down he swoops on them, like hawk on the
     heather,
  Strikes home with sure aim, and up-soars be-
     yond reach.
Or he sweeps all before him with whirling blade
     reeking ;
They fly helter-skelter, for shelter run shrieking,
    As waves wild and white,
    Driven mad with affright,
Are dasht into foam as they hide up the beach.

Watching o' nights in the cold, he remer bers
  The homes of his love in their ashes laid low ;
And hot in his heart Vengeance rakes up the
     embers,
  To warm her old hands at the wrathful red glow.
He has had torn from him all that was nearest ;

He has seen murdered his darlings the dearest;
　　　With all this and more,
　　　To the heart's crimson core
He kindles! and all flashes out on the Foe.

No Peace, Garibaldi, till Italy, stronger
　　Shall sit with free nations, majestic, serene;
And meet them as lovers may meet when no longer
　　The cold corse of one that was dead lies between.
For this, God was with you when perils were
　　'　　round you;
For this, the fire smote you not, floods have not
　　　drowned you;
　　　Their Sword and their Shot
　　　Have harmed you not,
And your Purpose croucht long for its spring un-
　　　seen.

On, with our British hearts all beating true to you;
　　All keeping time to the march of the brave!
I would to God we might cut our way through to
　　　you,
　　Gallantly breasting the stormiest wave.
Would the old Lion could leap in to greet you,
Just as our free blood is leaping to meet you,
　　　Stand by your side,
　　　In his terrible pride,
Mighty to shield, as You 're daring to save

Long was the night of her kneeling ; but surely
  Shall Italy rise to her queenliest height.
Many a time has the battle gone sorely,
  To make the last triumph more signal and
    bright.
Her foes shall be swept from her path like the
    stubble,
For now is *their* day of down-treading and trouble ;
    God tires of old Rome !
    Venetia cries " *Come.*"
On, on, Garibaldi, for Freedom and Right.

ONE OF GARIBALDI'S MEN.

A CRIPPLED Child, a weak wan
    Boy,
  Sat by his Mother's side, —
A widowed Mother's gentle joy,
  Her only wealth and pride : —
One of those spirits, sweet and sad,
  That breathe with burdened breath,
Are grave in life, but calmly glad
  Their faces smile in death.

With a weird lustre in his look,
  Over his books he pored,
Like one that, in a secret nook,
  Sharpens a patriot sword.
The story of his Country's wrongs
  Made his heart melt in tears ;
The music of her olden songs
  Rang ever in his ears.

Oft in his face, white as a corse,
  Brave soldier blood up-springs,

Hot as the warrior leaps to horse,
    When Battle's trumpet rings;
With spirit afloat and blood aflame,
    Where Freedom's banners wave,
To win a name of glorious fame,
    Or fill a Soldier's grave.

The leal heart of a loving Maid
    Ran over towards him,
Longing with kisses to be stayed
    There at the ruddy brim!
But husht the yearning in her breast,
    Nor murmur made nor moan;
She lookt as though she had found the nest,
    But, lo! the Bird was flown.

Suddenly, Freedom's thunder-horn
    The graveyard stillness broke;—
It was the resurrection-morn,
    And Italy awoke!
He felt her majesty and strength
    Lift up his spirit too:
To Manhood he had leapt at length,
    And almost stately grew.

Then came, with all they had to give,
    Each kneeling worshipper:
And he, too, not worth much to live,
    But he could die for her.

The Widow gave her only Child,
    And bade him help to win;
While outwardly her proud face smiled,
    She — dropping tears within !

The General lookt on this young life
    Held out in hands so small !
He could not, for the battle-strife,
    Take the poor Widow's all.
"*Poor Child!*" he said, "*rest you at home*
    For the good Mother's sake;
We'll not forget you when we come."
    It made his old heart ache.

'T was at the close of one great day,
    The Red Shirts raised their cheer,
For Garibaldi came to say,
    "*Well done !*"   One cried, "*I'm here!*
And wounded in the battle's brunt."
    "*What ! hit behind, my child ?*
But brave men wear their wounds in front."
    And playfully he smiled.

Again, at the Volturno's fight
    The boy led on his band;
Uplifted there on Capua's height,
    He saw the Promised Land,
As Pilgrims see their Mecca rise
    Over the desert's rim; —

He saw, — possessed it with his eyes!
 Enough, enough for him.

Proud of his Boys, the General rode
 Past faces all aflame,
And praised them; and their spirits glowed
 As if from heaven he came.
Then something caught his eye; he reined
 His horse, stooped like a grand
Old weather-beaten angel, stained
 With battle-smoke, and tanned!

With look more keen than cry or call,
 One staggered from the rest:
"*I 'm hit once more, my General,* —
 And" — pointing to his breast, —
"*This time — see! — 't is in the right place.*"
 His smile was strangely sweet:
He lookt in Garibaldi's face,
 And fell dead at his feet!

GARIBALDI AT ASPROMONTE.

THE Lion is down, and how the Dogs
    will run;
    Something above the level is their
     'delight
For insult; Asses lift the hoof to smite;
The Birds of darkness hoot, "*His day is done.*"

"*Would he had kept his attitude sublime!*"
    Cry some; "*With crossed arms held his heart at
     rest,*
    And left us his grand likeness at its best;
High on a hill up which the world might climb!"

"*Better for all had he been sooner shrined;*
    The old true heart, and very foolish head!
    A model Man — especially if dead —
Perfect as some Greek statue — and as blind!"

Friends talk of failure; and I know how he
    Will slowly lift his loving, cordial eyes
    And look them through, with mournful, strange
     surprise,
Until they shrink and feel 't is Italy

That fails instead.   The words they came to speak
  Will slink back, awed by his majestic calm,
  His wounds are such as bleed immortal balm,
And he is strong again; the friends are weak.

It is not failure to be thus struck down
  By Brothers who obeyed their Foe's command,
  And in the darkness lopped the saving hand
Put forth to reach their country her last crown.

He only sought to see her safely home ;
  The tragic trials end ; the sufferings cease,
  In wedded oneness and completing peace ;
Then bow his old gray head and die in Rome.

It is no failure to be thus struck back —
  Caught in a Country's arms — claspt to her
      heart —
  She tends his wounds awhile, and then will start
Afresh ! Some precious drops mark out her track.

No failure ! though the rocks dash into foam
  This first strength of a nation's new life-stream,
  'T will rise — a Bow of Promise — that shall
      gleam
In glory over all the waves to come.

Christ did not fail because he found a cross ;
  The work went on, although the Saviour died
  With two poor malefactors at His side :
Eternal gain repays such human loss !

We miss a footstep, thinking "*Here's a stair*,"
  In some uncertain way we darkly tread;
  But God's enduring skies are overhead,
And spirits step their surest oft in air.

His ways are not as our ways; the new birth,
  At cost of the old life, is often given.
  To-day God crowns the Martyrs in his heaven
To-morrow whips their murderers on our earth.

You take back Garibaldi to his prison!
  Why, that may be the very road to Rome;
  They would have said, "*She croucheth to her
      doom*,"
If Italy, in some shape, had not risen!

I say 't was God's voice bade him offer up
  Himself for Aspromonte's sacrifice;
  So, to that height, his countrymen might rise:
For them he freely drank his bitter cup.

It is a faith too many still receive, —
  Since the false prophecy of old went forth —
  "*The tribe of Judas yet shall rule the earth.*"
But he is one that never would believe.

His vision is most clear where ours is dim.
  The mystic spirit of eternity
  That slumbers in us deep and dreamingly,
Was ever quick and more awake in him.

And, like a lamp across some lonesome heath,
    A light shone through his eyes no night could
        quench :
    The winds might make it flicker, rains might
        drench ;
Nothing could dim it save the dark of death.

And if his work 's unfinished in the flesh,
    Why, then his soul will join the noble dead
    And toil till it shall be accomplishëd,
And Italy hath burst this Devil's mesh.

Easier to conquer kingdoms than to breed
    A man like Garibaldi, whose great name
    Doth fence his country with his glorious fame,
Worth many armies in her battle-need.

His is the royal heart that never quails,
    But always conquers ; wounded, pale, and low,
    He never was so dear as he is now ;
They bind him, and more strongly he prevails.

Greater to-day than Emperor or King,
    There, where, for throne, they seat him in the
        dust,
    The express image of sublimest Trust,
Crowned, consecrated by his suffering.

A sovereignty that overtops success !
    Nothing but heaven might bind his patriot-brow,
    And lo, the Crown of Thorns is on it now ;
With higher guerdon than our world's caress.

The vision of all his glory fills our eyes,
    And with one heart expectant nations throb
    Around him — with one mighty prayer they sob,
And wait God's answer to this sacrifice, —

Praying for one more chance at turn of tide :
    One blow for Rome, ere many setting suns ;
    One stroke for Venice, kneeling 'neath her Guns ;
All Italy abreast, and at his side ;

That he may stand, as Wellington once stood
    Victorious, looking from the Pyrenees,
    With France below him ; offering, on her knees,
The White flower Peace, sprung from her Root of
        Blood.

A LETTER IN BLACK.

FLOATING on the fragrant flood
  Of Summer — fuller hour by
   hour ;
  All the Spring-sweetness of the
   bud
Crowned by the glory of the flower, —
My spirits with the season flowed.
  The air was all a breathing balm ;
The lake a flame of sapphire glowed ;
  The mountains lay in cloudless calm :

Green leaves were lusty ; roses blusht
  For pleasure in the golden time ;
The birds through all their feathers flusht
  For gladness of their marriage-prime :
Listless among the lilies I threw
  Me down, for coolness, 'mid the sheen :
Heaven, one large smile of brooding blue ;
  Earth, one large smile of basking green.

A rich suspended shower of gold
　　Laburnum o'er me hung its crown :
You look up heavenward and behold
　　It glowing, coming in glory down !
There, as my thoughts of greenness grew
　　To fruitage of a leafy dream, —
There, friend, your letter thrilled me through,
　　And all the summer lost its gleam.

The world, so pleasant to the sight,
　　So full of voices blithe and brave,
And all her lamps of beauty alight
　　With life ! I had forgot the Grave ;
And there it opened at my feet,
　　Revealing a familiar face
Upturned, my whitened look to meet,
　　And very patient in its place.

My poor bereaven friend ! I know
　　Not how to word it, but would bring
A little solace for your woe, —
　　A little love for comforting :
And yet the best that I can say
　　Will only help to sum your loss ;
I can but look above, and pray
　　God help my friend to bear his Cross.

I have felt something of your smart,
　　And lost the dearest thing e'er wound

In love about a human heart:
  I, too, have life-roots underground.
From out my soul hath leapt a cry
  For help! Nor God himself could save:
And tears yet run that naught will dry,
  Save Death's hand with the dust o' the grave.

God knows, and we may one day know,
  These hidden secrets of his love;
But now the stillness stuns us so;
  Darkly, as in a dream, we move.
The glad life-pulses come and go,
  Over our head and at our feet;
Soft airs are sighing something low;
  The flowers are saying something sweet;

And 't is a merry world. The lark
  Is singing over the green corn;
Only the house and heart are dark, —
  Only the human world forlorn.
There, in the bridal chamber, lies
  A dear bedfellow all in white;
That purple shadow under the eyes,
  Where star-fire swam in liquid night.

Sweet, slippery silver of her talk;
  The music of her laugh so dear,
Heard in home-ways, and wedded walk,
  For many and many a golden year;

The singing soul and shining face,
  Daisy-like glad by roughest road;
Gone! with a thousand dearnesses
  That hid themselves for us and glowed.

The waiting Angel, patient Wife,
  All through the battle at our side,
That smiled her sweetness on our strife
  For gain, and it was sanctified!
When waves of trouble beat breast high
  And the heart sank, she poured a balm
That stilled them; and the saddest sky
  Made clear and starry with her calm.

And when the world with harvest ripe
  In all its golden fulness lay;
And God, it seemed, saw fit to wipe,
  Even on earth, all tears away;
The good true heart that bravely won,
  Must smile up in our face and fall;
And all our happy days are done,
  And this the end.   And is this all?

The bloom of bliss, the secret glow,
  That clothed without, and inly curled,
All gone.   We are left shivering now,
  Naked to the wide open world!
A shrivelled, withered world it is,
  So sad and miserably cold;

Where be its vaunted braveries ?
  'T is gray, and miserably old.

Our joy was all a drunken dream ;
  This is the truth at waking ! we
Are swept out rootless by the stream
  And current of calamity —
Out on some lone and shoreless sea
  Of solitude so vast and deep,
As 't were the wrong Eternity,
  Where God is not, or gone to sleep.

It seems as though our darling dead,
  Startled at Death's so sudden call,
With falling hands and dear bowed head
  Had, like a flower-filled lap, let fall
A hoard of treasures we have found
  Too late ! so slow doth wisdom come !
We for the first time look around
  Remembering this is not our home.

My friend, I see you with your cup
  Of tears and trembling — see you sit ;
And long to help you drink it up,
  With useless longings infinite ! —
Sit rocking the old mournful thought,
  That on the heart's-blood will be nurst,
Unless the blessed tears be brought ;
  Unless the cloudy sorrows burst.

The little ones are gone to rest,
  And for a while they will not miss
The Mother-wings above the nest;
  But through their slumber slides her kiss,
And, dreaming she has come, they start,
  And toss wild arms for her caress,
With moanings that must thrill a heart
  In heaven with divine distress.

And Sorrow on your threshold stands,
  The Dark Ladye in glooming pall:
I see her take you by the hands;
  I feel her shadow over all.
Hers is no warm and tender clasp;
  With silence solemn as the Night's,
And veilèd face, and spirit-grasp,
  She leads her Chosen up the heights:

The cloudy crags are cold and gray,
  You cannot scale them without scars:
So many Martyrs by the way,
  Who never reacht her tower of stars,
But there her beauty shall be seen,
  Her glittering face so proudly pure;
And all her majesty of mien;
  And all her guerdon shall be sure.

Well.   'T is not written, God will give
  To his Beloved only rest!

The hard life of the cross they live,
  They strive, and suffer, and are blest.
The feet must bleed to reach their throne,
  The brow must burn before it bear
One of the crowns that may be won,
  By workers for immortal wear.

Dear friend, life beats though buried 'neath
  Its long black vault of night! and see
There trembles through this dark of death,
  Starlight of immortality!
And yet shall dawn the eternal day
  To kiss the eyes of them that sleep;
And He shall wipe all tears away
  From tired eyes of them that weep.

'T is something for the poor bereaven,
  In such a weary world of care,
To think that we have friends in heaven;
  Who helpt us here, may aid us there.
These yearnings for them set our Arc
  Of being widening more and more,
In circling sweep through outer dark
  To day more perfect than before.

So much was left unsaid.   The soul
  Must live in other worlds to be;
On earth we cannot grasp the whole,
  For that Love has eternity.

Love deep as death, and rich as rest;
  Love that was love with all Love's might;
Level to needs the lowliest;
  Cannot be less Love at full-height.

Though earthly forms be far apart,
  Spirit to spirit may be nigher;
The music chord the same at heart,
  Though one voice range an octave higher.
Eyes watch us that we cannot see;
  Lips warn us which we may not kiss;
They wait for us, and starrily,
  Lean toward us from heaven's lattices.

We cannot see them face to face,
  But love is nearness; and they love
Us yet, nor change, with change of place,
  In their more human world above,
Where love, once leal, hath never ceased,
  And dear eyes never lose their shine,
And there shall be a marriage feast,
  Where Christ shall once more make the wine

WIDOW MARGARET.

POOR Margaret's window is alight;
  The Widow sits alone;
  Though long into the silent night,
  And far, the world is gone.
She lives in shadow till her blood
  Grows bitter and blackened all;
Upon her head a mourning hood;
  Upon her heart a pall.

The stars come nightly out of heaven,
  Old Darkness to beguile;
For her there is no healing given
  To their sweet spirit-smile.
That honey-dew of sleep the skies
  In blessed balm let fall,
Comes not to her poor tired eyes,
  Though it be sent for all.

At some dead flower, with fragrance faint,
  Her life opes like a book;

And old sweet music makes its plaint,
  And, from the grave's dim nook,
The buried bud of hopes laid low,
  Flowers in the night full-blown;
And little things of Long-Ago
  Come back to her full-grown.

Her heart is wandering in a whirl,
  And she must seek the tomb
Where lies her long-lost little girl.
  O, well with them for whom
Love's Morning-Star comes round so fair
  As Evening-Star of Faith,
Already up and shining, ere
  The dark of coming death.

But Margaret cannot reach a hand,
  Beyond the dark of death ;
Her spirit swoons in that high land
  Where breathes no human breath ;
She cannot look upon the grave
  As one eternal shore ;
From which a soul may take the wave,
  For heaven, to sail or soar.

Across that Deep no sail unfurled,
  For her; no wings put forth ;
She tries to reach the other world
  By groping down through earth..

'T was there the child went underground ;
  They parted in that place ;
And ever since, the Mother found
  The door shut in her face.

Though many effacing springs have wrapped
  With green, the dark grave-bed ;
'T was *there*, the breaking heart-strings snapped
  As she let down her dead ;
And there she gropes with wild heart yet,
  For years, and years, and years ;
Poor Margaret ! there she will let
  Her sorrow loose in tears.

All the young mother in her old voice
  Its waking moan will make !
A young aurora light her eyes
  With radiance gone to wreck !
And then at dawn she will return,
  To her old self again ;
Eyes dim and dry ; heart gray and dern ;
  And querulous in her pain.

" We never loved each other much,
  I and my poor good-man ;
But on the Child we lavisht such
  A love as overran
All boundaries, loving her the more
  Because our love was pent ;

Striving as two seas try to pour
  Their strength through one small rent.

" For children come to still link hands,
  When lives have ebbed apart ;
And hide the rift, when either stands
  At distance heart from heart.
So on our little one we 'd look ;
  Press hands with fonder grasp ;
As though we closed some holy book,
  Softly, with golden clasp.

" And as the dark earth offers up
  Her little winterling,
The Crocus, pleading with its cup
  Of hoarded gold, to bring
Down all the gray heaven's golden shower
  Of spring to warm the sod ;
So did we lift the winsome flower
  That sprang from our dark clod.

" Our little Golden-heart, her name !
  And all things sweet and calm,
And pure and fragrant, round her came
  With gifts of bloom and balm.
And there she grew, my queen of all,
  Golden, and saintly white ;
Just as at Summer's smiling call
  The lily stands alight.   .

" To knee or nipple, grew the goal
  Of her wee stately walk;
The voice of my own silent soul
  Was her dear baby-talk;
Then darklingly she dwined and failed;
  And looking on our dead,
The father wailed awhile and ailed,
  Turned to the wall and said —

" *'T is dark and still, our house of life,*
  The fire is burning low;
Our pretty one is gone, old Wife,
  'T is time for me to go :
Our Golden-heart has gone to sleep ;
  She 's happed in for the night ;
And so to bed I 'll quietly creep,
  And sleep till morning light.' "

Once more the Widow Margaret rose
  'And through the night passed on.
Long shadows weird of tree and house
  Made ghosts in the moonlight wan!
She passed into the churchyard, where
  The many glad life-waves
That leapt of old, have stood still there,
  In green and grassy graves.

"O would my body were at rest
  Under this cool grave-sward :

O would my soul were with the Blest,
   That slumber in the Lord !
They sleep so sweetly underground ;
   For Death hath shut the door,
And all the world of sorrow and sound
   Can trouble them no more."

A spirit-feel is in the place, .
   That makes the poor heart gasp ;
Her soul stands white up iu her face
   For one warm human clasp !
To-night she sees the grave astir ;
   And as in prayer she kneels,
The mystery opens unto her :
   She for the first time feels.

The spirit-world may be as near
   Us moving silent round,
As are the dead that sleep a mere
   Short fathom underground ;
And there be eyes that sce the sight
   Of lorn ones wandering, vexed
Through some long, sad, and shadowy night
   Betwixt this world and next.

Doorways of fear, are eye and ear,
   Through which the wonders go ;
And through the night with glow-worm light,
   The Church is all aglow !

There comes a waft of Sabbath hymn;
  She enters; all the air
With faces fills divine and dim,
  The Blessed Dead are there.

One came and bade poor Margaret sit,
  Seemed to her as it smiled,
A great white Bird of God alit
  In a forest marble-aisled.
"Look to the Altar!" there a spell
  Fixed her; she saw upstart,
A woman, like a soul in hell,
  'T was her own Golden-heart.

" It would have been thus, Mother dear,
  And so God took her, from
All trials and temptations here,
  To his eternal home;
And you shall see her in a place
  . Where death can never part."
She lookt up in the Angel's face;
  Found her own Golden-heart.

The lofty music rose again
  From all those happy souls,
Till all the windows thrilled, as when
  The organ thunder rolls;
And all her life was like a light
  Weak weed the stream doth sway,

Until it reaches the full-height;
 Breaks, and is borne away.

Her life stood still to listen to
 That music! then a hand
Took hers, and she was floated through
 A mystic border-land.
'T was Golden-heart! from that eclipse
 She drew her into bliss;
Two spirits closed at dying lips,
 In one immortal kiss.

Next day an early worshipper
 Was kneeling in the Aisle;
A statue of life that did not stir,
 But knelt on with a smile
Upon the face that smiled with light,
 As though, when left behind,
It smiled on with some glorious sight
 Long after the eyes were blind.

HYMNS,

AND OTHER LYRICS.

(SOME OF WHICH WERE WRITTEN FOR CHILDREN TO SING.)

17

AT EVENTIDE.

THOU infinitely merciful!
   Thy garment's hem in prayer we pull;
   Bringing our burdens on our knees,
   We take the hand that lends release:
Turn on us one forgiving look,
Before this day shall close its book.

So yearningly we seek thy face
When darkness is our dwelling-place.
Our foolish hearts, that daily roam,
Would nightly nestle with Thee at Home.
Be with us Here, and grant that we
Hereafter, Lord, may be with Thee!

Father! our inmost parts lie bare
To Thine own purifying air;
We spread our stains out in Thy sight;
O, Sun of Pureness, turn them white:
And make our spirits clear as dew
For thine own Self to lighten through.

Send down the Comforter, we plead,
For all who are in bitter need;
Let homeless Hagars find, we pray,
Some well of succor by the way:
With the Angel of Thy Presence bless
Poor wanderers in the wilderness.

God keep our darlings safe this night,
Though scattered, *one* still in Thy sight!
Lead on, by many ways, and past
All perils, till we join at last:
With us the broken links! with Thee
The circle perfect endlessly.

Now take us, Father, to Thy breast,
And still all troubled thoughts to rest;
Thy watch and ward about us keep,
That tired souls may smile asleep,
And, having been in heaven awhile,
May wake to-morrow with Thy smile!

OUT OF THE DEPTHS.

O dark the way, I cannot see :
    O, somewhere-smiling face Divine,
    Look down and make my night to
       shine !
So dark the way, I cannot see.
Dear Jesus, let me lean on Thee !

All night I stumble gropingly,
    Seeking the door in some blank wall,
    That shuts me from the light, and call
And listen, listen hopingly.
Dear Jesus, let me lean on Thee !

My burden bows me to the knee ;
    O Lord, 't is more than I can bear.
    Didst Thou not come our load to share ?
My burden bows me to the knee.
Dear Jesus, let me lean on Thee !

The Deeps will surely swallow me ;
    I cry with fainting strength : the waves
    Are gaping round in open graves :
The Deeps will surely swallow me.
Dear Jesus, let me lean on Thee !

Far off, so far, the Heavens be,
  With their wide arms ! and I would prove
  The close warm-beating heart of Love.
But so far off the Heavens be :
Dear Jesus, let me lean on Thee !

Father in Heaven, we cannot see
  Thy face, nor grasp the spirit-hand
  That leads us to the Unseen Land ;
But trustingly, though tremblingly,
Dear Jesus, let me lean on Thee !

One smile, and all my fears would flee ;
  One whisper, and the storm would cease ;
  And I should know Thee in the peace ;
The door would ope ; no dark could be.
Dear Jesus, let me lean on Thee !

JERUSALEM THE GOLDEN.

JERUSALEM the Golden !
    I weary for one Gleam
    Of all thy glory folden
      In distance and in dream !
My thoughts, like Palms in Exile,
    Climb up to look and pray

For a glimpse of thy dear Country
That lies so far away !

Jerusalem the Golden !
Methinks each flower that blows,
'And every bird a-singing
Of thee some secret knows ;
I know not what the Flowers
Can feel, or Singers see,
But all these summer raptures
Seem prophecies of thee.

Jerusalem the Golden !
When Sunset 's in the West,
It seems thy gate of glory,
Thou City of the Blest !
And Midnight's starry torches
Through intermediate gloom
Are waving with our welcome
To thy Eternal Home !

Jerusalem the Golden !
Where loftily they sing,
O'er pain and sorrows olden,
Forever triumphing ;
Lowly may be the portal
And dark may be the door,
The Mansion is Immortal — ·
God's palace for His Poor !

Jerusalem the Golden !
  There all our Birds that flew, —
Our Flowers but half unfolden,
  Our Pearls that turned to dew, —
And all the glad life-music,
  Now heard no longer here,
Shall come again to greet us
  As we are drawing near.

Jerusalem the Golden !
  I toil on, day by day;
Heartsore each night with longing,
  I stretch my hands and pray,
That 'mid thy leaves of Healing,
  My soul may find her nest;
Where the Wicked cease from troubling —
  The Weary are at rest !

THE ONLY ONE.

WITH tired feet, o'er thorny ground,
    My spirit made its quest;
  On wearied wing it wandered round,
    But could not find its nest;
Till at my Saviour's feet I found
    At last my Only Rest !

I went the downward way of Doom,
  With those that walk in night;
I stumbled on from tomb to tomb
  Of Joys that lured my sight;
Until He touched me through the gloom
  And smiled — my Only Light!

All gleams of glory, shapes of grace,
  My Saviour shines above :
He sits in Heaven for brooding-place .
  He comes down like a Dove !
I look up in His pitying face
  And know my Only Love ! ·

O, sweet the touch of hearts, and sweet
  The tie of Child and Wife !
And blessed is the home where meet
  True souls that shut out strife ;
But nestling at my Saviour's feet,
  I know the Only Life.

THE NEST.

BUILT my Nest by a pleasant stream,
That glided on with a smile in its gleam,
    Bringing me gold that was sum-
        less;
Ah me! but the floods came drowning one day,
And swept my Nest with its wealth away;
    I in the world was homeless!

I built my Nest in a gay green tree,
And the summer of life went merrily
    With us! we were Birds of a feather!
But the leaves soon fell, and my pretty ones flew,
And through my Nest the bitter winds blew;
    'T was bare in the wildest weather.

I built my Nest under Heaven's high eaves;
No rising of floods, no falling of leaves,
    Can mock my heart's endeavor;
Waters may wash, breezes may blow,
In the bosom of Rest I shall smile, I shall know
    My Nest is safe forever.

POOR MAN'S SUNDAY.

THE merry birds are singing,
  And from the fragrant sod
The Spirits of a thousand flowers
  Go sweetly up to God;
While in His holy temple
  We meet to praise and pray
With cheerful voice, and grateful heart,
  This Summer Sabbath Day!

We thank thee, Lord, for one day
  To look Heaven in the face!
The Poor have only Sunday;
  The sweeter is the grace.
'T is then they make the music
  That sings their week away.
O, there 's a sweetness infinite
  In the Poor Man's Sabbath Day!

'T is as a burst of sunshine,
  A tender fall of rain,
That set the barest life abloom;
  Make old hearts young again.
The dry and dusty roadside
  With smiling flowers is gay;
'T is open Heaven one day in seven,
  The Poor Man's Sabbath Day!

'T is here the weary Pilgrim
  Doth reach his House of Ease !
That blessëd House, called " Beautiful,"
  And that soft Chamber, " Peace."
The River of Life runs through his dream
  And the leaves of Heaven are at play ;
He sees the Golden City gleam,
  This shining Sabbath Day !

Take heart, ye faint and fearful,
  Your cross with courage bear ;
So many a face now tearful
  Shall shine in glory there;
Where all the sorrow is banisht,
  The tears are wiped away ;
And all eternity shall be
  One endless Sabbath Day !

Ah ! there are empty places,
  Since last we mingled here !
There will be missing faces
  When we meet another year !
But, heart to heart, before we part,
  - Now altogether pray
That we may meet in Heaven, to spend
  The Eternal Sabbath Day !

THE LIGHT OF THE WORLD.

BEHOLD me standing at the door,
　And hear me asking o'er and o'er,
With pleading voice above the din,
　" May I come in ?　May I come in ? "

I fought for thee with Death's grim wave ;
I burst his dungeons of the grave ;
I would my rightful guerdon win,
　" May I come in ?　May I come in ? "

Wearing the cruel thorns for thee,
I listen long and patiently,
To hear the footstep from within,
　" May I come in ?　May I come in ? "

Ye dream dark dreams alone by night,
And lo, I am the Living Light,
That smiles away all mists of sin.
　" May I come in ?　May I come in ? "

There 's surely room upon thy breast
For one more loving head to rest :
One empty place for kith and kin.
　" May I come in ?　May I come in ? "

I would not have thee beat in vain
Onr Father's door and plead in pain,
When Heaven and all its joys begin.
   " May I come in?   May I come in? "

GOING TO SCHOOL.

N Sunday morning early,
   While yet the grass is pearly;
     The air is bright and cool;
   All clad in our best graces,
With rosy morning faces,
   We go to the Sunday School!

To-day is Life in blossom:
Heartsease in every bosom,
   And all is beautiful.
A spirit within us springing
At Heaven's gate will be singing
   Thanks for the Sunday School!

We sun us in its brightness;
We clothe us in its whiteness,
   As doth the wayside pool,
That holds from Morn till Even,

Its little bit of Heaven —
  The gladsome Sunday School!

Here learn we how to lighten
The heaviest lot, and brighten
  The day most dark with dule,
And lay up Childhood's treasure,
To reap immortal pleasure
  Even in a Sunday School!

The summer Earth rejoices,
With hers we lift our voices
  And Heaven blends the whole.
And when God's Angels cover us,
Drawing the darkness over us,
  They bless the Sunday School!

PARENTS' PRAYER FOR THE CHIL-
DREN.

HRIST on Earth, in Heaven the King,
As we heard the Children sing :
How the thought within us smiled,
Thou wert once a little Child!

Hover near them, Heavenly Dove,
With thine overshadowing love ;
Keep them pure and undefiled :
Thou wert once a little Child!

See them playing on the sands,
'Twixt two tides, with helpless hands ;
Save them when the waves grow wild :
Thou wert once a little Child!

Bless them in their joyousness ;
Hear them, help them, in distress ;
Be their Shepherd when beguiled ;
Thou wert once a little Child!

Let their feet be firmly shod ;
Let them not go back to God

With immortal jewels soiled;
Thou wert once a little Child!

Take them, when the Peril 's past,
To thy Father's Home at last;
He remembers, and is mild,
Thou wert once a little Child!

CHILDREN'S EVENING PRAYER.

GRACIOUS Saviour! meekly crave
          your
        Little Lambs their fold to-night;
    Do Thou hear us, and be near us;
Through the darkness lead to light:
Fence our weakness with Thy might!

Night is nearing! timid, fearing
    Life is shrinking in its nest;
To Thy keeping take us sleeping,
    Gentle Shepherd, in Thy breast,
    Where we nestle and are blest!

Through the nightfall may Thy Light fall
    On us, safely hid apart,

18

When no change or passing danger
  Clouds us, with Thy smile at heart.
  Where the lambs are there Thou art!

White mists wreathing their soft breathing,
  Where the water-courses run,
From their hiding-place are gliding,
  Hanging dew-drops, one by one,
  To be lighted by the sun!

We too kneeling for Thy healing,
  Pray Thy dews may fall apace
In rich showers, that Thy Flowers
  May uplift their morning face,
  Glistening with Thy freshest grace.

May good Angels with evangels
  Glad our slumbers by one gleam
Of their covering white wings, hovering
  Down the ladder of our dream —
  Soft the hardest pillow will seem!

O Thou Solace of the weary;
  O Thou Rest for all that roam;
Nightless Sunshine for the dreary;
  For the Homeless endless home;
  To Thy waiting arms we come!

AND THEY SUNG A NEW SONG.

HEAR what the Saint in solemn dream
was shown
Through Heaven's own Gates of
Gold;
He saw them standing by the great White Throne;
He heard their raptures rolled!
Christ was the Sun of that new firmament,
And there was no more night,
While through the golden City harping went
The glorious all in white.

These, out of their great tribulation, came
To bow before the Throne!
These lifted up their foreheads from the flame
And by His name were known!
Some on the rack were living witnesses,
And many fell afield;
But Christ did greet His Martyrs with a kiss,
And all their hurts were healed.

These had to wrestle with wild waves of strife,
Long ere they reached that shore
Where they at last have won the crowns of life
They wear forevermore.

There do they drink of Life's all-healing Stream,
   And quench their thirst of years;
All star-like now the precious jewels gleam,
   They sowed on Earth as tears.

Help us, O Lord, to reach that Better Land,
   Afar from sorrow and sin,
And join that Blessed band all harp-in-hand,
   All safe with Christ shut in.   .
Feeble and poor the songs we sing! at most,
   Some selfish Prayer we raise ;
While the white Harpers on that Heavenly coast
   Hymn everlasting Praise.

THE ASPEN.

WENT out into the wistful night,
   Along with my little Daughter ;
Down in the valley the weird Moon-
   . light
With an Elfin shine lit the wan water.

The Trees stood dark in a flame of white ;
   A Nightingale sang in the stillness ;
It seemed the husht heart of the sweet spring night
   Brimmed over because of its fulness.

Not a breath of air in the region wide ;
   Not a ripple upon the river ;
Yet all of a sudden the Aspens sighed
   And through all their leaves ran a shiver.

My darling she nestled quite close to me
   For such shield as mine arms could give her ;
" *There went not the least waft of wind through the*
      Tree ;
Then why did the Aspens shiver ? "

I told her the tale, how by Kedron's Brook
   Our Saviour one evening wandered ;
 A cloud came over His glorified look
   As he paused by the way and pondered.

The trees felt his sighing ; their heads all bowed
   Towards Him in solemn devotion,
Save the Aspen, that stood up so stately and proud ;
   It made neither murmur nor motion.

Then the Holy One lifted His face of pain :
  " *The Aspen shall quake and shiver,*
From this time forth till I come again,
  Whether growing by Brook or by River."

And oft in the listening hush of night
   The Aspen will secretly shiver ;

With all its tremulous leaves turn white,
　　Like a guilty thing by the River.

So the souls that look on His sorrow and pain
　　For their sake, and bow not, may quiver
Like Aspens, and quake when He comes again,
　　Through the night forever, forever!

LEGEND OF THE FLOWERS.

THE Seraph faded into air;
　　The Snake glode underground;
As on the last step of Heaven's stair,
　　Poor exiled Eve lookt round.

Heartless as Death, and blind as Doom,
　　The heavens bowed with wrath:
Where God, betwixt the glare and gloom,
　　Stood in their backward path.

Two mourners following the hearse
　　Of their dead joy went forth,
To find the shadow of their curse
　　Fall lengthening over earth.

The memories in each other's eyes
  They cannot, dare not face;
Forlorn and vast the wide world lies;
  They see no hiding-place.

Then did the Flowers of Eden grieve;
  As though a low wind stirred,
They softly prayed to follow Eve;
  And God in Heaven heard.

As when some erring Child may see,
  The Father's face no more;
A Mother's love sends secretly;
  · Her heart keeps open door;

So were the Flowers from Paradise
  For missioned comfort sent;
All heaven in their sweet pitying eyes!
  And where Eve trod they went.

With dear drops of that gladness spilled
  In Eden, they came pearled;
Their cups with color of Heaven filled,
  To pour through all the world.

They kiss her feet; embrace her knees;
  About her dance and play;
They run before and climb the trees,
  To cheer her by the way.

On hills and moorlands golden fires
  Of gorse in beauty burn;
Into red roses break the briers;
  A flower for every thorn.

And ever since, their silent march
  Goes glowing overground,
And under Ocean's azure arch,
  In an immortal round.

The wee white fairies of the snow '
  May cover them awhile;
But from their hiding-places, lo!
  The world's young morning-smile!

They come back with their fragrant news,
  By brook, and field, and fell;
They wake, and in a thousand hues
  Their dream of beauty tell.

They bring the distant dearness of
  That dewy Eden youth,
Into the kindling nearness of
  Warm kisses on the mouth.

Our thoughts are with their fancies freakt,
  And delicately drawn;
With them our gray of life is streakt,
  Divinely as the dawn.

And ailing souls come forth to see,
　How the sweet Flowers reveal
The waving skirts of Deity,
　Which at a touch can heal.

Our dying eyes their balm beseech;
　Our dying fingers fold
Their coolness, when we cannot reach
　The flower; so near the mould.

Their roots like feeling fingers twine,
　About the lone grave-bed:
Stars of the ground, they kindly shine,
　Through that long dark o' the Dead.

Incense, pathetically sweet,
　Their little censers wave —
Standing all night at head and feet
　Of our wee Sydney's grave.

With mournful fragrance to my heart
　They pierce at times, until
The tears up in mine eyes will start,
　With airs of heaven athrill.

Still blooms with all its buried charms,
　That old lost land of ours;
Above its silent war of worms,
　Earth will laugh out in flowers.

LEGEND OF LITTLE PEARL.

 *"POOR little Pearl, good little Pearl!"*
　　Sighed every kindly neighbor;
It was so sad to see a girl
　　So tender, doomed to labor.

A wee bird fluttered from its nest
　　Too soon, was that meek creature;
Just fit to rest in mother's breast,
　　The darling of fond Nature.

God shield poor little ones, where all
　　Must help to be bread-bringers!
For once afoot, there 's none too small
　　To ply their tiny fingers.

Poor Pearl, she had no time to play
　　The merry game of childhood;
From dawn to dark she went all day,
　　A-wooding in the wild-wood.

When others played, she stole apart
　　In pale and shadowy quiet;
Too full of care was her child-heart
　　For laughter running riot.

Hard lot for such a tender life,
  And miserable guerdon;
But like a womanly wee wife,
  She bravely bore her burden.

One wintry day they wanted wood
  When need was at the sorest;
Wee Pearl, without a bit of food,
  Must up and to the forest.

But there she sank down in the snow,
  All over numbed and aching:
Poor little Pearl, she cried as though
  Her very heart was breaking.

The blinding snow shut out the house
  From little Pearl so weary;
The lonesome wind among the boughs
  Moaned with its warnings eerie.

To little Pearl a Child-Christ came,
  With footfall light as fairy;
He took her hand, he called her name,
  The voice was sweet and airy.

His gentle eyes filled tenderly
  With mystical wet brightness:
" *And would you like to come with me,*
  And wear the robe of whiteness? "

He bore her bundle to the door,
  Gave her a flower when going:
" *My darling, I shall come once more,*
  When the little bud is blowing."

Home very wan came little Pearl,
  But on her face strange glory:
They only thought, " *What ails the girl?* "
  And laught to hear her story.

Next morning mother sought her child,
  And clasped it to her bosom;
Poor little Pearl, in death she smiled,
  And the rose was full in blossom.

POOR ELLEN.

IS hard to *die* in Spring-time,
    When, to mock my bitter need,
All life around runs over
    In its fulness without heed:
New life for tiniest twig on tree,
New worlds of honey for the bee,
And not one drop of dew for me
    Who perish as I plead.

'T is *hard* to die in Spring-time,
   When it stirs the poorest clod;
The wee Wren lifts its little heart
   In lusty songs to God;
And Summer comes with conquering march;
Her banners waving 'neath the arch
Of heaven, where I lie and parch —
   Left dying by the road.

'*T is* hard to die in Spring-time,
   When the long blue days unfold,
And cowslip-colored sunsets
   Grow, like Heaven's own heart, pure gold!
Each breath of balm brings wave on wave
Of new life that would lift and lave
My Life, whose *feel* is of the grave,
   And mingling with the mould.

But sweet to die in Spring-time,
   When these lustres of the sward,
And all the breaks of beauty
   Wherewith Earth is daily starred,
For me are but the outside show,
All leading to the inner glow
Of that strange world to which I go —
   Forever with the Lord.

O, sweet to die in Spring-time,
   When I reach the promised Rest,

And feel His arm is round me —
  Know I sink back on His breast :
His kisses close these poor dim eyes;
Soon I shall hear Him say " Arise,"
And, springing up with glad surprise,
  Shall know Him and be blest.

'T is sweet to die in Spring-time,
  For I feel my golden year
Of summer-time eternal
  Is beginning even here!
" Poor Ellen ! " now you say and sigh,
" Poor Ellen ! " and to-morrow I
Shall say " Poor Mother! " and, from the sky,
  Watch *you*, and wait you there.

THE SUNKEN CITY.

Y day it lies hidden and lurks beneath
    The ripples that laugh with light ;
  But calmly and clearly and coldly as
        death,
  It glooms into shape by night
When none but the awful Heavens and me
Can look on the City that 's sunk in the sea.

Many a Castle I built in the air;
  Towers that gleamed in the sun;
Spires that soared so stately and fair
  They toucht heaven every one,
Lie under the waters that mournfully
Closed over the City that 's sunk in the sea.

Many fine houses, but never a home;
  Windows, and no live face!
Doors set wide where no beating hearts come;
  No voice is heard in the place:
It sleeps in the arms of Eternity —
The silent City that 's sunk in the sea.

There the face of a dead love lies,
  Embalmed in the bitterest tears;
No breath on the lips! no smile in the eyes,
  Though you watcht for years and years:
And the' dear drowned eyes never close from me,
Looking up from the City that 's sunk in the sea.

Two of the bonniest birds of God
  That ever warmed human heart
For a nest, till they fluttered their wings abroad,
  Lie in their chambers apart —
Dead! yet pleading piteously
In the lonesome City that 's sunk in the sea.

O, the brave ventures there lying in wreck,
    Dark on that shore o' the Lost!
Gone down, with every hope on deck,
    When all-sail for a glorious coast!
And the waves go sparkling splendidly
Over the City that 's sunk in the sea.

Then I look from my City that 's sunk in the sea
    To that Star-Chamber o'erhead;
And torturingly they question me —
    "What of this world of the Dead
That lies out of sight, and how will it be
With the City and thee, when there 's no more sea?"

THE LIFE BEYOND.

LTHOUGH its features fade in light of
        unimagined bliss
    We have shadowy revealings of the
    Better World in this.

A little glimpse, when Spring unveils her face and
        opes her eyes,
Of the Sleeping Beauty in the soul that wakes in
        Paradise.

A little drop of Heaven in each diamond of the
    shower,
A breath of the Eternal in the fragrance of each
    flower !

A little low vibration in the warble of Night's bird,
Of the praises and the music that shall be hereafter
    heard !

A little whisper in the leaves that clap their hands
    and try
To glad the heart of man, and lift to Heaven his
    thankful eye !

A little semblance mirrored in old Ocean's smile
    or frown
Of His vast glory who doth bow the Heavens and
    come down !

A little symbol shining through the worlds that
    move at rest
On invisible foundations of the broad almighty
    breast !

A little hint that stirs and thrills the wings we
    fold within,
And tells of that full heaven *yonder* which must
    here begin !

A little springlet welling from the fountain-head
    above,
That takes its earthly way to find the ocean of all
    love !

A little silver shiver in the ripple of the river
Caught from the light that knows no night forever
    and forever !

A little hidden likeness, often faded and defiled,
Of the great, the good All-father, in His poorest
    human child !

Although the best be lost in light of unimagined
    bliss,
We have shadowy revealings of the Better World
    in this.

IN A DREAM.

SHE came but for a little while,
    Yet with a wondrous gleam !
She left within my soul her smile,
    The Darling of my Dream !

O face too clear for sorrow or tear,
    Too real for masks that seem ;

I seek, but shall not find you Here,
 You Darling of my Dream!

I wonder do you wait for me
 Beside the glad Life-Stream,
Or under the Leaf-of-Healing tree —
 You Darling of my Dream?

O sometimes lift your veil by night,
 And let one beauty-beam
Fill all my life for days with light,
 You Darling of my Dream!

A CRY IN THE NIGHT.

DARK, dark the night, and tearfully I
 grope,
 Lost in the Shadows, feeling for the
 way,
But cannot find it.   Here 's no help, no hope,
 And God is very far off with His day.

Hush, hush, faint heart! why this may be thy
 chance,
 When all is at the worst, to prove thy faith;
Stand still, and see His great Deliverance,
 And trust Him at the darkest unto death.

Ofttimes upon the last grim ridge of war
    God takes His stand to aid us in the fight;
He watches while we roll the tide afar,
    And, beaten back, is near ns with His might.

We hear the Arrows in the dark go by :
    The cowering soul no longer soars or sings,
Or it might know His presence then most nigh,
    Our darkness being the Shadow of His wings.

No need of faith if all were visibly clear !
    'T is for the trial-time its help was given ;
Though clouds be thick, the Sun is just as near
    That shines within and makes the heart its
        heaven.

Amidst our wildest night of saddest woes,
    When Earth is desolate — Heaven dark with
        doom,
Faith has its fire-flash of the soul that shows
    The face of the Eternal through the gloom.

A SONG IN THE MORNING.

WAKE, poor Soul, the Shadows flee,
  Dawn kindles in the sky,
Lift up the drooping head, and see
  Redemption draweth nigh !

A little further we must bear
  The load, and do our best ;
Then take immortal solace where
  The Weary are at rest.

A few more Meetings on the Deep,
  And partings on the shore ;
And then in Heaven at last we keep
  Our tryst forevermore.

And we shall see the lifted head
  Once bowed to show His face ;
And feel the arms in death He spread
  Close round us in embrace !

The Devil, standing in our light,
  And darkening all our day,
Shall wave his wings for final flight,
  His shadow pass away.

Our Pilgrimage will soon be past,
  Our worst afflictions borne ;
Some weary Night, 't will be our last,
  And then Eternal Morn.

HIS BANNER OVER ME.

URROUNDED by unnumbered Foes,
  Against my soul the battle goes !
  Yet though I weary, sore distressed,
  I know that I shall reach my Rest :
  I lift my tearful eyes above, —
  His Banner over me is Love.

Its Sword my spirit will not yield,
Though flesh may faint upon the field ;
He waves before my fading sight
The branch of palm — the crown of light ;
  I lift my brightening eyes above, —
  His Banner over me is Love.

My cloud of battle-dust may dim ;
His veil of splendor curtain Him !
And in the midnight of my fear
I may not feel Him standing near :
  But, as I lift mine eyes above,
  His Banner over me is Love.

THE TWO HEAVENS.

THERE are two Heavens for natures clear
    And calm as thine, my gentle Love !
One Heaven but reflected here ;
    One Heaven that waits above :

As yonder Lake, in Evening's red,
    Lies smiling with the smile of Rest ;
One Heaven glowing overhead ;
    One mirrored in its breast.

HOW IT SEEMS.

STARS in the Midnight's blue abyss
So closely shine they seem to kiss ;
But, Darling, they are far apart ;
They close not beating heart to heart :

And high in glory many a Star
Glows, lighting other worlds afar,
Whilst hiding in its breast the dearth
And darkness of a fireless hearth.

All happy to the listener seems
The Singer, with his gracious gleams;
His music rings, his ardors glow
Divinely: ah, we know, we know !

For all the beauty he sheds, we see
How bare his own poor life may be;
He gives ambrosia, wanting bread ;
Makes balm for Hearts, with ache of head.

He finds the Laurel budding yet,
From Love transfigured and tear-wet;
They are his life-drops turned to Flowers
That make so sweet this world of ours !

ALBERT THE GOOD.

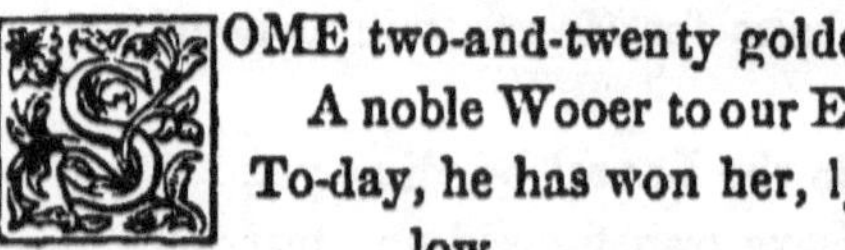OME two-and-twenty golden years ago,
   A noble Wooer to our England came ;
To-day, he has won her, lying pale and
   low.
  Albert the Good we write his royal name.

The Power that sits enthroned by open graves
   Hath risen to rule the air. His death-bell tolls,
And rolls upon us in dull heavy waves,
   Sepulchral shadows over living souls.

On every burdened wind the sound is borne,
   Invisibly swift the sparks electric slide ;
Till, under archways of full many a morn,
   The gloom of our great loss will visibly glide.

The meanest doorway darkens at this cloud,
   The poorest poor have lost a personal friend ;
Down to one level are the loftiest bowed ;
   In the large clasp of nature all hearts blend.

The gush of gladness in our eyes is dimmed;
　Christmas hath lost its glow of merry heart-
　　shine;
The Wassail-cup will pass as though 't were
　　brimmed
　With the red, solemn, sacramental wine,

And dark in His extinguished light we stand.
　In every face we read how much bereft!
A sterner pressure of the grasping hand
　Tells of our loss, and clings to what is left.

For he was one of those we never know
　Till they have left us, nor how great the love
We bore them; they are all too meek to show
　Their dearness, till they stand our praise above.

How should we mirror truly when a breath
　Set all the surface in a blurring strife?
We are calmer now! — touched by the hand of
　　Death!
　To hold the lustrous image of his life.

We met him coldly, and on looking back
　See all our dimness by his kindling glow;
The mist we breathed hath served to mark his
　　track.
　And make a starrier halo for his brow.

At last our clouds of earth are cleared away !
  Albert the Good goes patiently to God ;
Smiling back to us with his frank blue day,
  Leaving us shining footprints where he trod.

We know that when our mortal work is done,
  Few to the Master's keeping will return
A fairer copy of the life His Son
  Once left us, or a warmer " well done " earn.

Down goes the scaffolding, the work is crowned ;
  Much that was hidden from us may be read,
And for the first time we can look all round
  The Statue of his life now perfected.

The Flower of Chivalry upon the height,
  As featly could he bend to lowliest place ;
With something in his presence of the light
  That sweetly shone in Philip Sidney's face.

His natural kingliness made crowns look wan,
  Whom God had set amongst the Lords of Earth,
To show them how the majesty of Man
  May shine above the starriest badge of Birth.

He held forever hallowed the dear breasts
  Where nestling Love and its sweet babes had
    lain ;

Forever sacred kept Home's secret nest
　Of purest pleasure and of proudest pain.

A calm, high life, crowned with a quiet death!
　His robe of pain around him folding, he
Was not the man to waste his dying breath;
　Who nobly lives, can die with dignity.

The gentle spirit did not wish to hear
　The women moaning through the house for him,
But only sought to feel its darlings near
　Enough to bless them when 't was getting dim!

No need of courtly lies for comforting;
　For he can face the truth, though stern and wild:
Through spiritual rehearsal, he can wring
　The victory! and his soul within him smiled.

And 't is not near so hard for one to bow
　And enter the dark doorway of the Tomb,
Who has learnt to meet Death kneeling with bent
　　　brow;
　Whose inner light can pierce that inner gloom.

And while in sorrow here we dimly sit,
　We lift the head, to ease an aching breast,
And, looking up, behold the Stars are lit;
　And there 's another in the realms of Rest.

Rest, happy soul, in thy salvation deep;
  The top of life, and endless day for thee;
While in the valleys here we sit and weep
  Among the shadows of Eternity.

We can but kneel, and grope, and kiss His feet
  Who takes thee to His infinite embrace;
We feel transfigured if our touch may meet
  His garment's hem; but *thou* behold'st His face.

Poor widowed Queen! we see her as she trod
  The Aisle where Music's mellow thunders rolled,
And Heaven opened, and the smile of God
  In sunbeams crowned her head with saintly gold.

And how we listened — knowing she was blest —
  To the proud murmurs of the brooding dove;
Home-pleasures round the royal Mother pressed,
  And ·God gave many voices to her love.

And now the cloud of this calamity
  Darkens the crown we set on her young brow:
Ah, look up to the side next Heaven, and see
  'T is God Himself that crowns our lady now!

With all hearts aching for the folded face,
  We can but grasp His hand in prayer for her!
So lonely in her desolate, high place;
  And leave her with the Eternal Comforter.

Though two be parted in that shadow drear,
    Where one must walk alone, yet is it given
For the dear blessëd spirit to be near ;
    The human vision with the voice in Heaven.

It is my faith they friend us in our need ;
    With tender chords they draw us where they
        move ;
And often at the noon of night they feed
    With dews of Heaven the lilies of their love.

Warm whispers will come stealing like a glow
    Of God, to kiss the spirit's scalëd eyes
Till they be opened, and true love doth know
    Its Marriage Garden blooms in Paradise.

Here hearts may beat so close that two lives make
    Only one shadow in the sun we see,
But, in the light we see not, these shall wake
    One angel — wedded for eternity.

This morning shall be made majestic mirth ;
    This grief shall be a glory otherwhere ;
The music that we hear no more on earth
    Will help to make up Heaven when we are there.

The sap is swarth and bitter in the bark,
    That sweetens in the sunny fruit above,

And spirits yearning upward through the dark
  Shall reach and summer in their light of love.

And Thou, young Prince, whose Pilot saw thee
    tide
  Safe o'er the reefs beyond the harbor-bar,
Then left thee — beaconing o'er the waters wide,
  This Star of Morn shall rise, thine Evening Star.

May thy life flourish, ripen hour by hour,
  And heavenward draw the virtues of thy root;
Our eyes have seen the beauty of the flower,
  Do thou unfold the glory of the fruit.

We build his Monument, but men may see
  His steady lustre live in thee and thine;
And thou mayest bear, to Empires yet to be,
  The goodness and the glory of thy line.

Think of the dear face dark beneath the mould,
  And be thou to us what he would have been;
So shall the secret springs of sorrow old
  Give to thy future paths a gladder green.

This is a waiting hour of wonder for
  A world; our England looks across her waves!
Will the Dove seek her bosom, or red War,
  Whose footprints tread deep pits for gory graves?

Is it the kiss of Peace and Righteousness,
  That softly thrills the husht, grim silence
    through,
Or Battle's bugle-cry that makes us press
  All sail — send up our brave old bit of blue?

We know not. But, if foot to foot we stand,
  On slippery boarding-plank, or ruddied sward,
'T will be the sturdier stroke for our dear Land
  That holds another grave like this to guard.

And all is well that makes a People one,
  Even though the meeting-place be Albert's tomb:
We gather grapes of joy up in the sun,
  But our best wine must ripen in the gloom.

Many true hearts have mouldered down to enrich
  The roots of England's greatness underground;
Until, below, as wide and strong they stretch,
  As overhead the branches reach around.

And so our England's glory ever grows,
  And so her stature rises ever higher,
Until the faces of her farthest foes
  Darken with envy, overshadowed by her.

So climb the heavens, Old Tree, until the gold
  Stars glisten as thy fruitage — heave thy breast
And broaden till the fiercest storms shall fold
  Their wings within thy shelter and find rest.

COUSIN WINNIE.

HE glad spring-green grows luminous,
   With coming Summer's golden glow;
Merry Birds sing as they sang to us
   In far-off seasons, long ago:
The old place brings the young Dawn back,
   That moist eyes mirage in their dew;
My heart goes forth along the track
   Where oft it danced, dear Winnie, with you.
A world of Time, a sea of change,
   Have rolled between the paths we tread,
Since you were my *"Cousin Winnie,"* and I
   Was your *"own little, good little Ned."*

There 's where I nearly broke my neck,
   Climbing for nests! and hid my pain:
And then I thought your heart would break,
   To have the Birds put back again.
Yonder, with lordliest tenderness,
   I carried you across the Brook;
So happy in my arms to press
   You, triumphing in your timid look:

So lovingly you leaned to mine
  Your cheek of sweet and dusky red :
You were my "*Cousin Winnie,*" and I
  Was your "*own little, good little Ned.*"

My Being in your presence basked,
  And kitten-like for pleasure purred ;
A higher heaven I never asked,
  Than watching, wistful as a bird,
To hear that voice so rich and low ;
  Or sun me in the rosy rise
Of some soul-ripening smile, and know
  The thrill of opening paradise.
The Boy might look too tenderly,
  All lightly 't was interpreted :
You were my "*Cousin Winnie,*" and I
  Was your "*own little, good little Ned.*"

Ay me, but I remember how
  I felt the heart-break, bitterly,
When the Well-handle smote your brow,
  Because the blow fell not on me !
Such holy longing filled my life,
  I could have died, Dear, for your sake ;
But, never thought of you as Wife ;
  A cure to clasp for love's heart-ache.
You entered my soul's temple, Dear,
  Something to worship, not to wed :

You were my "*Cousin Winnie,*" and I
  Was your "*own little, good little Ned.*"

I saw you, heaven on heaven higher,
  Grow into stately womanhood;
Your beauty kindling with the fire
  That swims in proud old English blood.
Away from me, — a radiant Joy!
  You soared; fit for a Hero's bride:
While I a Man in soul, a Boy
  In stature, shivered at your side!
You saw not how the poor wee Love
  Pined dumbly, and thus doubly pled:
You were my "*Cousin Winnie,*" and I
  Was your "*own little, good little Ned.*"

And then that other voice came in!
  There my Life's music suddenly stopped.
Silence and darkness fell between
  Us, and my Star from heaven dropped.
I led Him by the hand to you —
  He was my Friend — whose name you bear:
I had prayed for some great task to do,
  To prove my love.   I did it, Dear!
He was not jealous of poor me;
  Nor saw my life bleed under his tread:
You were my "*Cousin Winnie,*" and I
  Was your "*own little, good little Ned.*"

I smiled, Dear, at your happiness —
  So Martyrs smile upon the spears —
The smile of your reflected bliss
  Flasht from my heart's dark tarn of tears !
In love, that made the suffering sweet,
  My blessing with the rest was given —
" *God's softest flowers kiss her feet*
  On Earth, and crown Her head in Heaven."
And lest the heart should leap to tell
  Its tale i' the eyes, I bowed the head :
You were my " *Cousin Winnie,*" and I
  Was your " *own little, good little Ned.*"

I do not blame you, Darling mine ;
  You could not know the love that lurkt
To make my life so intertwine
  With yours, and with mute mystery workt.
And, had you known, how distantly
  Your calm eyes would have lookt it down,
Darkling with all the majesty
  Of Midnight wearing her star-crown !
Into its virgin veil of cloud,
  The startled dearness would have fled.
You were my " *Cousin Winnie,*" and I
  · Was your " *own little, good little Ned.*"

I stretch my hand across the years ;
  Feel, Dear, the heart still pulses true :

I have often dropped internal tears,
  Thinking the kindest thoughts of you.
I have fought like one in iron, they said,
  Who through the battle followed me.
I struck the blows for you, and bled
  Within my armor secretly.
Not caring for the cheers, my heart
  Far into the golden time had fled :
You were my " *Cousin Winnie,*" and I
  Was your "*own little, good little Ned.*"

I sometimes see you in my dreams,
  Asking for aid I may not give :
Down from your eyes the sorrow streams,
  And helplessly I look and grieve
At arms that toss with wild heartache,
  And secrets writhing to be told :
I start to hear your voice, and wake.
  There 's nothing but the moaning cold !
Sometimes I pillow in mine arms
  The darling little rosy head.
You are my " *Cousin Winnie,*" and I
  Am your "*own little, good little Ned.*"

I wear the name of Hero now,
  And flowers at my feet are cast ;
I feel the crown about my brow —
  So keen the thorns that hold it fast !

Ay me, and I would rather wear
　　The cooling green and luminous glow
Of one you made with Cowslips, Dear,
　　A many golden Springs ago.
Your gentle fingers did not give
　　This ache of heart, this throb of head,
When you were my " *Cousin Winnie*," and I
　　Was your " *own little, good little Ned.*"

Unwearying, lonely, year by year,
　　I go on laying up my love.
I think God makes no promise here
　　But it shall be fulfilled above ;
I think my wild weed of the waste
　・Will one day prove a flower most sweet ;
My love shall bear its fruit at last —
　　'T will all be righted when we meet ;
And I shall find them gathered up
　　In pearls for you — the tears I 've shed
Since you were my " *Cousin Winnie*," and I
　　Was your " *own little, good little Ned.*"

A WINTER'S TALE FOR THE LITTLE
ONES.

 MERRY sound of clapping hauds,
    A call to see the sight ;
And lo ! the first soft snow-flakes fall,
    So exquisitely virginal.
'T is my wee Nell at window stands,
    And the world is all in white.

Her eyes, where dawns my bluest Day,
    Dance with the dancing snow !
I see delicious shivers thrill
Her through and through.   She feels the chill
Of Earth so white, and skies so gray
    Enrich our fireside glow.

" No Winters now, my little Maid,
    Like those that used to come,
Making our Christmas sparkle, bright
As crystallized plum-cake at night,
And Frost his Puck-like trickeries played,
    With fancies frolicsome.

" He fixed your breath in flowers, the Trees
    To Chandeliers would turn :
He pincht your toes, he nipped your nose,
And made your cheek a wrinkled Rose :
Perhaps at night you heard him sneeze,
    And the Jug was crackt at morn !

" The Snow-Storms were magnificent !
    And in the clear, still weather
Against the bitter wintry blue
And Sunset's orange-tawny hue
You saw the smoke straight upward went,
    For weeks and weeks together.

" At night the Waits mixt with our dream
    Their music sweet and low :
We children knew not as we heard,
Each, listening, nestled like a Bird,
Whether from Heaven the music came,
    Or only over the snow !

" No winters nowadays like those."
    And then my darling tries
To coax me for a *" tale that 's true :*
A story that is new — quite new."
And up the arch of wonder goes,
    Above the frank, blue eyes !

" *Once on a time* " — " *Do tell me when,*
   And where ? " says my wee Nell —
" *When Christmas came on Thursday — now,*
Some five-and-thirty years ago !
Superbly we were snowed-up then,
   Who lived in Ingle Dell.

" *His icy Drawbridge Winter dropped ;*
   The running springs he froze ;
The Roads were lost ; the hedges crossed ;
All field-work ceased through the ' Long Frost.'
But there was one thing never stopped —
   That was Grandmother's nose !

" *The snow might fall by day, by night,*
   The weather grow more rough,
And up to our bedroom windows heap
The drift, and smother men like sheep,
And wrap the world in a shroud of white —
   Old Gran must have her snuff !

" *So, Uncle Willie, then a lad*
   Not more than nine years old,
Upon the Christmas morn must go
And fetch her snuff, and face the Snow,
Which surely had gone dancing mad,
   And wrestle with the cold.

" Wrapt in his crimson Comforter,
   His basket on his arm,
He started.   Mother followed him
With her proud eyes so dewy-dim;
While kisses from the heart of her
   Within his heart were warm.

" How gentle is the gracious Snow,
   When first you watch her dance;
Her feathery flutter, winding whorls;
Her finish perfect as the pearl's;
She looks you in the face as though
   'T were unveiled Innocence.

" But now, 't is wild upon the waste,
   And winged upon the wind:
You see, just passing out of sight,
The Ghost of things in a swirl of white ! —
The Storm unwinkingly he faced,
   Though it snowed enough to blind.

" Fire-pointed, stinging, strikes and burns
   To the bone, each icy dart.
He stumbles — falls — is up again,
And onward for the Town a-strain;
Backward our Willie never turns,
   And never loses heart.

" *He looks a weird and wintry Elf*
　With face in ruddy glow ;
And all his curls are straightened out,
Hanging in Icicles about
A sparkling statue of himself,
　Shaped out of frozen snow.

" *He still fought on, for though the Storm*
　Might bend him, he was tough ;
And when the Blast would take his breath,
With kisses like the kiss of death,
One thought still kept his courage warm—
　It was Grandmother's Snuff !

" *At length with many a danger passed,*
　Unboding any to come,
He has got the Snuff.　Far more than food,
Or wine, 't will warm her poor old blood.
He has it safe at last, at last !
　And sets his face for Home.

" *He has the Snuff ; but it were well*
　If Granny had it too !
For early closes such a day,
And wild and dreary is the way ;
If dark before he reach the Dell,
　What can poor Willie do ?

" *Within the Town the blast is husht ;*
    The snow-flakes from you melt :
But out upon the pathless moor,
The storm grows wilder than before ;
And at him all its furies rusht,
    Till he faint and fainter felt.

" *His thoughts are whirling with the Snow :*
    His eyes wax dizzy and dim !
And on the path, 'twixt him and night,
Now dancing left, now dancing right,
It seems a white Witch-Woman doth go,
    With white hand beckoning him !

" *To the last stile he clung — maybe*
    A furlong from our door ;
Then missed his footing on the plank,
    And deep into the snow-drift sank.
O, my belovĕd Willie, we
    Shall never see you more !

" *Ah, they looked long and wistfully*
    Who waiting sat at home :
They strained their eyes through the deepening dark,
At every sound they leaned to hark ;
And wondered where could Willie be,
    And when would Willie come ?

" Through all that night of wild affright
They searched the road to Town ;
They called him high, they called him low,
They mocked each other through the snow,
And all the night, by lanthorn light,
They wandered up and down.

" They sought him where the waters plash
Darkly by Deadman's Cave !
They sought him at the Rag-Pit, near
The Mill, and by the lonesome Weir ;
At the Cross-Roads where ' Harry's Ash '
Grows from the Suicide's Grave.

" In Ingle Dell they locked no door,
Put out no light.   At such
A time you cling to a little thing
That 's done for neighborly comforting !
Old Grán thought she 'd take snuff no more,
And she took thrice as much.

" All night the Snow with fingers soft
Kept pointing to the ground.
Only too well they knew 't was there ;
But had no hint to guide them where !
And he so near.   They passed him oft,
Close by his white grave-mound.

" *And did he die ?* " cries little Nell.
  " *No, he was nestled warm.*
It seemed the white arm round him curled
And caught him in another world :
What other world he could not tell,
  But, out of all the storm.

" *And all was changed too suddenly*
  For him to know the place.
He swooned awhile, and when he woke
A lightning from his darkness broke.
Alone with the Eternal he
  Was standing face to face !

" *There in his grave alive, he knew*
  He stood, or sat upright !
With burning brain, and freezing feet.
And he so young, and life so sweet !
And, bitter thought ! what would Gran do
  Without her snuff that night ?

" *A long, long night of sixty hours*
  Did Willie pass.   I know
Not how he lived.   But Heaven can hold
A life as safe as Earth can fold
Her hidden life of fruit and flowers,
  Through her long trance of snow.

" ' T is Sabbath day.   How quietly gleams
    That snow-drift o'er him driven !
The winds are softly laid asleep,
In their white snow-bed covered deep.
The white Clouds all so still ! it seems
    Like Sunday up in Heaven !

" The Country-folk are passing near
    His tomb — no tale it tells —
Old Ploughmen in their white smockfrocks,
Old Women in long scarlet cloaks,
And Lad and Lass, — when on his ear
    There faints a sound of Bells !

" And, looking up, a tiny hole
    Was melted with his breath ;
Wherethrough a bit of God's blue sky
Was smiling on him like an Eye ;
A living eye with a loving soul
    Shone in that face of death !

" O joy !   He shouted from his grave,
    And finding room to stir,
He tooth and nail began to climb ;
He clutcht the top o' the bank this time ;
Thrust his hand through the snow to wave
    His good old Comforter !

"' I 'm here!' ' It 's me!' His flag they see,
  And know lost Willie's voice;
They quickly answer shout for shout,
And with their hands they dig him out,
And carry him home.   Oh! did n't we
  In Ingle Dell rejoice?

" There be some tears that smile, and such
  Were wept by Woman and Man.
But while they glistened in each eye,
He pulled the snuff out sound and dry;
Snow might cover him, cold might clutch,
  The Snuff was safe for Gran."

WILLIAM MAKEPEACE THACKERAY.

HE Merry Bells ring in the Christmas
Day,
While in our hearts a mournful knell
is knolled,
As other tidings through the land are rolled —
Telling of a great spirit passed away.

Another heart of English Oak gone down,
Like some three-decker striking with no word
Of warning; sails all set; all hands aboard;
When sunniest skies are smiling with their crown.

Low lies the stately form that towered so tall,
With life so lusty, and with look so brave;
The head thrown back, as if to breast the wave
For many a year — the wave that whelmeth all.

For all the sobs that rise, or tears that rain,
No more fond, fatherly words for Lad and Lass !
No more across his manly face will pass
The light of passion, or the shadow of pain.

We never told our love !   He would have thought
  We prattled prettily, amused the while ;
  And held us at a distance with his smile,
Until we hid the presents we had brought.

Now we might stroke the almost young, white hair,
  And even kiss the cold and quiet brow ;
  The heart may have its way, and speak out now !
He will not mock us, lying silent there !

A nature — not at first sight meant to win —
  That prickly for protection grows without,
  To safely fence its tenderness about,
And fold the sweet virginities within :

Just as you find a nest whose outer form
  Looks grimly rugged when the boughs are bare ;
  The birds have flown — you peep inside, and there
How softly it is lined ! how brooding-warm !

He had our English way of making fun
  Of those shy feelings which our hearts will hold
  Like dew-drops all a-tremble, and enfold
Them with our strength — sacred from storm and
    sun.

We listened to his voice, as some true Wife,
  Upon her Husband's breast may lean her head,
  While many things in her dispraise are said
By Him ; but she leans closer, life to life,

For, while the covert words sound on above,
  Their other, deeper meaning she divines;
  She hears the heart; knows its masonic signs;
And nestles in a bosom large with love.

So loud he cried, a Snake in Beauty's bower;
  A Worm that gnaws at life's most human root;
  A Wasp that revels in our rarest fruit;
So gently breathed the fragrance of the flower!

He kept his Show-Box — scant of Mirrors where
  You saw Eternity whose worlds we pass
  Darkly by daylight, but, with many a glass,
Reflecting all the Humors of the Fair!

The thousand shapes of vanity and sin;
  Toy-stalls of Satan; the mad masquerade:
  The floating Pleasures that before them played:
The foolish faces following, all agrin.

He slyly prickt the bubbles that we blew;
  He cheered us on to chase our thistle-down;
  Crowning the winner with a fool's-cap crown;
And *Bon-Bons* mottoed in quaint mockery threw.

Then in the merry midst some sad, strange words
  Would touch the spring of tears. His eyes were
    dry,

And, as your laughters ceased, were wondering
    why ?
Laugh on !   He had only struck the minor chords !

He was not one of those who are light at heart
    Because 't is empty in its airy swing :
    He found the world too full of sorrowing,
But showed us how to smile and bear our smart.

Many of God's most precious gifts are sad
    To tears, and, though no weeper, this he knew.
    So, in our merry wine, would steep the rue,
That with a manlier strength we might grow glad.

And, year by year, still kindlier to the last,
    He drew us towards him ; showing more and
        more,
    The heart of honey, human to the core,
That into Love's full flower ripened fast :

Thus Music sweetens to the latest breath,
    And closer draws the leaning, listening ear ;
    And still it whispers, from its heaven near,
Of some more perfect sweetness beyond death.

Large-hearted, brave, sincere, compassionate !
    We could not guess one half the Angels see :
    They found you out, Old Friend, ere we did !
        We
But reach the nobler justice all too late.

Soft, O Belovëd! be your early Rest,
  And sweet its quiet where the grassy green
  Shuts out so many and many a sorry scene :
Heaven sun the hoarded fragrance from your
      breast !

And may the Spirit that with us but gropes
  And stirs our earth, and yearns up through our
      night
  In strivings dumb, with you have found the
      Light
That giveth eyes to poor, blind human hopes.

For us — I know you would have us put away
  The tears; draw closer, fill the gap, and keep
  Old kindly customs; sing the sorrow asleep,
And all make merry, this being Christ's own day.

A ROYAL WEDDING CHIME.

MANY a time, from out the North,
    The fire-eyed Raven flew,
    And England watcht its sailing forth,
    With eyes of wistful blue;
Many a time her True-hearts stood
  All ranked and ready for
Grim welcome, should the Bird of blood
  Swoop down on wings of war !

To-day, another Norland Bird
  Comes floating o'er the foam ;
And England's heart of hearts is stirred
  To have the dear bird Home.
She comes soft-eyed, with brooding breast,
  On swift'ning wings of love ;
And England, to her bridal nest,
  Welcomes the gentle Dove.

She comes ; across the waters spread the sails ;
   Sho comes, to play her bravc, uncommon part ;
The Princess who shall wear the name of Wales ;
   The Woman who shall win our England's heart,
The Nation's life up-leaps to meet her ;
And England with one voice goes forth to greet
     Her !

Our Lady cometh from the North,
   The tender and the true,
Whose fire of darkest glow hath rarest worth ;
For love more inly nestles in the North,
To give, like fire in frost, its fervors forth ;
   Whose flowers can keep their dew ;
And a look in its women's eyes is good
As the first fresh breath of the salt sea-flood,
   Or the bonnicst blink of its blue :
And from its dark Fiords, with sails unfurled,
   Came those fair-haired Norsemen,
     The men that moved the world.

They were the pride and the darlings of Ocean,
   Rockt on her breast by a hundred storms ;
Tossed up with joyfullest motherly motion ;
   Caught to her heart again — claspt in her arms.
No Slaves of the Earth but Sea Kings, the rough
     rovers
   Took wings of the wind and flew over the foam.

Yet the old True-hearts, like faithfullest lovers,
  Came back with the fruitfuller feeling of Home.

Come! stir the Norse fire in us mightily!
Come, conquering hearts as they the heaving sea.
Come, wed the people with their Prince, and bless
Them from your neighboring heaven of noble-
      ness.
There 's nothing like a Beauty of the Blood
To set the fashion of a loftier good!
There 's nothing like a true and womanly Wife
To help a man, and make melodious life.
For she can hold his heart-strings in her hand,
And play the tune her pleasure may command,
And cause his climbing soul to grow in stature,
Trying to reach the heights of her diviner nature.

        Come in your beauty of promise;
          Come in your maiden glee;
        Let your sunshine scatter from us
          The shadow of Misery.
        Hearts in the dark have been aching,
        But now the clouds are breaking.
        Come as come the swallows
          Over the brightening sea,
        And we know that summer follows
          With the sunny days to be.

Come and give us your glad good-morrow,
  The Joy-bells shall ring,
  And the merry birds sing ;
Dumbly drooping the Bird of Sorrow
  Shall hide his old head under his wing.

And now a shining Vision blooms ;
  I see the rich procession glide
Serenely 'twixt the swaling plumes,
  All nodding in their pride :

Some gate of Dreamland opens wide ;
  We, for a moment, catch the sight
Within — the beauty of the Bride ;
  Her maidens all in white !

Walking with sweet precision, she
  Moves slowly onward, softly nigher
The Altar ; meek in purity,
  Yet filled with stately fire.

·The dawn upon her sweet young face,
  The dewy spring-light in her eyes,
And round about her form of grace
  The airs of paradise.

But lo ! a shadow dims the scene !
  We lift our eyes and sadly see

How lonely stands the wistful Queen ;
  No leaning-place hath she,

Who, in her darkness seeks to hide,
  While the wed pair move whitely on
As swans go gliding side by side,
  And all their splendors sun.

O Widow's gloom ! O wedding joys !
  O white fringe to the Mourning-pall !
With the dead Father's hovering voice
  In music over all !

This world is but a newer paradise,
To that glad spirit looking through the eyes
Of Love, that sees all bright things dancing to-
      ward
It, gayly coming of their own accord.
For 't is as though the lightsome heart should
      climb
Up in the head, to look from height sublime
And sing, and swing as it would never drop —
The merry reveller in the tall tree-top !
Where Life is with such lofty gladness crowned,
And all the Pleasures dance in starry circle round.
But may this love be true as Hers who sees
Ye, like a smiling future, at her knees :
The Wife who held God's gifts the richest wealth ;

Our Queen of Home who sweetened England's
    health;
The Widow in whose face we lookt to see
That great black cloud of our calamity
On the side nearest heaven, and markt her rise
In stature, calm to meet her sacrifice:
As one with faith to feel Death's darkness brings
Almighty Love on overshadowing wings.

True love is no mere incense that will swim
Up from the heart a lover's eyes to dim,
But such a light as gives the jewel-spark
To meanest things it looks on in their dark, —
A spring of heaven welling warm to bless
And sanctify each grain of earthiness.
True love will make true life, and glorify
Ye very proudly in the nation's eye.
Ah, Prince, a-many hopes upfold the wing
Within the Marriage-nest to which ye bring
Your Bride, the life ye live there will be rolled
Through endless echoes, mirrored manifold.

We charge you, when you look on your young
    Wife,
And watch the ascending brightness of new life
In the sweet eyes that double the sweet soul,
That ye forget not others' dearth and dole.

Just now, the north-wind wails
As though the cold were crying
Over the hills and over the dales,
And sinking hearts know well what ails
The sound of the wintry sighing:
It bears the moan of the dying;
Dying down in the starving Shires,
Without food, and without fires.

The bitter nights are cruel cold,
One cannot help but wake, and think
Of the poor milch-lambs of the human fold
That have no milk to drink.

A Royal Worker to his grave went down
A little year ago, without his crown.
He dreamed the time would come when Rich and
Poor
Might shake hands, strove to open wide the door.
He tried to till our waste-land, — sought to see
It glad in good, the stern world Poverty.
His was a heart that nobly beat to bless,
And heaved with double-breasted bounteousness
Like very woman's.

But, 't is ever so;
He 's gone where all our golden sunsets go;

Gone from us !   Yet his memory makes a light,
  Enriching life with tints of pictured bloom,
Like firelight warm upon the walls of night,
  An inner glow against the outer gloom.
Do thou but live, and work as Albert willed,
And he shall smile in heaven to see his dream ful-
      filled.
Heroic deeds of toil are to be done,
And lofty palms of peace are to be won.
Life may be followed by a fame that rings
With nobler music than the Battle sings,
When Death, astride the black Guns, laughs to see
That flashing out of souls, and grins triumphantly.

Love England, Prince ; for Christ's sake may ye be
Loyal to her, the glorious, great, and free !
Bear high the banner of her peerless fame,
And let the evil-doers fear her name.
We joy to serve her, least of all the race ;
Yours is the prize to fill her foremost place.

Like some proud River, stretching forth before ye
    Through all the land, your widening way doth
      lie,
Brimming and blessing as it rolls in glory,
    Broadening and brightening till it reach the sky.
A splendid Vision ! the green corn looks gay ;
    The Bird of Happiness sings overhead :

And may the autumn uplands far away
  Rise with the Harvest ripe in Evening's red ;
Your crescent Honey-Moon laugh out, — above
The gathered Sheaves it gilds, — at full, — with
    love.

PICTURES IN THE FIRE.

LD Winter blows, and whistles hard,
   To keep his fingers warm, while I
  Shut out the cold night, frosty-starred,
   Bleak earth and bitter sky;
And to the Fireplace nestle nigher,
And gaze on pictures in the Fire.

It has a soft, blithe, murmuring glow,
  As if it crooned a cradle-song;
Yet whispers of some awful woe
  Are on each flaming tongue
That may have licked up human life,
Quick, ruddy as a murderer's knife!

I see the Dead Men underground,
  Just as they found them rank on rank;
Old Mothers — Young Wives — red-eyed round
  The Corpses brought to bank;
I see the mournful phantoms flit
About the mouth of Hartley Pit;

And that poor Widow above the rest
  So eminent in Suffering's crown,
Who wearing sorrow's loftiest crest
  Is bowed the lowliest down;
Poor Widow with her Coffins seven,
Look down on Her, dear God in Heaven!

I hear that crash with sinking heart—
  Eternity has broken through!
I see him play his Hero Part,
  That leader tried and true,
Who faithful stood to his last breath,
And fell betwixt them and their death.

I hear him bid them trim their lamps—
  For Light hath not gone out in Heaven!
And through the dark, above the damps,
  He beacons them to haven:
Long in his eyes had lived the light
That should make starry such a Night.

I see the strong man's agony,
  That seeks to rend his ghastly shroud;
The touch of solemn radiancy
  That kindles through the cloud;
The trust that earned a nobler doom
Than such a death in such a tomb;

The valor that invisibly
  Lifted the bosom like a targe;

The hidden forces that must be,
　Ready for Life's last charge!
And all the bravery brave in vain,
And all the majesty of pain:

Visions of the old Home that flash
　With all the mind's last mortal power;
The tears that burn their way, to wash
　A soul white in an hour,
When thoughts of God go deeper than
The Devil at His utmost can.

I hear the poor faint heart's low cry
　That sickens at the sight of Doom;
The prayer of those that feel it nigh,
　And groping through the gloom!
They cower together hand-in-hand
At the dark door of the dark land.

Ghostly and far away life seems
　To one returning from a swound;
And sharp the sorrow comes in dreams
　When we are helpless bound;
But deathliest swoons, or ghastliest nights,
Have no such sounds, or spirit-sights.

The waiting human world is near,
　Yet farther off than Heaven for them

Who bow the doomëd head, to bear
  Death's cruel diadem,
With farewell words of solemn cheer
And love for those who cannot hear:

Old heads with hair like spray above
  A tossed and troubled sea of life;
Young hearts, just kissed to the quick by Love,
  That leave a one-day wife!
O pathos of a hopeless fate!
O pain of those left desolate!

'T is brave to die in Battle's flash,
  For the dear country we adore—
Struck breathless 'mid the glorious crash,
  When banners wave before
The fading eyes, and at the ears
We are caught by following Victory's cheers!

And sailor-blood that on the waves
  Can feel the Mother's heaving breast—
True sailor-blood no wailing craves
  Over *its* place of rest,
When souls first taste eternity
In those last kisses of the Sea:

And Death oft comes with kind release
  To win a smile from those that lie

Where they may feel the blessëd breeze,
  And look up at the sky,
And drink in, with their latest sigh,
A little air for strength to die:

But 't is a fearful thing to be
  Instantly buried alive; fast-bound
In cold arms of Eternity
  That clasp the breathing round,
And hold them, though their Comrades call
And dig with efforts useless all.

A tear for those who, in that night,
  Went down so unavailingly;
A cheer for those who fought our fight,
  And missed the victory!
Peace to the good true hearts that gave
A moral glory to that grave!

We know not how amid the gloom
  Some jewel of the just outshone;
With precious sparkle lit the tomb
  And led the hopeless on
To hope, and showed the only way
To find God's hand and reach his day.

We know not how in that quick hour
  Some poor uncultured human clod

May have put forth its one sweet flower,
   Acceptable to God ;
Or how the touch of Death revealed
Some bnried beauty life concealed :

We know not how the Dove of peace
   Came brooding on the fluttering breast,
To make the fond life-yearnings cease,
   And fold them up for rest ;
And into shining shape the sonl
Burst, like the flame from out the coal :

We only know·the watch-fires bnrned
   Long in their eyes for human aid,
And failed, and then to God they turned,
   And altogether prayed,
And that the deepest Mine may be,
For prayer, God's whispering Gallery !

That Christ still hangs npon the Tree
   To smile beneath His thorns, and say
" *This night, Soul, thou shalt sup with me,*"
   In His old loving way ;
And suffering men get back to God
By that same path the Savionr trod.

Deep, dark the deathly River is,
   But on before still walketh Christ !

His brightness over that abyss
  Is moving in the mist.
If they who pass the bridge of Dread
Look up, He goeth overhead.

Dear God, be very pitiful
  To these poor toiling slaves of men ;
Be gracious if their hearts be dull
  With darkness of their den :
'T is hard for flowers of Heaven to grow
Down where the earth-flowers cannot blow !

Their lives are as the Candle-snuff,
  Black in the midst of its own light !
Let hard hands plead for spirits rough —
  They work so much in night.
Be merciful, they breathe their breath
So close to danger, pain, and death.

The love-mist in a Father's eye
  Must rise, and soften much that 's rude
In his poor children — magnify
  The least faint gleam of good !
O, find some place for human worth
In Heaven, when it has failed on Earth.

PRIDEAUX AT MAGDALA.

NO Cross of Valor hath the Muse to give
His faithful breast, but she may bid him live
   In hearts of grateful glow,
Who went to bear his Message with last breath,
Nor changëd countenance at sight of Death,
   When Napier bade him go.

England, our Helen, watching from the wall
To cheer us fighting, mourn us if we fall,
   O'erlooks her gallant Son!
She hath so many lofty memories
To keep her lifted gaze; a deed like this
   So many would do — have done:

He did it! that poor Private in the "Buffs,"*
Though only one of her neglected "roughs," —
   All English, — life and limb!

* Moyse, an English soldier killed in China because he would not perform the *kotou*, said he would not prostrate himself before any Chinaman alive, — would see them, &c., &c.

He would not bow his head except to die;
He could not let our England's image lie
  Dishonored, shamed in him !

Duty, not Glory, is our proud password,
Who ask that we may prove for England's sword
  True steel at need — no more.
Yet worthy of his guerdon is Prideaux,
As if on board they had borne him, lying low
  For us who were safe on shore.

That large content with death for England's sake
In narrower hearts a nobler life shall wake
  To breathe with ampler breath,
And some poor soul, caught in as bitter strait,
Shall think of him, and sternly face its fate —
  Go on, and out-face Death !

Blow, winds of God ! and stir us to the root,
Shake down all wormy and unworthy fruit,
  There 's new life in your breeze !
Traitors may talk of England going down
(In quicksands that their coward selves have
        sown) —
  She swims in hearts like these !

SONGS AND OTHER BREVITIES.

SYLVIA MAY.

EART *of mine, so longing for rest,*
Better to build thy love-lined Nest
On a storm-swung bough than a Woman's
breast."

But this heart of mine still sayeth me, "Nay";
Shows me the picture of Sylvia May :
Wilful heart must have its way!

" Heart of mine, far wiser 't would be
To build thy nest on a wave of the sea,
Tossed and troubled perpetually."

But this heart of mine still sayeth me, "Nay";
And whispers the name of Sylvia May :
Foolish heart will have its way!

" Never was love I think like mine ;
Never was woman so nearly divine ;
Never could lives more perfectly twine."

And this heart of mine it murmureth, " Yea " ;
Wilful heart must have its way —
When will you marry me, Sylvia May ?

PARTING

TOO fair, I may not call thee mine .
   Too dear, I may not see
   Those eyes with bridal-beacons shine ;
   Yet, Darling, keep for me —
Empty and husht, and safe apart,
One little corner of thy heart ;

Thou wilt be happy, dear ! and bless
   Thee ; happy mayst thou be !
I would not make thy pleasure less ;
   Yet, Darling, keep for me,
My life to light, my lot to leaven,
One little corner of thy Heaven !

Good by, dear heart ! I go to dwell
   A weary way from thee :

Our first kiss is our last farewell;
  Yet, Darling, keep for me —
Who wander outside in the night,
One little corner of thy light!

OLD FRIENDS.

WE just shake hands at meeting
  With many that come nigh;
We nod the head in greeting
  To many that go by, —
But welcome through the gateway
  Our few old friends and true;
Then hearts leap up, and straightway
  There 's open house for you,
          Old Friends,
  There 's open house for you!

The surface will be sparkling,
  Let but a sunbeam shine;
Yet in the deep lies darkling,
  The true life of the wine!
The froth is for the many,
  The wine is for the few;

Unseen, untoucht of any,
  We keep the best for you,
               Old Friends,
  The very best for you !

The Many cannot know us ;
  They only pace the strand.
Where at our worst we show us —
  The waters thick with sand !
But out beyond the leaping
  Dim surge 't is clear and blue ;
And there, Old Friends, we are keeping
  A sacred calm for you,
               Old Friends,
  A waiting calm for you.

AUTUMN SONG.

THE summer days are ended ;
  The after-glow is gone ;
  The nights grow long and eerie ;
  The winds begin to moan ;
The pleasant leaves are fading ;
  The bonny swallows flee ;
Yet welcome is the Winter
  That brings my Love to me.

No voice of bird now ripples
    The air; no wood-walk rings!
But in my happy bosom
    The soul of Music sings
It sings of clearest heaven,
    And summers yet to be;
Then welcome is the Wintei
    That brings my Love to me.

A world of gathered sunshine
    Is this warm heart of mine,
Where life hath heapt the fruitage,
    And love hath hid the wine.
And though there 's not a flower ·
    In field, nor leaf on tree;
Yet welcome is the Winter
    That brings my Love to me.

SONNET.

LOVE a lady all so far above
Me, she can never hear the name of
    love;
I only whisper to my heart in low
Dark sayings what my lady must not know;
But, had I only a minute's space to live,

And she beside me, I would pray her give
Me on the mouth one dear and holy kiss;
And straightway a warm stream of paradise
Would gush and gladden all the gulf of death,

A calm of blessëd faces take mine eyes,
A hurricane of harpings take my breath:
All heaven would bend brooding down to meet
Me, in that gracious stooping of my Sweet;
And, at her touch, my soul should enter bliss.

HEIGH-HO!

EIGH-HO! She will never be mine:
   Never! never! I know.
  The grasp of gold
  My Jewel will hold:
She is Lofty and I am Low.

Heigh-ho! but my heart like a Bird
   On wings of the night will go,
  To make its love-nest
  In that heaven of her breast
   'Neath the heaven of her eyes all aglow!

Heigh-ho! in dreams she is mine,
   All mine: and how can I know

But she loves *me* in dream,
With no drawn sword agleam,
   'Twixt the kissing of Lofty and Low.

LOVE'S WESTWARD HO!

PLEASANT it is, sweet Wife of mine,
   As by my side thou art,
To sit and see thy dear eyes shine
   With bonfires of the heart!
And young Love smiles so sweet and sly,
   From warm and balmy deeps,
As under-leaf the fruit may try
   To hide, yet archly peeps:
Gliding along in our fairy boat,
   With prospering skies above,
Over the sea of time we float
   To another New World of Love.

One of God's Darlings is our Guide:
   Ah, how it makes us lean,
Hearts beating lovingly side by side
   That nothing may come between.
As yon brave ring of Stars doth fold
   Our world, so is it given

To this wee ring of wedding gold
   To clasp us round with heaven :
Gliding along in our fairy boat,
   With prospering skies above,
Over the sea of time we float
   To another New World of Love.

HOME SONG.

HE Larch is snooding her tresses
   In a twine of the daintiest green ;
With fresh spring-breath the Hawthorn
   heaves
His breast to the sunny sheen.
A shower of spring-green sprinkles the Lime ;
   A shower of spring-gold the Broom ;
And each rathe tint of the tender time
   Wakes the wish that my Lady were Home.

In the Coppice, the dear Primroses
   Are the smile of each dim green nook,
Gravely gladsome ; sunny but cool
   With the sound of the gurgling brook.
And by the wayside, in a burst of delight,
   From the world of fairy and gnome,
All the flowers are crowding to see the sight
   At their windows. My Lady, come Home !

The Country's growing glorious
  Quietly day by day;
The color of April comes and goes
  In a blush to meet the May.
And the spring-rains steal from their heaven of
    shade,
  In a veil of tender gloam,
With a splendid sparkle for every blade.
  Dear my Lady, come Home!

The Spirit of Gladness floating
  Goes up in a sound of song:
Robin sings in the rich eve-lights;
  The Throstle all day long:
The Lark in his heaven that soars above
  Each morn with a distant dome;
All sweet! but sweeter the voice we love.
  Come Home, my Lady, come Home!

Your Apple-blooms are fragrant
  Beyond the breath of the South;
Every bud, for an airy kiss,
  Is lifting a rosy wee mouth.
A greener glory hour by hour,
  And a peep of ruddier bloom,
But the leafy world waiteth its human flower.
  Dear my Lady, come Home!

Our thoughts are as the Violets
  Around the Ash-tree root,

That breathe the earliest hints of Spring
  At their lofty lady's foot,
And wonder why she still delays —
  When the sea of life is afoam
With flowers — to crown her in these glad days.
  Come Home, my Lady, come Home !

Come ! feel the deepening dearness
  About the grand old place.
Come ! let us see the cordial smile
  Once more in our Lady's face.
Winter was dreary : of waiting we weary :
  Best of all joy-bringers, come !
Spread, bonny white sails ! blow, balmy spring-
      gales !
  And bring my Lady Home !

EPIGRAM.

DO believe that Shakespeare hath re-
  vealed
To me that very *self* so long concealed !
But, if His soul my soul hath lightened
  through,
I do believe it was to glance at You —
  To find, with loving wonder in his looks,
One of his Women living out of his Books.

SEA-SONG.

OME, show your colors now, my Lads,
　That all the world may know
The Boys are equal to their Dads,
　Whatever blast may blow.

All hands aboard ! our country calls
　On her seafaring folk !
In giving up our wooden Walls,
　More need for Hearts of Oak.

Remember how that old Fire Drake
　Did singe the Spaniard's beard ;
\nd think how Raleigh, Nelson, Blake,
　Into their harbors steered.

Think how o' nights we cut them out !
　'T was many a time and oft —
Silence ! — a rush — a tug — a shout —
　And the old flag flew aloft.

Be it one to seven, — be it Hell or Heaven, —
　We fought our decks red-wet !
Be it hell or heaven, — be it one to seven, —
　We fear no foeman yet.

That secret in the Sphinx's eyes
  Must have solution stern ;
Another throw o' the Devil's dice
  And it may be our turn !

At every port-hole there must flame
  The same fierce battle-face :
All worthy of the old sea-fame —
  All of the old sea-race.

THE WHITE CHILD.

MOTHERS of Children three ;
  Two of them ruddy with glee ;
  One your White Child, your pearl !
  Do you feel as I feel with my Girl ?
For I peer in her tender face,
And I fear that its light of grace
Is too still and too starry a birth
For our noisy, dim dwellings of Earth.
She looks like a natural Child
Of the heavens — too lustrous, too mild
For us.   Other Roses are blowing
While mine seems upfolding and going, —
Dreamily happy in going.
Yet on it more soft is the thorn

Than the tiniest little snail's-horn,
And golden at heart is the Morn
Of a day that will never be born.

Just a spirit of light is my Girl,
Seen through a body of pearl;
A spirit of life that will fleet
Away, more on wings than on feet.
Her cheek is so waxenly thin,
As if deathward 't were whitening in,
And the cloud of her flesh, still more white,
Were clearing till soul is in sight.
She leans as the wind-flowers stoop;
All their loveliness seen as they droop!
Her eyes have the sweet native hue
Of the heaven they are melting into,
Blue as the Violets above
The grave of some tender babe-love
That back to us wistfully bring
The buried blue eyes with the Spring.
Her large eyes too liquidly glister!
Her mouth is too red.
     Have they kissed her—
The Angels that bend down to pull
Our buds of the Beautiful,
And whispered their own little Sister?

O Mothers of Children three!
Two of them bright of blee;

One, your White Child, your pearl !
Do you feel as I feel with my Girl ?
For I think I could give half her wealth
Of heaven for a little more health :
The halo of Saints for the simple
Blithe graces that dip in a dimple !
Nay, I feel in my heart I could revel
To see but a wee dash of devil ;
A touch of the old Adam in her ;
A glimpse of his fair fellow-sinner ;
Any likeness of earth that would give
Me a promise my Darling should live.
O my love !   O my life !   O my Maker,
Take ME too, if Thou MUST take her !

CHILDREN AT PLAY.

"OPEN *your mouth and shut your eyes,*"
 Three little Maidens were saying, —
"*And see what God sends you !*" little
  they thought
He listened while they were playing !
So little we guess that a light light word
At times, may be more than praying.

" I," said Kate with the merry blue eyes,
 " *Would have lots of frolic and folly* " ;

"I," said Ciss with the bonnie brown hair,
  " *Would have life always smiling and jolly* " ;
" *And I would have just what our Father may send,*"
  Said lovable little pale Polly.

Life came for the Two, with sweetnesses new
  Every morning in gloss and in glister.
But Our Father above, in a gush of great love,*
  Caught up little Polly and kissed her.
And the Churchyard nestled another wee grave ;
  The Angels another wee Sister.

SLEEP-WALKING.

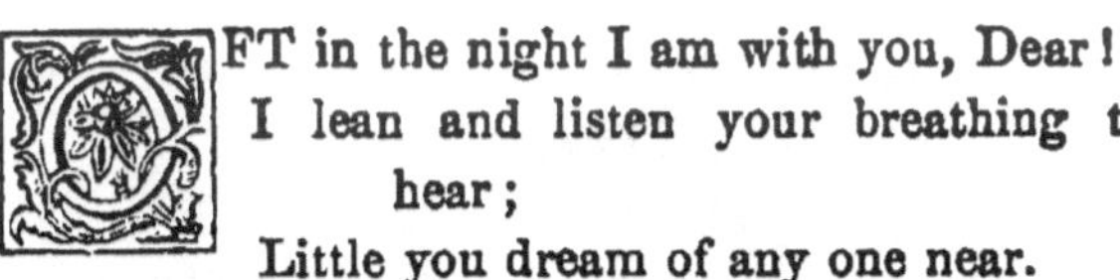

FT in the night I am with you, Dear !
  I lean and listen your breathing to
      hear ;
  Little you dream of any one near.

No one knoweth that I am gone ;
Curtains closely about me drawn,
When dreams dissolve at touch of Dawn.

Nobody meets me under the sky,
Only the staring Owl goes by
Softly as though the Night should sigh.

Under the moonlight, over the moss !
I need no bridge the river to cross,
Though winds awake and waters toss.

O sweet, so sweet the Nightingale's strain !
Is it her pleasure that works us pain,
Or her pain that with pleasure pierces the brain ?

Window or door I pass not through :
The way I never could show to you
By day. I enter as spirits do !

There you are ! lying cheek-on-palm,
Drinking of slumber's dewiest calm,
Filling your life with the rosiest balm.

The little wee bird that beats in the breast,
Hath folded its wings in a wee white nest,
Breathing the odors of sweet rest.

But the other night — see my blushes bloom —
Somehow I missed my way in the gloom,
And, thinking myself quite safe in your room,

I nestled my face, as I thought, in your bed
To kiss you, and — let me hide my head —
I kissed — I kissed — your Teacher instead.

AN APOLOGUE.

IN the olden day when Immortals
  Came oftener visibly down,
    There went a Youth with an Angel
    Through the gate of an Eastern Town:
They passed a Dog by the roadside,
  Where dead and rotting it lay,
And the Youth, at the ghastly odor,
  Sickened and turned away.
He gathered his robes about him
  And hastily hurried thence:
But naught annoyed the Angel's
  Clear, pure, immortal sense.

By came a lady, lip-luscious,
  On delicate tinkling feet:
All the place grew glad with her presence,
  The air about her sweet;
For she came in fragrance floating,
  And her voice most silvery rang;
The Youth, to embrace her beauty,
  With all his being sprang.
A sweet, delightsome Lady:
  And yet the Legend saith,
The Angel, while he passed her,
  Shuddered and held *his* breath.

THE GLOW-WORM.

THE Apes found a Glow-worm,
  Shining in the night, —
A little drop of radiance
  Tenderly alight;

Ho! Ho! shivered the Apes,
  Grinning all together,
We'll make a fire to warm us;
  'T is jolly cold weather.

With dry sticks and dead leaves,
  All the Apes came;
Piled a heap and squatted round
  To blow it into flame!

But fire would not kindle so —
  Vain their wasted breath!
Only they blew out the glow —
  Put the worm to death.

Glow-worms were meant to shine ·
  Apes can't blow them hot,
Just to warm their foolish hands, ·
  Or boil their flesh-pot.

So the World would serve the Poet,
With his light of love.
Probably his use may be
Better known above.

MY NEIGHBOR.

OVE *thou thy Neighbor*," we are told,
" *Even as Thyself.*" That creed I hold;
But love her more, a thousand-fold!

My lovely Neighbor; oft we meet
In lonely lane, or crowded street;
I know the music of her feet.

She little thinks how, on a day,
She must have missed her usual way,
And walked into my heart for aye.

Or how the rustle of her dress
Thrills through me like a soft caress,
With trembles of deliciousness.

Wee woman, with her smiling mien,
And soul celestially serene,
She passes me, unconscious Queen!

Her face most innocently good,
Where shyly peeps the sweet red blood.
Her form a nest of Womanhood !

Like Raleigh — for her dainty tread,
When ways are miry — I could spread
My cloak, but, there 's my heart instead.

Ah, Neighbor, you will never know
Why 't is my step is quickened so ;
Nor what the prayer I murmur low.

I see you 'mid your flowers at morn,
Fresh as the rosebud newly born ;
I marvel, can you have a thorn ?

If so, 't were sweet to lean one's breast
Against it, and, the more it prest,
Sing like the Bird that sorrow hath blest.

I hear you sing !   And through me Spring
Doth musically ripple and ring ;
Little you think I 'm listening !

You know not, dear, how dear you be ;
All dearer for the secrecy :
Nothing, and yet a world to me.

So near, too ! you could hear me sigh,
Or see my case with half an eye ;
But must not.   There are reasons why.

A POET'S LOVE–LETTER.

OU ask me, Friend, to tell you of my
    Wife !
And on what stair or landing-place of
    life
I met, as 't were, God's Angel coming down,
Or mine ascending, for her marriage crown ?

I say you sooth, however strange it seem,
The first time that I saw her was in dream :
A vision of the night did clearly glass
Her living lineaments.   I saw her pass
Smiling, as those may smile who feel they hold
At heart safe-hidden, secret fold on fold,
The sweetest love that ever was untold.
Aad as it went the Vision flasht on me
A moment's look ; a lifetime's memory.
But little could I dream that this should prove
The whole wide world's one lady of my love.
I had never seen that face or form, and yet
I knew them both by daylight when we met.

Blind World! to pass, and pass my darling by,
My lily of the vale, where she did lie
Snug in her own green leaves, and never see
The flower veiled and waiting there for me,
With cloudy fragrance all about her curled;
And yet, my blessings on thee, O blind World!
It is so sweet to find with one's own eyes,
Led by divine good-hap, to her surprise,
Our Perdita, our Princess in disguise!
The eye that finds must bring the power to see;
(Says Goethe's doctrine, comforting to me!)
And now she 's found, the world would give me much
        much
Could I but tell it of another such.

Is she an Angel?
        Let us not forget,
My Friend, that WE are scarcely Angels yet.
At least my modest soul would not be pledged
To call itself an Angel fully fledged:
Flesh is so frail! nor am I very sure
Of being, in spirit, altogether pure!
Snags of old broken sins torment me still
With pains that Death itself will hardly kill.
If not an Angel, let the truth be told,
I have not grasped the glitter — missed the Gold.
And lucky is the man who gets the gold,
Refined and fitted for the marriage mould!

Still happier who can keep it purè to bear
The finer features of immortal wear.
She is of Angel-stuff; but I 'm afraid
The Angels are not given us ready-made :
In other worlds, this wife of mine may be
The perfect public Angel all may see ;
At present she 's a private one for me —
My household deity of Common Things,
That into lowly ways a beauty brings,
Just as the grass comes creeping, making bright
And blessëd, with its ripples of delight
And quiet smiles, all pathways dim and bare.

Is she a Beauty ?
                Well, I will not swear
A thousand beauties with her beauty blend ;
A thousand graces on her Grace attend ;
Or that she is so piteously fair
Each passer-by must turn, or stop, or stare,
And he on whom she looks feels instantly
As one that springs from dust to deity.
Nor can I sing of outward symbols now
The swan-white stately neck; the snow-white brow ;
The lip's live rose ; the head superbly crowned ;
Eyes, that when fathomed, farthest heaven is
        found !
I chose for worth, not show, nor chose for them
Who want the casket richer than the gem.

That Wife is · poor, whate'er her dower may
    be,
Who hath no beauty save what all may see :
No mystery of the human and divine ;
No other face to unveil within the shrine,
Up-lighted only for one worshipper,
And to one love alone familiar ;
No veil to lift from the familiar face
Daily, and show the unfamiliar grace.
Eyes shine for others, but divinely dim
And dewy do they grow only for him !
And her dear face transfigured he doth find
All mirror to the marvel in his mind !

The beauty worn by Bird and Butterfly
Lives on the outside, lustrous to the eye :
But still as nobler grow hue, form, and face,
More inward is shy Beauty's dwelling-place.
And there 's a beauty fashioned in the mould
Transmitted from the Beautiful of old,
That from some family-face its best doth win :
But my love's beauty cometh from within ;
The loveliness of love made visible,
To feature which the sculptor Form is dull :
Not the mere charms of cheek, or chin, or lip,
That vanish on a week's acquaintanceship ;
But that crown-beauty which we cannot clasp,
The beauty that eludes Death's own grave-grasp.

At forty, what we seek for in a Wife
Is a calm haven amid seas of strife :
One fresh green summit in the waste of life,
That gathers dew of heaven and tenderly
Turns it to healing drops for you or me ;
A spring of freshness in the desert sand ;
A palm for shadow in a weary land ;
A being that doth not dwell so far apart
That we can find no entrance save at heart ;
One that at equal step with us may walk,
And kiss at equal stature in our talk ;
And scale the loftiest life, still arm-in-arm,
As well as nestle in the valleys warm.

And here 's my Rest, where sun and shadow meet
O'erhead, the small flowers budding at my feet ;
Green picnic places peeping from the wood,
Where you may meet the spirit of Robin Hood
Crossing the moonlight at the old deer-chase ;
A brooding Dove the Spirit of the place ;
Gleams of the Graces at their bath of dew ;
An earthly pleasaunce ; heaven trembling through ;
My Darling sitting with her hand in mine,
Here, where 'mid the lush grass the large-eyed
          kine
Ruminant, stolid, statelily behold
The milky plenty and the blossoming gold :
And with glad laugh the tiny buttercup

Its beaker of delight brimful holds up ;
And prodigally glorified, the mead
Is all aglow with red-ripe sorrel-seed,
And quick with smells that make one long to be
A-gathering sweets, bloom-buried utterly.

The sylvan world's old royalties around
With all their summer beauty newly crowned :
Broad beeches, that have caught alive the swirl
O' the wind-wave — shaped it in their branches' curl ;
Proud oaks, from head to foot all feudal yet ;
And whispering pines, that have in worship met, —
Their delicate Gothic sharp against the shine
Of sunset heaven's honeyed hyaline —
As dark and still and plumëd, as the Hearse
Of day's departed glory, are those Firs
When Venus, glowing in the Lift above,
Laughs down on lovers with the eye of Love,
Luminous in her loveliness, as though
The Goddess' self were coming from the glow.

I brought my Love here happy months ago,
Her winter prison, amid miles of snow.
Poor bird ! she felt that she was caged at last,
Her forest far away, its freedom past :
Her eyes made mournful search, mine laughed to
    see,
She would have flown, and knew not where to flee.

The little wedding ring had grown a round
Large hoop about our lives, and we were bound!
Useless was all petitionary quest,
No outlet!— so she nestled in my breast;
And may we always be as wise, my dear,
When things look dark around, or foes are near.

And now the fragrant summer-tide hath come
And isled us in a sea of leaf and bloom.
And now the tremulous sweetness, restless grace,
Have settled down to brood in the dear face
That lightens by me, fair and privet-pale,
Soft in the shadow of the bridal veil:
The sunny sparkle of Southern radiance
That in her English blood doth bicker and dance,
Hath steadied to the still and sacred glow
Which hath more inner life than outer show.

So many are the mishaps and the griefs
In marriage, like Beau Brummel's Neckerchiefs;
Armfuls of failure for one perfect tie!
And *have we hit it?* do you say or sigh.
Time was when life in triumph would have run,
And faster than the fields catch fire o' the sun,
Or light takes shape and feature in the flowers,
My answer would have blossomed with the hours.
I should have felt the buds begin to blow
With my love-warmth, another dawn to glow;

Heard all the bells in heaven ring quite plain
Because young blood went singing through my
      brain :
Like vernal impulses the verses came ;
My soul on tiptoe and my words aflame.
I should have sung that we had reached the land
Where milk and honey flow o'er golden sand,
And that far *El Dorado* we had found
Where nothing less than nuggets glad the ground.
But 't is no more the lyric life of youth,
When fancy seemëd truer than all truth,
And standing in that dawn, the sun of love
Hung dewy rainbows on each web we wove,
·And to the leap o' the blood we felt it given
To scale the tallest battlements of heaven ;
Poor was the prize of wisdom's proudest dower
Beside that glory of the flesh in flower !

And now I cannot sing my Ladye's praise,
Lark-like, as in the morning of those days
When at a touch the song would upward start,
And, half in heaven, empty all the heart.
'T is August with me now and harvest-heat,
And in the nest the silence is so sweet ;
Moreover, love is such a bosom thing,
In words its nestling nearnesses take wing ;
Nor flower of speech could ever yet express
The married sweetness or the homeliness ;

We cannot fable the ineffable;
The tongue is tied too, with the heart at full:
Music may hint it with her latest breath,
But fails;—her heaven is only reached through
     Death.

The stirring of the sap in bole and bough —
Mere feeling — will not set me singing now!
I thank my God for all that he hath given
And ope the windows of my soul to heaven;
I think, in bowed and very humble mood,
I must be better, He hath been so good.
So would I journey to the land above,
Clothed with humility and crowned with love.

I look no more Without, and think to win
The treasures that are only found Within;
And, after many years, have grown too wise
To search our world for some lost paradise;
Or feel unhappy should we chance to miss
The next life's possibilities in this.
'T is here we follow — but hereafter find
The goal all-golden miraged in the mind.
That Age of Gold behind us, and the Isles
Where dwelt the Blessèd are but as the smiles
Reflected from a heaven that onward lies,
The Gold of sundown caught in orient skies.

And yet, if any bit of Eden bloom
In this old world, 't is in the WEDDED HOME
And, what a wonder-world of novel life
Do these two range through, hand-in-hand, as Wife
And Husband; in one flesh two spirits paired;
Their joys all doubled, all their sorrows shared:
Two spirits blending in one heavenward spire,
That soars up fragrant from an altar fire;
Two halves in one perfection wed to prove
The shaped Idea of immortal love!

We cannot see Love with our mortal sight,
But lo! the singing Angels come some night
To bring His tiny image in the Child
Wherewith from out the darkness He hath smiled;
The tender voice whereby the All-loving breaks
His silence, and in human fashion speaks;
The gentle hand put forth to draw us near
The heart of life whose pulse is beating here.
Though seldom do we guess, so dim our eyes,
That God comes down in such a simple guise,
And yet of such the kingdom of Heaven is;
Through them the next world is revealed in this!

And how they come to us to bring us back
What we have lost along the dusty track:
The sweetness of the dawn, the early dew,
And tender green, and heaven's unclouded blue;

The treasures that we dropped upon the ground,
And they, in following after us, have found !

Ah, Love, my life is not so bare of leaf
But we can find a nest for shelter if
The bounteous heavens should bless us from above
And in our branches cradle some wee dove.
Nor will my darling lack a touch still warm
To finish that fine sculpture of her form ;
For if Love dwell in me, the Angel-Elf
Shall kiss her to some likeness of himself.

At the hill-top I reach my resting-place,
To find clear heaven and feel it face to face ;
Firm footing after all the weary slips,
To hold the cup unshaken at the lips.
The meaning of my life grows clear at last,
And all my troubles smile back now they 're past:
The clouds put on a glory to mine eyes,
My sorrows were my Saviour in disguise :
And I have walked with angels unawares,
And upward mounted, climbing over cares,
A little nearer to the home above.
Here let me rest in the good Father's love
Embodied in these arms embracing me,
Serenely as the sea-flowers in deep sea.

'T is true, just as we feel our foreheads crowned,
And all so glorious grows the prospect round,

It seems one stride might launch us on heaven's
    wave,
Thenceforth our steps go downward to the grave.
What then!   I would not rest till spirit rust,
And I am undistinguishable dust:
And if Love bring no second spring to me,
This is the fore-feel of a spring to be;
If no new Dawn, yet in the evening hours,
Freshly bedewed, more sweetly smelt the flowers;
And round my path the glow of love hath made
Gentle illumination for the shade.

Something, dear Lord, thou hast for me to say,
Or wherefore draw me toward the springs of day,
And make my face with happiness to shine
By softly placing this dear hand in mine
Even while I stretch it to Thee through the dark:
A something that shall shine aloft and mark
Thy goodness and my gratitude upon
This Mount Transfiguration when I'm gone?
If thou hast set my foot on firmer ground,
Lord, let me show what helper I have found;
If Thou hast touched me with thy loftier light,
Lord, let me turn to those that walk in night
And climb with more at heart than they can bear,
Though but a twinkle through their cloud of care.
Only a grain of sand my life may be,
But let it sparkle, Lord, with light of Thee!